MW01243636

Nobody Drowned

Book II of the Awan Lake Series

PETER KINGSMILL

NOBODY DROWNED
Awan Lake Series Book II
A Frank Anderson novel by Peter Kingsmill
Cover design by Rae Ann Bonneville

All characters are fictional, and any similarity to people living or dead is purely coincidental.

Copyright © 2019 Peter Kingsmill

:

DEDICATION

For my beautiful granddaughter Tiana,
whose passionate soul and gentle ways
are reflected in her poetry,
already recognized in her own right:
Who's the bully
...I am the kid who gave these kids their names
I know they have names...
They all have names.

08:35 JULY 30

Anderson didn't like burying people, but he was fond of Suzy. That, he reflected as the Airbus A319 banked into its final approach to the airport at Nanaimo, is why he was here, in the middle of the summer when he could be back home finishing off a small dock-construction project that would net the revenue this flight was costing him. Two days earlier, he had received a call from a tearful Susan Kirkpatrick in Campbell River, telling him that Keith had been killed in a machinery accident in the bush. The funeral was tomorrow, and she had asked him if he would give the eulogy for his long-time friend and former Coast Guard colleague.

The Coast Guard days had been many years – decades – earlier, but this was a request he couldn't refuse. Frank Anderson, and Keith and Suzy Kirkpatrick, had been very close, both at the Coast Guard station (where Suzy worked in the dispatch office) and off-work when they used to fish from Keith's decrepit little outboard cruiser, then enjoy barbecuing the catch along with steaks, beer and music on the deck of their mobile home. Keith played banjo, Suzy played mandolin and Anderson the guitar. They loved old country and folk songs, and Suzy sang them in a soft velvety voice that warmed everyone who heard her. Despite many requests, they only took the music off the porch to play for the annual Coast Guard staff party. Mostly it was just for fun.

The double thump of the wheels hitting the tarmac shook Anderson out of his memories and relieved the tightness that was creeping in behind his eyes. "Well, that was smooth," he joked to his seatmate.

"They always land here like they're in a hurry," his neighbour responded. "Don't know why – it's like they're landing at Toronto with a wind off the lake. You taking the shuttle to Campbell River?"

"Nope. I've booked a rental. I need a car to get around up there anyway."

The men shook hands at the departure gate and wished each other luck – Anderson with the funeral and his seat companion with a technology assessment contract for an ore refinery near Port Alberni.

***

A small aluminum fishing boat droned slowly through

the gray calm waters of Awan Lake in Ontario, about two miles off the east shore. Its old-model 20 horsepower outboard engine seemed barely up to the task, and the two young people onboard were probably not fishers or they would have known that this far offshore on Awan Lake in an early-morning fog was a poor place to be in such a small craft.

They were, however, wearing lifejackets. The young woman yelled back to her male colleague who was operating the motor: "There's no frickin' cell service out here. I can't even text anymore!"

"Well, let's hope we don't need help from the prof and that our protocols work out. Is your GPS working okay?"

She rummaged around amongst the equipment boxes on the bottom of the boat and pulled out a black plastic case, which she set on a seat and opened. She put the mushroom-shaped antenna on the seat beside her, attached two wires to a battery, turned on the instrument, and waited.

"Yup, seems okay," she yelled back less than a minute later. "I think I have about 16 satellites, and it shows I'm on Awan Lake."

"Cool! Can you back out the screen and find our targets? As I remember I think we input three."

There was a pause while she fiddled with the screen

adjustments. "Yup. Maybe head a little away from the shore. I'm guessing we're about two miles from the first one. Maybe we'll get this part done today after all... then, just the other side of the lake and into the river tomorrow, and we're done. I sure as hell hope so: I have a wedding to get to next weekend."

"You the bride?"

"Hell no... it's my girlfriend and that's even worse. Perfectly nice chick has turned into bridezilla."

"Where's the wedding?"

"Sarnia."

"You've got some travelling to do."

***

The Chevy Equinox rolled contentedly along Highway 19 north of Nanoose Bay. Anderson had chosen to rent the SUV because it seemed to fit his heavy-set six-foot frame better than a car, especially after several hours trying to conform to economy class airline travel. The SUV also had Bluetooth, so Anderson used it to call Marjorie.

"Hi there, it's me."

"Hi Frank! Good flights?"

"Yes, but have I ever told you how much I hated

airports?"

"Endlessly. Wendy and I were laughing about you after we dropped you off. But you got there safely, apparently!"

"Safely landed in Nanaimo and now I'm chasing a whole lot of traffic. Thank heaven it's Sunday and not on a long weekend – traffic's bad enough! Are you guys settled back in your Toronto house?"

"Yes, although settled isn't exactly the word. Are you missing your old haunts out there on Vancouver Island?"

"No, I'm kind of a 'today and tomorrow' guy, not a 'yesterday' guy. I'm just driving someone else's car along a road I used to travel, feeling like there's somewhere else I'm supposed to be."

"Sort of the same here, and it's weird. Wendy is in a state... confused over John who she really likes but can't relax with him, and feeling all worked up over mining companies, lakes and swamps. Not the usual city girl I've known all my life! And as for me, somehow the home I grew up in seems, well, sort of empty. It's like the shades of our parents have vanished from the house... not very comforting somehow. And you're not here to talk to, something that would have not even occurred to me two weeks ago. Unfair for me to burden you with this, though... how about you? You may be the "today" guy but you had to kill someone less than five days ago. How are you doing, really?"

"I'm fine... really. Several people died that day, and I figure it was all that dummy's fault, so taking him down was a blow for the good guys. Stuff happens. You're okay?"

"Uh huh. There's an ugly three-second video that pops into my head every now and then, but I'm fine. And it distracted me from my boob-squash this morning."

There was a pause... "Boob squash... I take it that's not a gently-rounded garden vegetable?"

Marjorie laughed: "Mammogram, you nitwit!"

Anderson paused again, longer this time. "Nothing wrong, I hope?"

"Nah, it's just that when you get to be an old lady – like over 35 – you're supposed to have the girls checked regularly. Kinda like you guys should get your prostate checked every year."

"Huh? You're kidding, right?"

"Not at all kidding! Do I have to make you an appointment too?"

"We can discuss that when I get home. Under the circumstances, that's just too much morbid stuff to think about."

"Yeah, I do understand, so I won't call you 'sissy' – yet. But we will talk about it soon!"

"Without meaning to change the subject at all, my seatmate on the flight into Nanaimo was a computer tech guy on a contract for Robertson Mines, here on the island. This guy was no junior techie playing video games during the flight; he's so high up in computer technology he doesn't even carry a laptop. Far as I can tell all he carried was a shaving kit and a cellphone. He had some interesting opinions about his client."

"Small world... never even thought they might have an operation out there. Did he know anything about the Robertson facility at home here at Awan Lake?"

"I don't think so, not specifically, but he was well aware it was a huge company. He was grumbling that their security protocols were more like you'd expect at the CIA in the States than at a mining company. When he goes in to work, he has to leave his phone at the desk and gets searched with a wand like they do at the airport. Coming out, same thing but he's strip-searched too."

"I'll tell Wendy. She'll be thrilled to add that to the conspiracy theory she's building!"

Anderson's phone began crackling as the connection cut in and out. "Hey Marj, I'm going to lose you here – cell service is crappy. I miss you, pretty lady. I'll call you in the morning if not before."

"Mmm, okay. Miss you too! We'll catch...." and her voice disappeared.

"Damn." He pushed the button to cancel the call. *Three weeks ago I'd never have thought I would miss talking with someone. It's always just been me, my boat, my lake and some good neighbours. Things change, I guess.*

10:00 JULY 31

OPS Sergeant John MacLeod was at his desk in the detachment office in Maple Falls. It was 10:00 a.m., but his third cup of black coffee still hadn't woken him up and as he sat there sorting a week's worth of paper, he reflected he was still feeling pretty beat up. The work of a detachment boss in rural Ontario doesn't usually involve too much in the way of international drug smuggling, helicopters and multiple murders all piled into one day. He had lost one officer and almost lost his own life if it hadn't been for the quick response of his new civilian friend Frank Anderson. *I wonder how Anderson's doing out there on the island, anyway. On top of all the other stuff last week, he just lost an old friend to a violent death, albeit one caused by a piece of road-building machinery, not a gunshot. I don't imagine he'll find that an easy eulogy to deliver.*

His thoughts were interrupted by one of his staff: "Sergeant, when do we need to get back out there to find that chopper and pull it out of the drink?"

"It'll wait until Anderson gets back from B.C., maybe

later this week. There's no boat around here better than his to find it and get it out of there, and I'm not going to push the guy until he's back and gets a couple of days to rest. I expect he'll be back here tomorrow."

"Understood sir. Just wondering."

***

At 2:00 p.m. Arnold Jamieson drove to the commercial wharf, stopping to check the locks on Frank Anderson's house and shop before walking out on the dock and checking the locks, mooring ropes and chain on *The Beaver*, Anderson's converted coastal lobster boat which he used to make a living as a contractor serving the Awan Lake's island cottagers. Over the last two weeks the boat had played an active role in a criminal investigation and – ultimately – something like a one-boat navy. Arnold stepped onto the narrow deck beside the wheelhouse and examined some splintered wood by one of the windows. He could actually put his finger into the hole the bullet had made as it entered the cabin just under the window.

Anderson's gonna have to get some plastic wood and paint to fix that little sucker. Maybe he'll even have to replace the frame.

***

It was 7:15 Monday evening, thirteen days before the Spirit River Board of Trade would host a public event where internationally-recognized water expert Dr. Sebastian Horowitz would talk about how the waters of Awan Lake were possibly under threat from a proposed mining development. Arnold and his wife Marion had just finished setting up the small banquet room at the Spirit River Inn for tonight's event planning meeting.

"Anderson was chuckling Saturday before he left, saying it was kinda odd that a small-town board of trade would be taking an anti-development position," said Arnold. "I wonder how he's doing out there on the wet coast. He hates going anywhere, and I'm convinced he left the coast because of the rain. He hates it!"

"Well, we all know that our board of trade is not officially taking an anti-development position. It's supposed to be a fact-finding event, and the goal is to protect our lake in support of our tourism industry," responded Marion. "At least, that's our story and we're sticking to it!"

"Well, they must believe that down in Ottawa because that LaChance fellow at Environment Canada has been ignoring what we're doing."

"Well, not quite. He did call on Friday just to confirm the legal name of our Board of Trade and to clarify it had been in existence for decades before the Protected Shorelines Project started up. I read him the details from the original charter, and he seemed very pleased. Then, of course, he was all over me about Wednesday and the killings and arrests. Seems like Spirit River was big-time in the news last week, even in Ottawa."

"Yeah, bad news travels fast, apparently..." Arnold paused and turned to the first arrival at the meeting. "Hi Adumbi, glad to see you. Thanks for coming... is Cyndi coming too?!"

Adumbi Jakande was an African-born Masters student in biology who was working as an intern with the community's Protected Shorelines Project, along with Cyndi Johansson, an undergrad summer student.

"Hello Arnold – and Mrs. Jamieson – I am glad to be here." He continued, his well-schooled British accent somewhat of an anomaly in a small Ontario town: "And no, Cyndi asked me to tell you that she has resigned from the PSP and won't be back. Between us, she was very scared last week. Both of us were, I guess, but she said she couldn't take it anymore."

Marion went over to Adumbi and shook his hand. "We

were all scared, believe me, so I don't blame her. We're just glad you're staying."

She turned to Arnold: "Sorry, Mr. J. I forgot to tell you that Cyndi quit on Friday. I gave her her last paycheque and she left as fast as she could. She was still pretty shook up about Wednesday."

Marion was the community's designated "everything to everybody" person. Nobody knew when she inherited that position or who had it before; it just seemed like she was always there, like the towering spruce in the forest, or the Spirit River itself. She and Arnold ran the Main Street Garage, where Arnold fixed everyone's cars and she – apart from keeping the books, answering the phone and pumping gas – kept track of life in the community and made sure people – neighbours and visitors alike – were okay. And, she was also secretary to the meeting tonight.

Over the next few minutes a dozen or so more people drifted into the room and settled themselves around the collection of round banquet tables that had been pulled together near the centre of the room. One couple, dressed in expensively casual slacks and hooded sweaters, came over to Arnold: "I don't see Frank tonight," said the tall elderly gentleman. "I do hope he is alright after last week's excitement. I can imagine it was tough on him?"

"Hi, Mr. (and Mrs.) Barker. Yeah, Anderson's okay. He's one tough old bird, but his week didn't get any better after the dust settled. An old friend from his Coast Guard days was killed in a bulldozer accident on Thursday and his widow asked Frank to delivery the eulogy at the funeral, which is tomorrow. The Webster girls drove him to the airport very early this morning, then stayed over at their place in the city."

"Geez, I'm sorry to hear that. He didn't need that on his plate. And Arnold, my name is Tony and this is my long-suffering spouse Jean."

"Really glad to meet you, and can't say enough how grateful we are for your contribution to help make this event possible."

"And please don't think we're here tonight to watch over you. We really just want to show our support as people, more than money. And of course, I was hoping we'd see Anderson – he has become a good friend, not just a great contractor. As you likely know, he has helped us out with a number of improvements out at the island. He's really good at his job and he doesn't charge enough!"

Arnold was about to reply when a very attractive dark-haired young woman bounced into the room, made a beeline for Adumbi Jakande and delivered him an enthusiastic hug.

"Adumbi! I thought I'd never see you again. You're still here!"

"Anita! I'm so happy to see you! Every one of us thought we'd never see you again! You look just great... especially since we had all considered that you were dead in a ditch somewhere!"

"Nah, I'm too tough to kill! Actually, without the help of a lot of folks around here that bastard might have got it done anyway. Uncle Arnold, is Wendy – the sister of the lady Mr. Anderson was hanging around with – coming to the meeting?"

"Nope. The girls are in Toronto and Anderson is out on Vancouver Island for a couple of days."

Anita ducked her head momentarily, then: "Oh. I thought she was bringing some posters she was working on. We were looking at the design on Friday night."

"That's okay – the posters are done, pretty much. The committee has to approve them tonight then she'll get them printed and bring them up early this week. They look great... nice to have a few artistic folks around here!"

By now all the seats at the meeting tables were filled up, and folks were pouring themselves coffee. Arnold looked at Marion and shrugged his shoulders. "Might as well get started," she said, and the two of them settled near one end of the main table.

Arnold cleared his throat and rapped his knuckles on the table: "Okay folks, thanks for coming out tonight – the weather is 'way too nice to be stuck inside so we appreciate the good turnout anyway. I'll try to keep this short; there are some new faces around the table since last meeting so we'll go around the table with introductions... I'll start: I'm Arnold Jamieson, vice-chairman of the Board of Trade, filling in for our chairperson Florence from the Inn who couldn't get away tonight. To my left is Marion Jamieson, who everyone here knows. She is the board's secretary and – poor lady – is also my long-suffering wife! We'll keep going clockwise around the table... Jeremy?"

Jeremy Forbes gave his name as a retired village resident; he was an elderly man who showed all the signs of having had a life of hard work and likely too much alcohol. And so it went, around the table: Sam from the "Zoo" (the restaurant on Main Street), the Barkers, Adumbi and Anita, Jim from the marina, Pete from the Co-op, and a half-dozen island cottage-owners including Dave Bradshaw, a Ryerson University professor who had suggested this event with Dr. Horowitz in the first place, and had made the initial contacts to get it started.

Four men were seated at a table a bit off to the side,

watching politely. Arnold looked across at one of the group, a short, stout man in his sixties, and spoke rather more loudly: "So, Mr. Mayor, I guess we all know you but could you introduce your friends?"

Spirit River Mayor Ronald Klassen introduced the other three men as representatives of property owners in the village and surrounding county. "They would like to know more about who put together this event in two weeks. They have concerns about possible long-range impacts it might have on property values in the area."

Arnold looked over at Marion, glanced around the table and replied, "Thanks, Ron, and welcome folks. We'll proceed with the meeting so you have an understanding of our plans and I'll make sure you have an opportunity to ask questions afterward." Turning back to his wife, he continued, "Marion, do we have an agenda for tonight?"

"Yes, but it's pretty short so I didn't print one out. There are two items: approving the poster and finalizing the schedule for August 13th. I'll add questions from the floor after that."

Arnold glanced around the table again and – seeing no questions or objections – helped Marion circulate the suggested Love Our Lake event poster. According to the immediately-favourable comments, Wendy – and apparently

Anita too – had done a great job. One of the cottagers wondered at the use of 24-hour time on the poster, and after a couple of jokes at Frank Anderson's expense, it was decided to use 12-hour time along with "a.m." and "p.m."

"Good thing Frank is away tonight," Arnold laughed. "He'd have a fit; I'd probably have to smack him upside the head – then feed him beer – to settle him down!" Arnold was missing his friend. As their friendship had grown over several years, Arnold had remembered from his school days the biblical story in Exodus about Moses and Aaron, each with different skills and always supporting the other.

Settling the details and schedule for the August event took longer – about 45 minutes – and then it was time for questions. The Mayor started: "The board of trade has been dead for at least ten years, with no membership, and now all of a sudden it's putting on a big event for environmentalists. Who is behind all this?"

"You're such an asshole, Klassen. You know perfectly well what's going on. Your council approved using the fairgrounds just last week... I was at your damn meeting!" The speaker was Jeremy Forbes, not generally known for subtlety or good manners.

"Jeremy, can we maybe keep this civil? There are ladies present, and this is a community meeting." The disheveled old man went back to staring at his coffee cup and clicking his ballpoint pen. Arnold thought for a moment and continued with a response to the mayor: "Yes, Ron, you are right, the board of trade hasn't done much for a number of years, probably because most of us in business thought we had it just about perfect. Great community, an active but not crazy tourism industry, all the services we need between here and Maple Falls, and a well-run village. But the village, the small cottage developments and the tourist industry could all fall apart if the lake was threatened. So, what better time for the board of trade to get together so we can all learn if there may be problems with the lake?"

***

"So, Mum, what did you think of that?"

Arnold and Marion had left the Spirit River Inn and gone home right after the meeting. When Anderson was around, they usually joined a few stragglers at the bar, but tonight they agreed – even without speaking together – to avoid any further discussions in public that night.

"Meeting was good, all things considered," Marion replied. "And since when did you become a diplomat? You sat Klassen back on his fat butt without allowing him room for an argument at all. I think we were all impressed!"

"I think he could see that – since most of the village's business folks were there – he had no room to say much. Wouldn't want to piss off too many influential voters, y'know!"

It had indeed been a useful and pleasant meeting, all things considered, and Marion wanted to send off an email to Wendy Webster to approve the slightly-changed poster so she could get them printed up Tuesday morning. She also wanted to do a couple of online searches for property-owners in the district: turned out that, of the three men who came in with the mayor, apparently only one was a village resident, and all three owned good-sized tracts of land along the shore outside the village boundary. And, all three worked in management positions at Robertson Mines.

08:12 AUGUST 1

The redeye flight from Vancouver touched down seventeen minutes late in Toronto, for no apparent reason that Anderson could figure. He dialled Marjorie immediately to confirm that she would meet him outside the arrivals doors to save parking: "Hi Marj... sorry I'm late, but we've landed! Have they bumped you around the loop yet?"

"Nope. I parked anyway. I'll meet you at Timmy's on the arrivals level, where I am sipping coffee. I'm in city mode, so it's a latte. You don't have to stop for baggage, I assume?"

"No, just the same suitcase I left with. I'm on my way."

After leaving the plane at the gate, he walked what felt like halfway across Saskatchewan to the escalators down to the arrivals area and found the Tim Hortons. Of course, at this time of morning it was full, but he immediately spotted Marjorie who had scored a table in the back corner. She had already picked up a black dark-roast for him, and sat there proudly with a big grin.

Anderson wedged his way through the several serving

lines to her table, and they shared a lingering hug before settling down. The coffee was good, although his stomach was crying out for something to eat. That could wait; Marjorie had news: "I went and registered Dad's old Jeep Wrangler that he was so proud of, so that's what we're driving today. Wendy will be headed to the lake later with the car, since she has to wait for the Spirit River posters to be printed. Sounds like they had a good meeting last night!"

"Wow... how long has it been since you ran that thing?"

"About three – maybe four – years. Wendy and I used it once to move some stuff up to the lake. I called Arnold about it yesterday and he suggested I add a can of Sea Foam to the gas tank, which I did. Seems to run fine – despite its age that old Jeep only has about 60,000 kilometers on it. It was Dad's pride and joy and it has always lived in the garage. He called it the Black Beast... it's black with tinted windows! But enough of that. How did yesterday go?"

"Fine, at least as fine as a funeral can go anyway. I do know that I am eternally grateful to your sister for helping me put the eulogy together. She found the right words to reflect my blatherings about Keith and the facts that Suzy gave us. She was very grateful, and made sure to tell me to be nice to you!"

"Aw, that's very sweet! I'll remember that advice if you

ever decide to beat me: 'remember Suzy? She said don't do that!' Is she very sad?"

"Yes, very. She adored Keith and they always did stuff together. She does have a job as a senior emergency services dispatcher which she enjoys – not the same as Coast Guard days, but she likes it anyway and has lots of friends, so she'll be okay. It'll just take some time."

Marjorie and Anderson decided to leave the airport and stop along the highway somewhere enroute to Awan Lake for bacon and eggs.

***

In a private office in the management section of Robertson Mines' Awan Lake facility, four men gathered around a well-finished oval table. The big window looked west across the lake, beyond the chain-link fence and concrete breakwall at the foot of the massive building which rose nearly ten stories from the shore. The mid-morning sun shone brightly on the sparkling blue-green waters of the lake.

A tall, spare man with closely-cropped blond hair was still standing, leaning back against a leather-covered desk. "So, gentlemen, did Mr. Mayor finally agree to take you to the village meeting last night, and were you able to learn anything more?"

"Well, Maurice, I'm not sure that we really accomplished anything, except to learn that a local organization has indeed engaged that damned Horowitz to speak in the village on August 13 – Sunday afternoon. They have some professionally-designed posters going up this week, and with that much forethought, I expect there will be accompanying media releases."

Maurice Bonner was General Manager of the Awan Lake operations for Robertson Mines, and he was obviously less than thrilled with this news. "That mayor is not about to do anything about it, I gather. Who's leading the charge?"

One of the three who attended the meeting last night – Charles Morrell – stood up and took off his crested work jacket, placing it on the small sofa on the east wall. "Even though I actually live in the village, I never hang around there except to go for an occasional beer and a hamburger at the Inn when the wife's in the city. It's a bit hard to tell who leads what around there. The chairman of the meeting – Jamieson – is a rough-cut businessman and mechanic who runs a local garage. He is surprisingly eloquent and folks listen to him. His wife is a tough old broad, well-connected in the village and smart as hell, and she was taking the minutes. There were some other business folks there, and some cottagers, but the only one who kind of stood out from that bunch was a guy who's a professor at Ryerson. Seems like he's behind some of this."

"Was that guy with the big boat there?"

"No, he wasn't. Sounds like he was away at Nanaimo or near there... somewhere on the island anyway."

"Would he have gone to our mine out there?"

"No, no, I doubt it. I heard someone say he was giving the eulogy at a friend's funeral. Why? Does he have something to do with this?"

"Perhaps, but I'm not at all sure. He was certainly involved with that fuss last week, using his boat to help shut down those idiots with their drug-smuggling operation. Seems like he has friends in the OPS. He is also somehow connected with that wildlife project with the college kids who count frogs and birds around the lake every summer."

"I hear that our famous 'Gerry Gatekeeper' was involved in the drug thing."

"Gerald Giordano? Yeah, silly old bugger even got arrested and held overnight without charges. They let him go in the morning and delivered him back out here. They could have kept him as far as I'm concerned... he's a pain in the ass anyway. But his buddy from the campground actually got himself killed, along with another guy from north of here."

"Cops get them?"

"I don't think so – one of the other gang members I expect. I heard it was execution-style, somewhere out on the lake. Anyway, that's now old news. We need to figure out what to do about this Horowitz bullshit. There's gonna be television cameras all over this place; that guy draws a bigger crowd than Garth Brooks. I'll give head office a call... they'll definitely want to know. Thanks for going to the meeting last night. As soon as I find out I'll let you all know what's next."

The three men stood up and left the room. Bonner went back around his desk, sat down and picked up his phone. He sighed, and stabbed his vice-president's contact button.

***

The old Jeep wagon was a surprisingly comfortable ride. Anderson and Marjorie had taken their time over a couple of Denver Omelettes at a pleasant roadside café about an hour south of Spirit River and stopped at a fruit stand for some fresh vegetables a few miles later. "It's almost afternoon coffee time at the Zoo. Let's stop in and show Arnold the Black Beast. He'll get a kick out of it, and more importantly it will introduce the Jeep to the village so folks will adopt it as one of theirs, instead of a strange vehicle in town."

Marjorie laughed: "It's always coffee time in Spirit River! Good idea though. Wendy's about two hours out – maybe more because she was going to stop in at Maple Falls and put up some posters. Somewhere in the next hour or two we can unload that stuff in the back into Polly and I'll make arrangements for an extra place to park this thing."

"You are more than welcome to leave it at my place. It would be an honour to have Marjorie Webster's Black Beast in my ample parking lot!"

"Really? You have room?"

"Duh."

"Okay, that would be perfect. I don't want to impose.

"The only time you ever imposed was when you knocked on my door three weeks ago. It's been all uphill since then!"

She leaned across the front seat and punched him on the arm. He grabbed her hand and kissed it. "Settled, then."

They drove by the Main Street Garage, where Anderson bellowed in the door, "Coffee time at the Zoo!" and they drove up the street to the restaurant. Sam greeted them when they walked in, and when he delivered their coffees to Anderson's favourite table in the back he told Anderson he was sorry to hear about his friend.

"Hey Frank – what's with the old black Jeep with tinted windows? You starring in a 60s crime movie now?" That was Arnold speaking as he and Marion walked in.

"Gimme a break, man... it's a 1980's Jeep, not a 60s, and it belongs to Marjorie, not me."

"Geez, Marjorie – that's what you called me about yesterday? That's a pretty cool ride for a young lady like you!"

"Listen to the old bugger now. Only time he ever sees a good woman is when she has a nice car!" That was Marion.

Sam, the Zoo's owner and Chef, brought the rest of the coffees and quietly asked Anderson to join him in the kitchen for a moment. "Frank, I have to say that I was not at all unhappy that old man Mistraika managed to get himself killed last week. He really was a nasty man. But you need to know that his two young nephews are not much better. They're now driving around in that old white crew-cab of his, bullying kids in town and even slashing tires. They know better than to come in here, but they are old enough to go to the Inn where they seem to like making trouble for Georgina and Florence. I thought you should know that they are trouble."

"Thanks Sam, I'll keep that in mind. I don't want any

trouble for those ladies."

"Well, you should also know that they were at the Inn last Wednesday night. Because of the probable connection between the guy you shot and their uncle's death (both on the same day), I expect they really know who you are!"

"Hmm. Yeah, thanks. I'll pay some close attention to that, too."

***

Down at the marina, the Webster sisters' outboard skiff shared a covered slip with a small classic cedar-strip runabout of similar size. Anderson and Marjorie were unloading the Jeep into the skiff when the marina owner Jim Russell came across from the marina store.

"Hi Ms. Webster! Frank, I intended to catch up with you at the meeting last night, but of course you weren't there. I was sorry to hear about your friend; that's tough luck. Could you and I get together for a chat?"

"Sure Jim – maybe tomorrow sometime? Say, ten in the morning? That is, unless the cops want me out on the lake first thing. I understand we have a chopper to find."

"Great. Can we meet at your place? This gets busy here sometimes. I'll give you my cell number in case it doesn't work out."

"No worries. I already have it, Jim – on speed-dial in case the marine radios crap out!"

They both laughed and Russell headed back to his store. "Wonder what that's about," he said to Marjorie. "We get along okay but in twenty years we've never really talked longer than a couple of minutes here and there. He always seemed to resent me a bit, like he was afraid I wanted to compete with him."

They headed back along the short narrow road between the marina and Anderson's combined house and workshop, an old but well-maintained wooden building a few yards up the street from the commercial docks where he kept his workboat.

"Well, did you?"

"Did I what?" Arnold unlocked the house and they were going in.

"Did you ever want to have a marina?"

"Hell no. It's an interesting business but you have to be good with the public."

"You're a lot better with the public than you admit, Mr. Anderson."

"I'm also not sure that I even like the public, Ms. Webster!"

Marjorie tapped him on the shoulder while he was

setting up the coffee maker and they shared a long hug. "Well, this member of the public missed the hell out of you and I'm awfully glad you're home."

"Hell, you ain't public – you're family. And yes, it's awfully good to be with you, and at home!"

While the coffee brewed, Anderson emptied out his suitcase, mostly into an already-full plastic tub in the corner of the room behind his bed. "I can see it's laundromat time very soon. From the looks of that pile I only have one change left!"

Marjorie's cellphone began to play Gordon Lightfoot's *If You Could Read My Mind.* She took it out of her pocket and read the text message. "So, Wendy's made it to town and is wondering where we are. I'll tell her to come by here."

"Sounds good. We can sort out the rest of the day – what's left of it – once she gets here. Obviously she'll want you to go with her to your cottage on the island and get settled back in, but I was hoping you and I could have dinner together. Maybe I could pick you up later? Might be a late dinner, but that's okay."

"That sounds like a plan to me. Wendy will understand, of course and... here she comes! That was quick – she must have been just up the street!"

The Webster sisters' Accord pulled up by the door, and Wendy was not alone. "Hi sis, and hi Frank – glad to see you home! Marj, this is Anita - Anita Antoine. Frank already knows her of course but I don't think you and she have met. And we have a plan: Anita and I are going to spend the evening with a couple of laptops doing all the media stuff for the 'Love Our Lake' event. I kind of figured you two would want to spend some time together and maybe have dinner, so we'll just take all the stuff out to the island, have an omelette and a glass of wine and get to work. Then you don't have to worry about me."

Anderson and Marjorie glanced at one another and shrugged happily. "That's perfect," said Anderson. "Marjorie and I were planning to have dinner anyway, either at the Inn or I had thought maybe at that little place by the locks in Maple Falls. Anita – it's really good to see you, and I'm happy to see you're all revved up to help out with the event. I was gonna ask if you'd had a chance to keep up that *Friends of Awan Lake* page on Facebook... I have to confess I haven't checked it recently, but you've got a great following there and it could be especially useful over the next few weeks."

"Yes, I've been checking it out even when I was in hiding, but over the last few days I put a some more time into it. Wendy and I have been back and forth about it on Messenger already... she also wants to use it to promote Love Our Lake day."

Anita paused for a moment, then continued: "Mr. Anderson, I don't really know what to say except that I know I owe you my life and I've probably never thanked you enough for believing in me and not giving up."

Anderson reached out and squeezed her shoulder. "You can thank me best by calling me Frank, or Anderson, but not Mr. Anderson. What little I did was part of a whole bunch of people who believe in you. Just take care of yourself. And thanks for believing in us and your community... I don't expect that's always been easy."

Wendy wanted to get going out to the island, so together all four went to the marina and finished loading the skiff. Marjorie and Anderson then waved the two women off the dock and out onto the lake before walking back to the house to refresh – and re-heat – their coffees. "That was more words in one sentence than I've ever heard Wendy speak," remarked Anderson.

"She gets that way when she's excited. I'm glad to see it, I have to say. She was pretty scattered this week, emotions all over the place. Helping out with the Love Our Lake project has given her a mission, and that's good. It's also nice that she has a new buddy to share her enthusiasm. Anita seems like a real sweetie, if maybe a bit buzzy!"

"Yeah, a bit buzzy would be right. But she has brains and talent to spare, so they're well-matched that way. So, what do you think? Maple Falls by the locks for dinner? I'm not sure if I'm up to going to the Inn tonight. It's not that the memory of my first (and hopefully only) 'kill' has me choked up, but I'd rather not have to explain what happened a week ago to everyone in the bar. Not yet anyway... I don't need to re-live it in technicolour."

"I'm the same, and yes, Maple Falls sounds perfect. We can take the Jeep."

"Cool. Which reminds me: Sam told me this afternoon that there are a couple of kids in town – little more than teenagers – who could be making trouble. That collector's item car of yours, tinted windows and all, is bad-boy bait, so for awhile let's park it inside the shop at night. Better to be safe."

"Maybe a good idea. You got room in there?"

"Oh yeah, it's not as messy as it looks."

"Really?"

"Really."

***

The restaurant at Maple Falls was named, appropriately, 'The Old Lockmaster's House', and was tiny. The proprietors lived on the second floor of the one-and-a-half storey stone house, which was a heritage building presumably leased from the government. For years now, the Lockmaster (and his assistant) have lived elsewhere in town and only used the separate office and storage shed right at the top of the double set of locks along the river. The three rooms that made up the dining area were small, so the maximum seating area was perhaps 20, although in nice weather – like tonight – the big veranda across the front of the house could seat another ten plus a couple of tables on the lawn.

Arnold and Marjorie chose to sit inside, in the smallest room. Their server, a tall middle-aged man dressed in elegantly casual black slacks and button-down shirt with a white tie, introduced himself as Richard and delivered a folder which included the short menu and wine list. "I really like the look of that wine list," said Anderson.

"Me too. Pick one," said Marjorie.

"I am fully experienced with wine varieties. Some are red, and some are white. You choose, please," said Anderson.

Marjorie laughed: "I'm not that much better at this. I am

a passionate believer in eating and drinking Canadian, though, so why don't we ask Richard to suggest a Canadian wine of the colour of our choice. Tonight, I'll go for red."

"Perfect. We'll start with a bottle of red, then."

Richard returned with water and a small note-pad to take their wine order. When Anderson proposed that he choose a nice not-too-sweet Canadian red, he paused for a moment before telling his guests that actually, the restaurant was proud to serve Canadian wines only, and that he recommended a Merlot from Nk'Mip cellars in the Okanagan.

"Thank-you, Richard. Sounds like that would go well with this item: *An 8-ounce rib-eye steak topped with crab and shrimp in a mild cheese and wine sauce, garnished with asparagus tips?*"

"That would indeed be my choice, mademoiselle: a perfect match. Will you be having the same, sir?"

"Sounds great. Steak rare for me please."

"And me. Thank-you. Frank, would you share a plate of scallops for an appetizer?"

"Oh yeah. Any day!"

"Thank you. I'll bring your wine right away and get this order to my husband, who is our chef tonight."

"Thanks Richard," said Anderson. "And the washrooms

are... where?"

The server indicated a short hallway off the main room, and headed for the kitchen.

"I was going to say it's not very busy here this evening, but I see two couples have just sat down together on the porch, and a third couple is settling into the next room, so they do have some customers even on a Tuesday night. Good for them!"

"Well, I imagine they get quite a lot of trade from cruisers coming through the locks and tying up overnight. Awan Lake is the turning point on their cruise – there's nowhere else to go – so they'll maybe spend a day or two on the lake then head back downstream."

"Don't those cruisers have kitchens?"

"Well, yes, but most of the cruisers that come up this way are only 30 or so feet long. There is only so much joy in cooking endless meals in a galley the size of a broom closet. These folks are on vacation, so they'll only do what feels like fun. Most, though not all by any means, have lots of disposable income or they wouldn't be here at all, so a place like this, dear as it is compared to the Zoo, will seem like a marvellous bargain to them if their home is Toronto, or Montreal, or even somewhere in New York!"

***

Marjorie and Anderson spent two hours over dinner and another hour or better after dusk at a table out on the lawn where they sipped brandy (for her) and Southern Comfort (for him) with coffee and cigarettes.

They talked at length about the house in Toronto that had meant so much to the sisters. They had grown up there, to be sure, but it had seemed to embrace – perhaps even dominate – them ever since. "I don't believe in ghosts, really, but it always felt like we had to ask Dad if we wanted to paint a wall," Marjorie had said. "I'm not sure I want to live in his shadow anymore, and certainly Wendy feels the same way, especially now that she is seriously thinking about getting out of her business. That whole episode three weeks ago, when she became aware of her client Robertson Mine's ethics with regard to the environment, snapped a string in her mind somewhere, and that only got worse when it appeared they were also turning a blind eye to international drug trafficking and people were getting killed. That stuff is not her, it never was Dad, and it ain't mine either, so we have been sort of thinking about new directions, in a rather scattered way."

"That could explain her growing passion to help with the Love Our Lake event and the Protected Shorelines

Project," Anderson commented.

Marjorie agreed: "Exactly. And it's cute to see her excitement, too. She's fun again, not all serious about her staff and her work and her clients all the time."

As Anderson drove them back from Maple Falls, he was quiet for a few moments. "You okay?" she asked.

"Oh, yeah. Sorry... my mind had wandered back to the whole Robertson Mines thing. Like Wendy, maybe, I'm putting two and two together and thinking about just how seriously they are taking this event we're planning. It's going to be very public with all sorts of television I expect, but do we know whether it really might impact a multi-million dollar project. Is the project even on the drawing board, or is it just a discussion at corporate headquarters somewhere? Are they really pissed off or just grumbling 'cause that's what corporations do? Of course I'm concerned about the lake and all that (without knowing a lot about environmental impacts) but right now I am concerned about the community and the people like Wendy and Anita – and Marion and Arnold for that matter. Maybe I should have a chat with Arnold – and Sergeant John – tomorrow."

It was Marjorie's turn to be quiet for a few moments. "I'd like to be able to say there's nothing to be concerned about, but now that you mention it, I wonder. Let's make those calls, in the morning. For now, let's curl up together in your nice warm bed... I'm beat and tipsy, but not too tired or drunk to want to cuddle up to your naked body!"

Which is exactly what happened, but not before Anderson stuffed Marjorie's jeep into the workshop and locked the doors.

06:37 AUGUST 2

Marjorie woke slowly, with a slight headache. She gently removed the hand which enveloped her left breast and slithered out from under the big arm that held her pinned to the bed. She turned over and stared at the man who lay beside her, snoring gently. *Yesterday, I wondered if I was falling in love with this guy, but this morning I know I am.* She smiled to herself, remembering her parents – who were always fiercely in love – moving into separate bedrooms because of his snoring; she and Wendy had been devastated, until they realized it had nothing to do with love or lack thereof: it had to do with getting a good night's sleep. *Maybe, if I am lucky, that will be the story for us. But not yet!*

At 06:43, her thoughts were interrupted by a persistent and loud knock on the front door. She shook Anderson by the shoulder and quickly got out of bed, looking something to wear... well, a blanket for now. She peered out the window and saw Arnold on the porch step.

"Frank, Arnold is here. He looks worried." She shook

him again, wrapped herself up in the blanket and headed for the door as Anderson rolled over and said "Huh?"

"It's Arnold... better get up!" She unlocked and opened the door. "Morning, Arnold! We're a bit late this morning!"

"I am so sorry, but we just have to talk! Wake the old bugger up and I'll put on the coffee. I really am sorry, Marjorie!"

Anderson was already on his feet, pulling on his blue jeans, socks and a t-shirt. He came across to the big table: "Hi Arnold, what's up?"

"Marion is getting threatening phone calls, voicemail and texts. There was one early last night but we didn't consider it to mean anything and just turned off her phone. There were a bunch more when she turned it on this morning. The only thing we could figure out was that someone is getting Marion's number off the Love Our Lake poster, some of which went up in Maple Falls yesterday afternoon. Sergeant John called a few minutes ago to say that he saw a poster when he picked up his coffee, and someone had written all over it in black marking pen. Just two words: 'Socialist Bullshit'. Oh, and the Sergeant is coming directly here in a few minutes. I told him to bring donuts 'cause we were gonna have to wake you up. Nothing more dangerous than waking up a hungry bear!"

"Poor Marion," Marjorie called from the bedroom corner of the loft-style single room house. "She must be pretty upset... she should at least make sure her voicemail message doesn't have her name."

"Actually she changed it a few years ago – it only gives back the number. I wondered why back then and she just said she was tired of giving the political robo-call geniuses any more information than they already had. Good decision, it turns out. And Frank, this morning Sergeant John mumbled about needing to talk to you this morning anyway – something about getting that helicopter off the bottom of the lake."

"Yeah, no rest for the wicked, I guess. I had promised him I'd get at that project as soon as I got back from the coast."

"And here he comes!" Having put on some clothes, Marjorie was pouring herself some coffee. "Guess I'll pour him a cup too – he says he likes your coffee better than Timmy's."

Sure enough, Sgt. John MacLeod's white and black cruiser had pulled up to the house beside Arnold's battered old truck, and the Sergeant was soon knocking at the door. Anderson called out, "Hey John, it's open – come on in!"

"Good morning folks... Marjorie, Frank, glad to see you

47

back. How was the wet coast?"

"Surprisingly dry, actually. Had sunshine both days. Regardless, I'd much rather be back here, even if we have the occasional 'Awan' day."

"'Awan' day?"

"Yes. 'Awan' is, after all, the word for 'foggy' in Ojibwe and they call this Awan Lake. So yeah, often enough it lives up to its name!"

The Sergeant plopped down a large box of fresh donuts, on top of which were a couple of slightly crumpled glossy posters. "Looks like they only marked up two of the posters. I saw a couple of others around The Falls this morning and they were okay. And then there's Monday afternoon's tire-slashing exercise out behind the Zoo here in the village. That's all kid stuff, but I'm treating these as connected events somehow. Just a hunch... the young folks whose tires were slashed were pulling a small boat on a trailer, and had been out on the lake doing something for Ryerson University, apparently."

"The late Mr. Mistraika's nephews, I think. Sam told me about them yesterday when Marjorie and I stopped in at the Zoo on our way home. Warned me they were trouble, and he did mention something about tire slashing in the village. That's why Marjorie's Black Beast is parked in my shop instead of out beside the house."

"Black Beast?" Something I need to know about?"

"Relax, John! Marjorie's father had a black 1980s Jeep Wagoneer with tinted windows, which she re-registered so she and Wendy could have separate vehicles up here. It's in beautiful condition and purrs like a kitten. It's perfect kid-bait, so we stuffed it into the shop."

"Likely a good move, in any case. Yeah, those boys are Rodney and David Mistraika, and they are trouble. They traded high school in The Falls for a year of juvie in North Bay a couple of years back. I'm not allowed to tell anyone this, of course, so your lips are sealed, right?"

"Never heard a word. But – tell me a bit more about those kids from Ryerson. Any idea what they were doing on the lake?"

Arnold shook his head: "No details, but they said they were taking water samples for the university. That was Monday afternoon that I talked to them, and Dave Bradshaw from Ryerson was at the meeting that night and didn't mention anything. Which makes me think... Frank, remind me to tell you about the meeting – which I wish to hell you could have been at. You, especially, would have enjoyed the part that featured Ronnie the Mayor and the Three Stooges!"

"Oh good grief. I wondered when that idiot was going

to turn up long enough to find out what was going on in his village. Who were the stooges?"

"Three local landowners. Actually, only one of them is a village resident, but all of them have potential development land nearby."

"Figures. And the paranoid in me says that Awan Lake, defaced posters, slashed tires and threatening messages may all have a connection."

"No, you're not paranoid. You're just beginning to think like a damn cop! It's a condition we all share," added the Sergeant.

Marjorie had been listening quietly, and wandered across to refuel the coffee maker. "Would you like me to call Dave Bradshaw? I don't have his contact, but I actually know him, and could probably get out of him what he might know about those research kids and the water tests."

"That would be great, Marjorie. Arnold, do you have Dave's contacts?"

Arnold suggested she give Marion a call, as he was sure she had Bradshaw's cell number in Monday's meeting minutes.

Anderson, in the meantime, had become deeply involved with a jelly-filled donut. "Do they still call these things 'Bismarcks'? I love 'em, but I'm gonna need a bath towel and a bucket."

***

Just over two hours later, Anderson's workboat was nearing a long sparsely-treed island some fifteen miles south of the village. His passengers were Marjorie and a young OPS officer whom the Sergeant had detailed to assist Anderson with the search for the helicopter. On their way, a couple of miles south of the village, they had met up briefly with Wendy and Anita who were enroute back to the village in the Webster sisters' outboard skiff. They had apparently had a busy and enjoyable night preparing media releases they wanted to send out this morning, but the internet and cell connection had been vandalized and had not been replaced, so they were going to Marion's office to use her computer.

The Sergeant had decided he should stay onshore to attend to what was a growing pile of potential problems, so he had called for his newest recruit to be part of the chopper search. Officer Bradley Foreman was a compactly-built man in his mid-twenties, friendly but quiet with dark eyes which looked everywhere and seemed to miss nothing.

"I set a waypoint on the GPS pretty close to where the chopper sank. We were right there because we were rescuing the crew, but setting the waypoint was not a priority in all the fuss and there was a stiff breeze blowing with waves to match, so I could be a couple of hundred meters out. It's a lot nicer out here today, so I'll do my best to run a grid with the sidescan sonar turned on and hope we don't take all day out here before we nail it. Brad – and Marjorie – there is about 100 feet of light rope coiled up over there, with a chunk of steel for an anchor and a red float. That's what we'll use as a mark when we do find it."

Anderson throttled back the engine in stages until they were right at the waypoint, moving dead slow. "Okay folks, like I explained away back when we started, the GPS is showing over two screens now, one small in front of me and a bigger one to the side. You guys choose one, and stay glued to it. I'll be mostly driving and watching the grid... I'm counting on you two to be my underwater eyes."

"Glub," said Marjorie. Bradley-the-cop smiled.

The boat was headed east after the third turn on the grid, and not far from the waypoint when the two sets of eyes spoke up, almost in unison: "There's something!"

Anderson pulled the transmission shift into neutral immediately. He could now see the irregular shape on the bottom, appearing to rise perhaps eight feet off the sandy floor. "Okay – get ready with that marker. We're almost right over it and I want the anchor and rope well clear because the next step is dragging with hooks." There was a short pause as they prepared to send over the anchor. "Okay, in about ten seconds... now!"

Anderson put the boat in gear and moved a few yards further east, and downwind, before putting it back in neutral. He checked over the engine instruments, joined the others on deck and took a pack of cigarettes out of his pocket. He offered them around, and lit one for himself. "That's one of the fastest searches I've ever experienced. Usually it takes hours, sometimes days. Just got lucky setting the waypoint in the middle of all the fuss last week, I guess. I've been known to stab the button and not have it set."

"No kidding," Marjorie remarked. "Looking around, all I see is blue water for miles and a long, low, gray, scrubby – and featureless – island. The world is somewhat short of landmarks around here, so let's hear it for technology!"

"Yeah, it's kind of shapeless, isn't it," put in the young police officer. "Not like that little island we passed that you live on, Ms. Webster. It looks like an old fashioned ship from a distance."

"Exactly!" chuckled Anderson, "That's why I call it 'Ship Island' but everyone looks at me like I'm nuts. Say, Brad, is that a satellite telephone you're carrying? Or can you reach one of your coms towers from here? Maybe let the Sergeant know we've located his chopper."

"Does anyone live on this big island here?"

Anderson was rummaging around in one of the hatches, so Marjorie answered, "No, apparently it's a wildlife sanctuary, mostly birds I expect. Nobody is supposed to land on it."

Anderson had produced two coils of half-inch nylon rope, to which he quickly tied two awkward-looking four-point hooks about ten inches across. They were made of concrete reinforcing rod and were designed so they would drag behind the rope and hook onto anything they could snag underwater. He set one set of rope and hooks at each corner at the stern of the boat and fastened the loose end to the mooring cleats.

"Okay, we're ready for the next step, dragging the bottom to see if we can hook onto the chopper. Any luck reaching the office, Brad?"

"Yup... they were going to pass along the message. The boss is out on the road somewhere."

"Cool, thanks. Might as well get at this. I've tied these ropes to the boat, but if you could each hold the rope with a bit of slack so you can "feel" the bottom, that would help. Whatever you do, don't hang on tight... just let it go if it snags. I'm pulling two grappling hooks, about 11 feet apart, which may be stupid because it would be easy for them to tangle. And we'll pull them up every time we turn because I sure don't want the ropes tied up in the propeller. I'll turn around, get aimed in the right direction and tell you to drop the hooks. And I am going to be going really slow 'cause I don't want to hook something and break the rope, either!"

Once they were dragging, Bradley and Marjorie could feel the hooks roll around and jump on the bottom which (according to the sonar) was sandy gravel with a few small rocks and no boulders. On the fifth pass, just north of the marker they had put down, Brad's rope snapped taut and he yelled forward. Anderson pulled the lever into neutral and yelled back, "Okay Brad, keep tension on the rope, just like you're playing a big Muskie. I'll be there in a sec..."

Before he left the wheelhouse he checked the sonar: yes, the screen showed they had just passed over the wreckage. "According to specs, these EC135s weigh about 3500 pounds empty so it should be easy to bring the chopper up under the boat using that electric winch over the transom. Getting it onboard may be harder – I have that hydraulic crane behind the wheelhouse which has that kind of capacity as long as the lifted object is not too far from the side. It's worth a try – bringing the barge out here is a longer process.

I've put some dunnage onboard here to avoid banging up the boat too bad if we get to dragging the chopper over the side."

***

Three hours later, they had managed to pull the helicopter, minus one rotor blade, over the side of the 40-foot workboat, lashed it on to the deck and were almost back at the village. There were indeed a few new scrapes on the boat. Marjorie had thoroughly rope-burned her hands pulling on a tagline that almost got away, and Anderson had cut his arm on a chunk of broken aluminum. The young police officer had worked like a beaver to help at everything, all the while taking photos and make notes as his commanding officer had directed.

Anderson had used the officer's satellite phone to call the Sergeant, and suggested that he have a truck and a picker crane down at the dock to lift off the chopper and get it away from curious onlookers as soon as possible. Sure enough, as they neared the village they could see the necessary equipment in place, plus two police cruisers parked in such a way that onlookers were discouraged from getting too close. When they landed, they could see the Sergeant among the officers, and they stepped forward to help tie up the workboat and its awkward-looking cargo with the OPS logo in plain view.

"That one ain't gonna fly again anytime soon," he commented to Anderson and the somewhat weary crew. "At least, not from the bullet holes I can already see along the side, through the tank and up to the motor. They peppered her pretty good! We brought along a big tarp to secure it away from prying eyes for travel to the compound. It's just a wrecked airplane, but it is evidence after all."

The crane operator knew his job well, and after the long afternoon it seemed like only minutes to get the wreck clear of the deck and onto a waiting flat-bed trailer. The Sergeant came over to Anderson privately and asked, "How was our new recruit?"

"He was really good, worked his buns off and seems very responsible. And he has a sense of humour too!"

The Sergeant then went to his young officer and told him to oversee tying down the cargo to the trailer, take photos and notes and follow it to the OPS compound to offload it. "Make sure you document the chain of custody. And... thank-you Brad. Sounds like a job well done."

"We left one rotor blade on the bottom," Anderson said, "probably roughly in the same place. I left my marker buoy over the site, and of course I still have it on GPS, just in case you need to send a diver down for some reason."

"Good to know. I doubt we'll need more scrap from the bottom, since the bad guys were never in contact with it. And you have pulled up the engine, fuel tank and transmission, so there'll be no more leakage. Thanks, Frank. And... can we get together after you're shut down and tied up?"

"You bet. We'll need maybe half an hour. Things are kind of a mess onboard."

***

Anderson had to be pretty stern to get Marjorie to head up to the house and put some ointment on her hands, which were red and blistered, but she did agree to go. He spent the next twenty minutes coiling ropes, putting things away under hatches, "folding" the hydraulic crane back against the wheelhouse, and checking over his engine fluids including fuel which, surprisingly, was at two-thirds of a tank. He wrote in the ship's log for a few minutes, locked the wheelhouse and the safety chain, and walked home.

The Sergeant was already there – along with Wendy, Arnold, Marion and a case of beer. He walked in his front door and said, "Hey, party-time!"

They all looked rather serious for people who were

supposed to be relaxing after a long day. "Open a well-deserved beer and let's talk. I am not a hundred percent sure if this is a police matter – yet – but I have not been wrong over the last few weeks listening to hunches from you folks in Spirit River, so I hesitate to write off what I am hearing as paranoia. Arnold and Marion, why don't you start by telling us about a couple of the calls you have received today."

Arnold nodded. "Frank, you will remember meeting that LaChance fellow from Environment Canada at Gatineau about three weeks ago? Pierre?"

"The nice guy who read us the riot act about the Protected Shorelines Project, then took us out to Starbucks and gave us some off-the-record suggestions? Yes, I do. That was the birth of the Love Our Lake event."

"Okay, just after lunch today I got a call from him, saying he wanted to see us, in private and confidentially. He planned on driving out here. I asked him if I could reach him on his cell, and he said no, he was on a burner, and definitely not to call his office or regular cell numbers. He said he expected to be in Spirit River by supper time, and that he would call me."

"Wow, that's just plain weird for a government guy," piped up Wendy. "I've read about that kind of stuff, but thought it was only fodder for spy mysteries. However, also today, I had a call from my assistant – who I hope like hell is buying my company any day now – who wanted to pick my brain about what's going on at the senior management level of my former client, Robertson Mines. She told me they're weird, which is not news to me. And, I didn't tell her anything she didn't already know, which isn't much. Apparently they are trying to find out from her why I had resigned as their public relations consultant, and if I had shared inside information about the firm with her."

It was Marion's turn: "So it's my turn to talk about creepy stuff. I didn't get any more threatening calls like last night, but I got one that is even scarier. At about two o'clock (sorry Frank, 1400 hours) I got a call from an over-friendly lady from the Clean Water Association of Canada Incorporated. First I figured she was fund-raising – like most of those outfits – then I figured she wanted in on the Love Our Lake event in two weeks, but soon I realized she was trying to get information – not money. She wanted to know all about who is putting on the event, who are the major players on the board of trade, were there any clean-water research projects going on, and so on. I played really dumb and said I would get our chairperson to call her back. She left me a number, which I immediately called back and it went to a generic 'out of service' message. Incidentally, her calling number had been blocked on my call-display."

Wendy was giggling: "No organization – non-profit or otherwise – would ever register a corporate name like that! Look at the acronym: CWACI, which reads out-loud as "See Whacky". Can't take that seriously, which means we may need to take it seriously for other reasons." Wendy was glancing down at her phone: "FYI, I just looked it up and no, it doesn't exist. So who, and why, is someone snooping around anonymously?"

Marjorie also had something to add: "I reached Dave Bradshaw from Ryerson half an hour ago. He told me he had persuaded a doctoral student to put together a targeted water-quality research project on Awan Lake. He said he wasn't the project supervisor, so he couldn't be certain, but it was very likely those young folks with the boat and trailer were post-grad technicians on the project. He also said he'd make more enquiries."

The Sergeant seemed lost in thought for a long moment. He checked his watch and stood up: "Okay, there is a lot to talk about, and a few wait-and-sees. I need to get out of here, because when that LaChance guy gets here, seeing a police cruiser parked outside the door will likely give him a heart attack! I think that whatever information he brings will answer a lot of questions about all this stuff. Typically, career bureaucrats don't buy burner phones and drive their private cars three hours down a secondary highway to meet people off-the-record, so we can be pretty sure something is shaking, somewhere, big-time."

"I agree." Arnold looked across at Anderson: "Should we meet him here, or at the Zoo or the Inn maybe? And should it just be you and I, since just the two of us met him last time?"

"Let's make it easy for him – when he calls, we can meet him at the Zoo, which is not an unusual place to meet someone. Depending on what we learn in the first ten minutes, we can suggest we come back here and meet privately with the people who are close to the project, like Marjorie and Wendy – and you too John, if you can stay."

The Sergeant smiled. "Thanks for that thought, but outside this circle of friends, I may get jammed into reporting up the ladder. I'd rather you folks include me informally with what you learn, and we can keep everything in context. You be SMEEs, I be cop!"

"SMEE's"? asked Wendy.

"S-M-E, or Subject Matter Expert."

"Ah. I see."

***

As it turned out, they met Pierre LaChance at the Zoo and he didn't want to see anyone else at all. The three of them had ham quiche for supper, and in fact LaChance only met with them for a short hour. Once LaChance's car had turned the corner onto the highway back to Ottawa, Anderson turned to Arnold: "Wow! That guy was as nervous as a bunny rabbit at a beagle convention."

"Considering what he told us, I'm not surprised. We'd better fill in the three ladies – I texted Marion once we knew he wanted to meet alone and I suggested they head to the Inn for supper, so I think we'll find them there, munching on burgers and sipping on wine."

Twenty minutes later they had re-joined Marjorie, Wendy and Marion. They had been joined by Anita, and the six of them were the only customers in the Inn's lounge. Georgina Antoine – Anita's mother – was serving, and she said they had beaten the evening post-supper crowd. "They usually don't come in until closer to 9:30 or 10:00."

Before Anderson could begin, Wendy flapped her hands: "So, before you two tell us what's up in Ottawa, I have news from Toronto, just in the last half hour. Remember I told you earlier about my former assistant being quizzed by the folks at Robertson Mines? Well, the shit must have really hit the fan because she was told an hour ago that the General Manager of Operations at the Awan Lake facility – Maurice Bonner – had just been fired, around noon. Of course Jenny wasn't told any official reasons, but she did say it sounded like he was simply incompetent, allowing staff to get embroiled with drug trafficking and for hiring local goons to intimidate people."

Anderson chuckled. "Thank-you, Wendy, that sorta makes my day! Although, I guess we'll never know whether his incompetence was in allowing those things to happen, or in getting caught and becoming the company fall guy."

"It's strange," Marion chimed in, "that as a village – officially – and as a community of neighbours we have so little knowledge of who is living around here and what they do. Robertson Mines is our biggest employer, and we didn't even know the name of the boss until he gets fired."

"Careful, woman," Arnold laughed, "you're beginning to sound like you want to be our next mayor!"

"Don't listen to Uncle, Aunty Marion. You'd be wonderful! You'd be 'way better than Klassen!"

Anderson grinned at Anita: "That's not exactly a resounding endorsement, Anita! There's a tomcat down the street who has more imagination that our current mayor!" He held up his hand: "Okay, hang on folks, we'd better share what we heard from our Ottawa visitor. It's fascinating, but it sure ain't very good."

Georgina brought beer for the boys, wine for two of the girls, and ginger ale for her daughter. "Her idea," she shrugged. "Probably a good one."

"Yup, one glass of wine per day," laughed Wendy, "and she's already had it!"

Anderson began: "First and worst, we will be served tomorrow with a document that shuts down our Protected Shorelines Project immediately and demands a reimbursement of the advance for this year's student and intern salaries..." The sense of shock around the table was palpable. "Bastards!" someone muttered. Anderson continued, "...and the official reasons are 'endangering the well-being of student employees' and 'improperly managing the protection of vulnerable persons'."

Anita was on the edge of quivering with rage: "It's that fucking bitch Cyndi. She's such a wimp! The cry-baby probably wouldn't admit..."

"I think they played her – I agree she seemed like a bit of a wimp, but I think they played her because they needed something more politically defensible than the real reason they dumped us."

"And that is?"

"Corporate pressure from the Robertson Group, playing

on cabinet ministers from B.C. and Quebec. And foreign affairs was getting poked by the American government as well. Makes me wonder if that local firing of the general manager was just a cover action, not that I wouldn't agree the local guy was possibly incompetent. This was away above his pay grade anyway."

Arnold had been silent so far, but he turned to Marion: "Can we manage to give Adumbi some work for awhile? He's awfully useful and willing, and he is well on top of the event planning."

"Yeah, we can make it work. Frank, you got anything out there?"

"Yup, I can think of a few projects that he could do, and that I never get around to. If we're going that way, let's get him in first thing in the morning so he doesn't hear about this from someone else first. And, I wonder how long we have to pay that money back – it's probably five or six grand, right Marion?"

"Probably. Not to worry, though, I'm pretty sure we have enough in the Project account."

Wendy was busy scribbling in her ever-present notepad. "You guys are amazing. You believe in what you're doing, and you believe in each other, things that have not been part of my line of work over the last twenty years." She was on the edge of tears, and both her sister and Anita put a hand on her arm. She smiled at them, and continued: "However, the media-relations-crafty-sneaky part of me wonders how we can make sure we're on top of any advantage, and ready to get out ahead of any story. I wonder if the feds will do a release, or if not, what is their back-up position if the press gets on their case."

"LaChance came to warn us what was going down, and I believe he kinda hoped we could make something out of it that might help the cause. He came today because he, too, believes in what we are doing and doesn't want us to fail. So yes, Wendy, Anita, everybody... let's give this some serious thought over the next day or so. Marion, the document will be served to the Project at our office in the garage, in the morning. That's the only physical address they have. Annette Dubois will come out to serve it... we know her pretty well. She'll be disappointed, she really liked the work we've been doing."

10:00 AUGUST 3

Anderson put on a fresh pot of coffee in anticipation of his meeting with Jim Russell from the marina, a meeting he had postponed yesterday because of the chopper search. Twelve hours ago, Anita had gone home with her mother; Wendy and Marjorie had got into their skiff and gone back out to their home on Ship Island; and Anderson had come back to his house, checked the emails he hadn't looked at for almost a week, and gone to bed. Today he had to meet Jim, then Sam at the Zoo, then he was headed out to Ship Island to check out the repairs needed on the Webster sisters' cottage and dock and make a list of needed materials. At 10:02, Jim Russell tapped on his front door.

"Hi Jim, come on in. Coffee's just about ready, so let's sit here at the table."

"Man, that's a lovely big table. Where did you find it, or did you make it?"

Arnold chuckled: "No way did I make it. I'm not good at stuff that I can't build with a chainsaw and a big hammer! Actually, I bought it at an auction at Maple Falls just after I got here. It was a rectory table from the old monastery that used to be just north of town, and I guess I was the only person bidding who actually had room for it!"

"You've done nice things to the old Awan Lake Boat Works shop. Nice to see it being used instead of torn down. And this part that's your house – it's huge, like a loft – just one room!"

"Thanks Jim, it works for me. Not sure if it's a great place to raise a family, but fine for a grumpy old bachelor! So, what's on your mind?"

"I'll get right to it: have you ever wanted to be in the marina business?"

Anderson was pouring coffee, but he didn't even hesitate: "Good grief no! I don't have the patience with people that you have, and I don't want to work the endless hours that you work!"

"But you work for the same people all the time – cottagers and tourists, and they love you!"

"There's a difference, a big difference, Jim. Everything I do out there is a one-off, or maybe I get several jobs from good customers, but all those jobs have a start and end point. They don't live in my pocket hour by hour, day in and day out. It must drive you crazy... it would me!"

Anderson paused a brief moment, then asked, "Are you trying to sell? Getting tired of it after all these years? You've been here longer than I have."

"Well, in fact I don't have much to sell anyway. Back in 2000, there was a real dip in the economy around here when Robertson Mines shut down for a couple of years and laid a bunch of folks off. I remember you had just moved here a couple of years before. Anyway, I almost went under but someone – I think Florence Dubois at the Inn – told her brother-in-law Leonard Hamilton and he offered to invest in the marina, at the same time he took over control of the Inn. The mine started back up again, and things went well after that. We made pretty good money, but it seemed I was never in a position to buy back control – Leonard still owns 51%"

"So some Ottawa bureaucrat owns the Inn and has you and the marina by the short and curlies?"

"Well, kind of, yeah. And Leonard added his wife's name to his and became Leonard Hamilton-Dubois, because he thought it would help him move up in the civil service. Must have worked – he's an ADM at the Ministry of Natural Resources. He's been there for years, and apparently makes buckets of money from investments. He's certainly made his pound of flesh from me each year, and I think the Inn makes him good money too!"

"Geez. Who knew! So now, you're trying to retire and need to sell your shares, or what?"

"Yes. My old lady inherited a nice little farmhouse near Arnprior and we'd just like to get off the treadmill. Trouble is, Leonard gets to approve or reject whoever buys me out. A few weeks ago he even suggested I talk to you – he sure as hell doesn't want to run it himself. I told him at the time that I thought your reaction would be pretty much what you just said, but he pushed me on it – so here I am!"

"Well, Jim, I really don't think anything would change my mind, and on top of what I said, I know I don't want to run something like that as a minority shareholder. I'll think about it a bit, but if I were you I'd keep looking for someone else!"

Jim drank down his coffee and stood up. "Thanks for hearing me out, Anderson. You've always been a good neighbour, even if we don't talk much. I gotta get back to the store, but maybe we can talk again."

Anderson reached out and shook hands. "Thanks for thinking of me, Jim. It ain't like its a bad idea, but probably not a good fit for me. Too much going on at the moment!"

After Russell had gone, he sat down on the porch with his coffee and a cigarette, and thought carefully about what he had learned. *Bureaucrats. Never have trusted them, and the higher up they are in the food chain, the scarier they get. And Mr. double-barrelled-last-name is in the natural resources ministry and has money. Things to think about.*

Twenty minutes later he headed up to the Zoo. It was still morning coffee time but Sam had a young student serving his customers so they went out on the back stoop where they could talk.

"Mr. Anderson, the only trouble with having a restaurant in a small town is that I get to hear things. Sometimes that's fun, and sometimes it's sad, but sometimes it's also scary. I was taught in my culture that nice people mind their own business, but even really nice people never do."

"Don't get all philosophical on me, Sam," Anderson laughed, "and please call me Frank. And tell me what seems scary."

"People. Groups of people in suits, and expensive cars. I know lots of our summer people here have expensive cars and they probably have expensive suits too but they never wear them around here. These people come in here and talk quietly, and then go outside and talk some more standing beside their cars. They never talk to anyone local. Oh, they are polite, almost friendly and they tip well, but they just seem, well, strange!"

"How long has this been going on?"

"Two or three weeks maybe, since before all that stuff

happened."

"You have a camera over the counter aimed at the door. Do you keep the video keys or disks?"

"Oh heavens no. It's a fake. I just have it so strangers don't hassle the staff."

Anderson paused a moment, then: "If it's okay with you, Sam, I'd like to change that. I'd like to put in a real camera. There is some strange stuff going on, and of course there's that big event coming up in ten days. Might be a good idea to be able to check up on stuff. Those things aren't expensive, so I'll pay for it – I need to get one for my house too. Is that okay?"

"That might be a good thing. Much better than a fake, anyway."

***

At the Arlington Seafood and Steak House near the Ronald Reagan National Airport south of downtown Washington, DC, the late luncheon crowd were beginning to settle their tabs and head back to their offices, or perhaps to make their afternoon tee times. Three men in summer suits were finishing their main course at a corner table: Jeremiah Lawrence, CFO of the Global Conservation Society; James Karsh, President of Water Source International; and Harold

Benson, Chief Executive at Robertson Group International. Benson raised his cocktail glass and tilted it toward each of his guests in turn: "Thank-you for agreeing to meet me here today. Jeremiah, you know how much we at Robertson Group International value the terrific work you do to raise the importance of good environmental conservation measures around the world, and often in regions where we have branches and facilities!"

Turning to the man on his left, he continued: "And James, it is a pleasure to meet you for the first time, in your new capacity as President. The growth of Water Source International has been an inspiration to your colleagues in the business world. Seldom has a five-year start-up had such a steady growth curve, matching your business model to the greater goal of ensuring that people the world over will be able to feel they have a safe and secure source of drinking water. Welcome to your new leadership role in moving society's global interests forward!"

"There is a cloud on the horizon, however... at the moment just a blip on the radar, but it has the potential to distract us along our shared journey. You are both aware, I am sure, of the single-minded campaign against us led entirely by one man: Dr. Sebastian Horowitz. I always chuckle at the "Doctor" thing, because he is a doctor of medicine in pediatrics, not a PhD in aquatic science, or even biology. The media, of course, fawn all over him because he is – admittedly – a passionate speaker. His speeches and books have never really caught fire in the USA and Canada, because his focus points usually touched on South America and Europe. However, that cloud I mentioned now has the potential to create a storm in the heart of North America – Ontario – and a scant hundred miles or so from Toronto, Canada's only metropolis and indeed one of the largest cities in North America."

Benson paused before continuing, ensuring he had eye contact with each of his guests: "I know you will agree with me when I say we need to meet this head on, and we don't have much time because he is giving a major speech in less than two weeks, and media is already beginning to talk about it. The most obvious way forward, in my view, is to thoroughly discredit Horowitz, and the best way to do that will be to have real scientists – statisticians perhaps – from the world's foremost conservation society call into question his credentials, pointing out that his enthusiasm is welcome but he could not possibly – given his lack of scientific training – understand the global implications of his over-simplistic viewpoint. I trust, Jeremiah, that you are following me here?"

The GCS representative paused for a moment, then said quietly, "Yes, I follow exactly, but nonetheless I am concerned that it may be difficult to persuade our academic and research chairs to speak critically of a man who has been a widely-acknowledged opinion-leader for conservation."

Benson took a sip from his water glass and continued: "Understood, of course, and you raise an important point. Remember that our corporation also engages the services of scientists – full-time as well as on contract – who assess the impacts of our projects worldwide, and also remember that neither the public nor the media are able to contribute to GCS at the level you need to continue with your important work. This is a big-picture issue, and the media needs to be fed, as does your society in a different way. Forward-thinking corporations such as Water Source International and the Robertson Group like to work with organizations we can count upon to look at the larger picture."

James Karsh of Water Source shifted slightly in his chair. He was very new to this job, and had been a financial leader in his former positions and so had not dealt so much with the cut-and-thrust of inter-corporate politics. But he was not totally naive: "You make a really good point, Harold. This has huge implications for us all – and for the future of the conservation initiatives of GCS as well – if we don't find a way to move appropriately and quickly."

"Well said, James. Alright, I think we all understand each other. James, would you work out an action plan with Jeremiah by week's end so we can put it in place on Monday? I have to travel this afternoon to Argentina for two days of meetings, but nevertheless I'll be following up on this closely over that time. You both have my contacts.

"And now," he closed," glancing at his watch, "I do need to get to Dulles International in time for my flight. Thank you again, gentlemen, for meeting with me. Our tab is all taken care of."

***

After consuming a plate of fish and chips at the Zoo, Anderson drove his battered Chevy S-10 pickup over to the Spirit River Co-Op where he loaded the slip-tank with diesel and headed down to the dock. Wendy had called him from the island to ask him to pick up Anita and bring her with him, so he detoured a couple of blocks to pick her up at her parents' home on Willow Road.

When they got to the dock, Anderson topped off the workboat's fuel tank, checked the motor-oil levels on the main engine and generator and the reservoir level for the pump that operated the hydraulic crane. He started both engines, checked the gauges and recorded the information in the boat's logbook before casting off and heading out of the harbour toward Ship Island.

Anita had been leaning against the side of the wheelhouse, gazing out across the lake. Anderson set the autopilot on the course to the island and joined her on deck. "It's so beautiful out here on the lake," she said above the growl of the diesel engine. "Whenever I'm out here, I imagine myself the luckiest person in the world. The only sad thing is that all the people I went to school with have gone off to the cities to work. And for most of them it wasn't because they had some big plan or wanted to go to university, but because they simply wanted to get away from here. I think they're dummies!"

Anderson smiled at his young passenger. "Well, from this viewpoint, I have to agree with you. But folks go through changes. I spent years and years at everything from Coast Guard to logging to driving semis and even working in an office before moving and settling here. Now, like you, I can't imagine being anywhere else, but life out there in the big bad world taught me stuff I still find useful."

"I learn stuff all the time. Mostly from books, but also by talking with people from that big bad world. Perhaps that's why I admire Wendy so much. She has lots of life to share and her brain never stops thinking!"

Anderson chuckled aloud: "Yeah, I don't think my old brain could keep up with Wendy. She's always got something going on in that head of hers. You guys are well-matched!"

"And she's a sweetie, too. Maybe I shouldn't tell stories out of school, but she thinks you're the best thing that ever happened to her sister!"

"Poor Marjorie – her sister must have set the bar pretty low! I'm 'way past my best-before date, but I do have to say I am really glad we've met."

It was a hot afternoon without any perceptible wind. The normally deep blue lake shimmered silver, with clusters of tiny dark ripples from invisible breezes skating here and there across the surface. The drone of the diesel and the steady swish of the bow-wave made it seem they were almost still, and that Ship Island was approaching them instead of the other way around. The illusion was somewhat intoxicating, and Anderson forced himself to snap out of it and attend to slowing down the boat, giving a couple of short blasts on the horn, and preparing to land.

The dock was sort of an illusion too. The wooden cribbing was in rough shape, and the walkway twisted and sagged throughout its length to the shore. It was just fine for the little outboard skiff the Webster sisters used, but Anderson was always more than cautious landing his several-ton boat alongside. By the time Anita had helped him tie up, Marjorie and Wendy – both in bright red bathing suits and sandals – had made it to the dock to greet the new arrivals. "Well, Anita," Anderson remarked loudly as they stepped onto the rickety platform, "this must be how the other half lives. All that's missing is the cocktails!"

"Didn't wanna spill 'em... they're up at the house on the porch!" Marjorie stepped up to Anderson and firmly planted a warm kiss on his lips. "And there's a big slab of ribs marinating in the kitchen for supper, too!"

"Mr. Anderson – Frank – told me he was coming out here to work," laughed Anita as she gave Wendy a quick hug. "Didn't know it included cocktails and barbecued ribs!"

"Actually, I didn't know that myself, or I would have dressed for the occasion. Standing around in work boots, blue jeans and a dirty t-shirt, surrounded by elegant half-dressed ladies is not a daily experience for me!"

"Hey, I'm wearing blue jeans too!"

Wendy giggled: "Yeah, so you are, but have you looked in the mirror at that tank-top you're almost not wearing? I'm surprised Frank could see to drive out here!"

"Never noticed a thing. I'm just too old to be anything

but well-behaved."

"Well, maybe. Marjorie did say you were very well-behaved."

"Right. I did say something like that, I recall."

***

Marita Juarez was a new hire at the Global Conservation Society, working as an executive assistant to the new CFO, Jeremiah Lawrence. Last night, she had just finished reading *Healthy Water: a Human Right and a Global Imperative* by Dr. Sebastian Horowitz. It was a bit of a doorstop, she reflected, at some 1200 pages. A lot of that, she admitted, was an extensive bibliography on water issues worldwide. In any case, she was a believer in the cause, one of the reasons she applied for her current position.

So it was with some surprise that she found Dr. Horowitz's name on her desk after only a week on the job. The memo called for her to flag for instant response correspondence from three GCS Robertson Group International scientists regarding a memo which may put Horowitz's credibility in jeopardy. The scientists were to contact her boss directly, and as soon as possible.

Marita found this unsettling. Having slugged through over 900 pages of Horowitz's text, and being fundamentally in agreement with his point of view, she felt a closer allegiance to the author than to her new employers. She didn't want to risk her dream job, and above all she didn't want to risk her own – and her child's – potential American citizenship. Her own mother had been 25 years in the USA illegally, and Marita (and her child) had only recently been given temporary status under DACA.

She walked alone around the block during her short afternoon break, and came up with a simple plan. She would find Dr. Horowitz's telephone number, and when she reached home she would call and leave him a simple message of warning. The wording of that message would consume much of her thinking that afternoon.

***

It was late afternoon, and the fourteen-foot aluminum fishing boat was headed upstream along the channel through the thick vegetation in the marsh where Awan Lake empties into the Spirit River. The young students in the boat – a man and a woman – had been having trouble with the boat's outboard engine yesterday, and a day off for repairs at the marina had already forced the woman to be late leaving for her friend's wedding in Sarnia. She was not at all pleased, and had spent much of the day sulking, sitting on her companion's lifejacket on the bottom of the boat and playing with her cellphone. To make matters worse, they were only able to travel at six miles per hour in the channel so that, too, was taking more time.

A big heavy 1970s era jetboat came around a bend in the channel ahead and passed by them, going very fast. "Those guys have to be crazy," her companion shouted to her over the noise of their own engine. "I couldn't even see them coming, the reeds are so high!"

"Idiots!" she shouted back and returned to her cellphone and the stream of texts and calls she had been answering all day. She never saw the jetboat turn around behind them and speed back in their direction, veering to the left as if to pass and then turning hard right into the side of the boat, sliding over top as the light aluminum crumpled and rolled underneath.

The jetboat straightened out and continued up the river. The young man steering the boat was not wearing a lifejacket. His neck was snapped and his right leg was broken and wedged under his seat in the twisted aluminum wreckage. The woman had been knocked clear of the wreckage. She was wearing a lifejacket, but the blood flowing from the gash on her head was already turning her white sweatshirt to pink. Her cellphone was still ringing, but it was on its way to the bottom of the channel where it, too, would shortly die.

***

Five miles south of the channel, a Ryerson professor was having his second pre-barbecue beer at his cottage on the north west shore of Awan Lake when the telephone rang. He muttered something to his wife about people not understanding the true meaning of the word "vacation", and picked up: "Hello, Dave Bradshaw here..."

It was Sebastian Horowitz, and he sounded upset. "Sorry to bother you Dave, but there's some weird stuff going on and I think it is somehow connected to my upcoming presentation at your little lake. Otherwise I wouldn't bother you with it, because I am always being hassled and my papers and speeches are always being challenged so I am used to that."

"No problem, Dr. H., I'm always happy to hear from you. In fact, we were just talking about you yesterday, because apparently we have a couple of students on a Masters project doing some full-spectrum water quality tests out here. I think they were done collecting Wednesday, or maybe today. So who's out to get you now?"

"Well, of all the options, this seems one of the most

unlikely. The Global Conservation Society – GCS – has some people – statisticians I think – trying to discredit my position that industrial contamination of global fresh water reserves is on the verge of becoming irreversible, or 'terminal' as I choose to call it."

"Have the statistics scientists reached out to you about this, or refuted your writings with their own documented findings?"

"No, and that's the odd part of this. I learned about this through an anonymous phone call this afternoon – just now in fact – from a woman who works in the GCS office in Washington. I get lots of anonymous calls, of course, and often enough nasty ones, but this lady is actually on my side, and – as much as I could discern by asking her questions – she checks out. She sounded extraordinarily nervous, but she does indeed work there and she knew the right names and details when I quizzed her."

"Was she aware of the Awan Lake event?"

"I don't think so. Her concern was for maintaining the credibility of the work I do, not because of some particular event. In any case, I have no wish to cancel, but I thought I'd give you a heads-up that if you think there is public controversy now, just wait a moment – it's likely to get a whole lot more so! The focus, unfortunately, will switch from Awan Lake to the larger issues, which is fine for me but not so great for you folks."

"No worries on our account. Our people here, with remarkably few local exceptions, are looking forward to you coming and they're pretty well organized. Are you sure you don't want me to pick you up at the airport on Saturday?"

"No, I'm looking forward to a nice relaxed drive in lake country! I would appreciate you're letting me know if you hear any repercussions from all of this, and I'll call you if I hear any more at my end. Go back to your beer!"

"Thanks Dr. H. How did you guess about the beer?

"You're a university guy. It's almost 5:30 where you are. And you're on holiday. Have a good evening, Dave!"

***

Back on the island where Marjorie and Wendy had their cottage, Anderson, too, had opted for a beer, leaving the ladies with their bottle of white wine. He and Marjorie poked around the tiny cottage with a pen and paper as he made notes, and took the odd photo. Most of the damage from last week's break-in had been to the main door (totally destroyed) and one window pane which needed replacement. The thieves had stolen the (new) 32" TV and satellite receiver as well as a good-sized computer monitor, router and a cheap printer. Of course, they had rummaged through all the bureau drawers and the medicine cabinet. Marjorie looked at him with a mischievous grin and whispered "buggers even took Wendy's vibrator!" He grinned and whispered back that maybe he wouldn't tease her about that because he really wanted some of those barbecued ribs.

After taking door and window pane measurements, they went back to the front deck where Wendy and Anita were chattering away about nothing in particular, the wine having apparently started to do its work. Marjorie said she'd go online from Anderson's house in the morning and price out the electronic replacements from Dell, which had always been their source for computer stuff and which usually had good delivery, although she was inclined to buy locally from a store in Maple Falls that she thought might supply better support. Frank would figure out the costs of replacing the door and fixing the other miscellaneous damage, and Marjorie would add it all up, get a statement from the OPS, and make an insurance claim.

Wendy began to giggle – she was obviously enjoying the wine: "I suppose Marjorie told you that those crooks stole my favourite vibrator!"

Anderson was trying to finish off the bottle of Stella Artois he had been drinking, but lost most of the last mouthful down the front of his shirt and turned a gentle shade of beet red. All three women collapsed in laughter, and Wendy went to the cottage's tiny pantry and got him another beer. "Here, Frank, looks like you'll need this if you're hanging around here for supper!"

06:15 AUGUST 4

Anderson and Marjorie had left the island to return to the village right after a relaxed but giggly feast on tastefully marinated and barbecued pork ribs with fresh garden salad and a loaf of homemade bread that Georgina had sent out with Anita earlier in the day. As they motored the 40 minutes across the water to the harbour, they were doing their own share of giggling about Wendy and Anita who had spent the evening like schoolgirls enjoying a pre-teen crush: "They were kind of all over each other, weren't they!" And Marjorie had responded that yes, they were. Anderson wondered if she thought "something is going on there" and Marjorie replied that it wouldn't surprise her, saying that Wendy had always been a bit of a free spirit when it came to relationships. Marjorie had wondered if that would be a bad thing for Anita, who was quite a few years younger, and Anderson thoughtfully replied that Anita had been in a series of affairs with married men, druggies and bad-news party boys, and if she had a fling with Wendy it might be the best thing for her: "I think she just wants someone who'll love her and treat her with respect."

Once ashore, Frank and Marjorie had quickly enough rolled into bed themselves, and soon the giggles were over and they were fast asleep.

Until Anderson's cellphone jarred them awake just after 0600. "Crap," he muttered as he looked at the phone, "it's our friendly police sergeant again!"

"Morning, John! Don't you ever sleep?"

"I'm really sorry Frank, I really am, but this is an urgent call. I need you and your boat to recover another body. At least with this one there's no search... we know pretty well where it is. I am about 15 minutes away from your place, and I have an old guy out there in a fishing boat with his cellphone, waiting for us. Can we saddle up right way?"

"Okay. Yup, we'll be ready. We'll head down to the boat within five minutes."

"This one may be kind of gruesome – the lady was apparently killed violently. May not be something Marjorie needs to see first thing on a Friday morning."

"Thanks for the heads-up. I'll let her know. See you in a few minutes," and he clicked off.

"You'll let her know what?" piped up Marjorie who was pulling on the fresh change of clothes she had brought in from the island last night.

"Got a body to pull out of the lake, and I guess it's not

pretty – she was killed, not drowned. You okay with that, or would you rather stay back?"

"Travelling around with you is a fascinating way to live: great sex one minute, sudden death the next," she laughed. "No worries, Frank. I'm good to go! I'll make a thermos of coffee while you fire up *The Beaver*... meet you down at the dock. I hope our human alarm clock with the stripes on his sleeve brings donuts!"

Twenty minutes later, *The Beaver* was clear of the dock and moving at near-full throttle toward the marshes where Awan Lake empties into the Spirit River. Sergeant John was sipping Marjorie's coffee and all three were munching the Sergeant's fresh-baked Timmys' donuts while they peered out the wheelhouse windows into a wispy fog. Visibility varied from two or three hundred feet to a quarter mile and Anderson's attention was fully focused on what was ahead of his boat, shifting back and forth from the windscreen to the radar screen.

The Sergeant was talking to Marjorie at the wheelhouse door: "We got the cellphone call at around 0600 from some old guy out doing some early-morning bass fishing in the marsh. He said he found the body of what looks like a woman in a lifejacket floating along the edge of the channel. The old boy was able to give me coordinates from his cellphone. He also said it looked like her head had been thumped with a sledge hammer, so it seems that right away this becomes at least a suspicious death and probably a homicide." He poked his head into the wheelhouse: "How long until we get into that area, Frank?"

"Twenty minutes or so. I'm spanking *The Beaver's* tail about as hard as I can and hoping that fog doesn't suddenly close up. I'm following a course on the GPS and the new radar unit works great, but normally I'd rather not be at full throttle this close to the channel and the marsh. Lots of little fishing boats play around out here and they are close to invisible even to this radar."

"I have the coordinates on Google Map on my phone, and the icon shows we are now about two miles away from our destination. Do you want to punch the coordinates into your GPS on the boat?"

"Nah, I'll get there using your information, then set a waypoint once we arrive." He reached up and pulled the air-horn lanyard for one prolonged blast. "That'll let the old boy know we're getting close."

The Sergeant's phone rang: "This is the guy, he's likely letting us know he heard the horn... Hello? Mr. Watson? Yes, we just gave the horn signal. I think we're about a mile away from your location. We've just passed a navigation buoy and it seems we are starting into the marsh."

Anderson slowly dialed back the throttle until they were snuffling along at about two knots. He asked Marjorie to lift open the forward window so they could see – and hear – more clearly. It wasn't many minutes before they could see the small car-topper fishing boat, slightly off to starboard along the edge of the tall reeds. The occupant waved, then pointed into the reeds.

Anderson reached up and unclipped the loud-hailer microphone from its place above his head on the wheelhouse wall, thumbed the key, and said, "I'm going to go past you, make a slow turn and come up to you against the current. I'll hand the microphone to Sergeant MacLeod."

"Good morning Mr. Watson! Thanks for your call, and for waiting for us here. I can see the body in the lifejacket now, so if you could leave space for our boat to come between you and the lifejacket, that would be a big help."

The elderly man nodded and began to move his boat further out into the channel. Anderson turned the boat slowly around, keeping his eyes on the spot where he had seen the orange and blue lifejacket in the reeds, brought the boat close in with the tall reeds slithering along the port side of the hull and stopped. The Sergeant used a boathook to gently snag the lifejacket and pull it close to the side, where he was joined by Anderson.

"That would indeed seem to be a woman, and no, she is not a pretty sight. Somebody – more likely some thing – had to really hit her hard to have taken out one eye and it looks like part of her skull. I'd better get a rope around under her arms so we don't lose her out from under the lifejacket straps." Anderson opened a hatch and retrieved a 50-foot coil of half-inch line.

"We need to use gloves as much as possible," said the Sergeant. "I can do that part – maybe best that I do. Marjorie, can you get Mr. Watson to bring his boat over and tie up to your boat for a few minutes? Once we get the body secured, I'll want to talk to him."

Anderson went forward and dropped the anchor over the bow, cleated the rope short, and came back to hold the boathook while the Sergeant pulled on a pair of blue latex gloves and, leaning far over the side, fed one end of the rope around under the corpse's arms and tied a loop with a slip knot to ensure it would stay tight around the victim's chest no matter how hard they pulled. He tied the rope to a cleat long the gunwale, and turned his attention to the elderly gentleman who's skiff was already tied alongside with Marjorie's help.

Marjorie crossed to join Anderson, and stared intently at

the body for a moment before calling to the Sergeant: "John, could I interrupt you for a moment? Can I use one of your gloves... I want to get a look at the lettering on the woman's sweatshirt. I'll tell you why in a moment."

The Sergeant reached in his jacket pocket and fished out another pair of latex gloves and handed them to her. "You're one tough lady," he shrugged. "Try not to touch anything you don't need to," then he turned back to   Mr. Watson.

Anderson shook his head and watched while Marjorie pulled on the gloves, leaned over the side and gently pulled the blood-stained material straight where it protruded above the lifejacket. Immediately he saw what Marjorie must have suspected: clearly visible was one word in capital letters: RYERSON.

"Yuck. I need to swallow something before I throw up." Anderson quickly stepped into the wheelhouse and grabbed a half-full coffee cup and gave it to her. She took a couple of swallows and said, "Thank-you. I'm okay now." She paused: "I think we'd better call Dave Bradshaw."

"Yeah, exactly. Let's check with John first, but yes. Smoke break!" He pulled a crumpled pack of Number Sevens from the breast pocket of his jacket, took out two cigarettes, lit them both and passed one to Marjorie who had been peeling off the blue gloves.

Several minutes later, Mr. Watson started up his outboard and headed off somewhere to continue fishing. The Sergeant came across to where Marjorie and Anderson were sitting on the gunwale and asked, "So, what did you find out, Marjorie?"

"We're almost certain that yesterday, this poor gal was a Masters student from Ryerson University taking water samples from the lake. Dave Bradshaw, a professor from there who we think was part of directing that project, has a cottage right here at the lake. I think we should contact him as soon as possible."

"Makes sense. How far away does he live?"

"No more than five miles, straight south of here," said Anderson. "He has a speedy little runabout and I bet he would be here within twenty minutes if we can get him on his phone at the cottage."

"By all means, give it a try. We can work at getting her out of the water and into a body bag while we're waiting. And, we need to take some more photos. I got a few before we hooked onto her."

"I have his number on my phone," said Marjorie, "I just spoke with him a couple of days ago, after the meeting in the village. I'll try him now." She went into the wheelhouse, sat at the small navigation table and dialed.

Anderson and the Sergeant turned and stared at the lifeless figure tied beside the boat. "Frank, she's not very big, but she will be totally waterlogged. Probably the three of us could use ropes and roll her over the side, but I want to do as little damage to her as possible. I know that seems bizarre, considering she is already battered, but it's about maintaining the integrity of the evidence. Do you suppose we could sling her over the side using that neat little crane of yours?"

"Sure, we'll make up a couple of slings and I'll fire up the hydraulics and stretch out the crane."

Marjorie came out of the wheelhouse: "Dave is on his way. I warned him to leave his wife and kids behind, and why. I told him we were just downstream from that channel marker at the edge of the marsh."

Anderson gave her a one-arm squeeze and chuckled: "Wow, you're talking like you've been on the lake all your life... I am impressed!" She grinned back at him.

It didn't take him long to unfold the articulated crane and center the hook about three feet over the body. Wearing fresh sets of blue gloves, they soon had a couple of slings in place, lifted the body clear of the water and let it drain as much water as possible over the side while the Sergeant prepared a body bag on the deck.

"That vision defines the word 'macabre'," muttered Marjorie. "That poor twisted body hanging off a crane in a swamp. What a way to end your life!"

Soon enough, they had the woman – lifejacket and all – down on the deck and zipped into the black bag well before Dave Bradshaw came into view from the lake side of the marsh. They had already topped off their coffees and were sitting smoking by the door of the wheelhouse.

"I think there was a helluva collision out here on the lake," Anderson was saying. "The woman was dressed in work clothes and boots, so she wasn't holidaying and if she was on that water-testing boat, it's likely only a foot or two longer than Mr. Watson's little fishing boat."

The Sergeant went back into the wheelhouse and returned with the box of donuts. "If there was a collision, then, where is the boat? Would it still float? If she had a companion, where is he (or she)?"

Bradshaw knew Anderson's boat from the village, and pulled his speedboat alongside and tied up immediately. "Good morning Marjorie, we meet in strange places..."

"Hi Dave. You know Frank, of course, and this is OPS Sergeant John MacLeod."

Bradshaw shook hands all around and accepted a cup of coffee from Anderson. "I assume the person Marjorie was talking about is in that black bag on the floor," he said, eyeing the bag from as far away as he could get on the small deck.

"That would be correct," said the Sergeant. "Is it at all likely you would know her if she is indeed from your university?"

"Not very likely, certainly not very well. If she had been a student I worked closely with, I would have known she was out here in the first place. While testing Awan Lake was my initiative, I was not the project's lead, so not the technicians' direct supervisor. How sure are you that there is a connection, anyway?"

"Well, we have learned that there was a small boat and two people from Ryerson out on the lake earlier this week. And of course Marjorie spoke with you earlier about that. Frank here has speculated – probably quite accurately – that from what we know they had a 12 to 14 foot aluminum boat with a small to medium sized motor. I have no way at the moment of knowing for certain when this lady was killed, but I'll guess at more than 12 and fewer than 24 hours ago. Frank?"

"For what it's worth, my guess is that they were returning from taking samples on the river yesterday afternoon, later than earlier or she would likely have been found by other boaters. I also think they were in a collision with a much bigger boat – maybe even a cruiser on its way up from the locks in Maple Falls." He paused. "Only thing is, not even the dumbest tourist would be running his toy ocean liner up the river and through the marsh on autopilot, and almost certainly not at a speed that would have crushed our victim's head so badly. So in my mind it's most likely to have been some idiot in a wakeboard boat charging up into the lake at full speed, and simply running over the smaller boat and whoever was onboard. The idiot had to have been aware he had hit something, but was likely too scared to stop and check, let alone report the accident."

"Sergeant!"

Everyone spun around to see Mr. Watson's boat coming alongside. "Hello sir," called the Sergeant. "Did we forget something?"

"Nope, but there's something in the weeds about half a mile up the channel you might want to see. I guess it's a wrecked boat kinda like mine, but it looks more like someone twisted up some tinfoil and threw it in the water. Only a small part of it is sticking out."

Anderson was already on the foredeck pulling up the workboat's anchor and Marjorie was standing ready by the wheel. First the Sergeant called out to the old man, "Will you please lead us there, Mr. Watson?" then he spoke to the professor: "Dr. Bradshaw, can you follow us along in your boat? We still have lots of stuff to talk about with you, and this may mean we have more stuff!"

"Thanks Marjorie," Anderson called through the wheelhouse door, "Can you put her in forward, no throttle, and let her ease out into the channel? I wanna check for weeds in the prop before we speed up."

After he was assured the prop was running free, he went back to the wheelhouse and planted a kiss on Marjorie's left ear. "Thank-you. I can take the wheel now, or – if you like – you can turn us around and follow Mr. Watson. He seems to be the only one who knows where he's going this morning!"

"Sure, I'll do that. But when we get to wherever that is, please take over because I'm not up to manoeuvring anything this big in tight spaces. Not yet, anyway!"

A quarter hour later, Mr. Watson stopped his boat and waved toward the reeds on the opposite side of the channel. Anderson grabbed his binoculars off their hook behind the helmsman's seat and scanned the opposite side as Marjorie throttled back the engine and took the transmission out of gear. After they had drifted along for about a half-minute, Anderson could see something glinting in the morning sun, which had finally dispersed the early morning fog.

"Over there," he called out and pointed. He went and relieved Marjorie at the wheel, put the transmission and engine into slow forward and pulled around so the workboat again faced upstream. As they got closer, it became obvious that Mr. Watson had found a severely twisted and crumpled aluminum boat, very likely the one they were looking for.

The Sergeant shouted "Thanks Mr. Watson!" across the water, and waved him off before grabbing the boathook, extending its adjustable length and reaching across to the wreckage. It was easy enough to hook onto the aluminum, but only part of the boat was above water and it became obvious that it wasn't going to cooperate. "Frank, is there any way we can get closer?"

"Maybe we don't have to. I'll get us one of the grappling hooks we used on the chopper, shackle it to a short piece of chain and hang that from the crane hook. Then with that boathook and a little fooling around, I bet we can snag something well enough to drag it out of the weeds. After that I may have to go in the water to get a chain around it but I'd rather not go swimming in the weeds with the alligators."

"We don't have alligators in Ontario." The voice belonged to Dave Bradshaw, who had brought his boat alongside.

"You may have spent a lifetime in Ontario, but you

have obviously never spent thirty seconds in my head," laughed Anderson as he fished a grappling hook out of the port stern locker, along with a coffee can full of various-sized shackles.

It worked. Within a few minutes of shoving and poking and pulling, they had snagged enough aluminum to very slowly ease the crumpled skiff closer to the side of the workboat. Leaving the winch cable tight, Anderson went to the wheel and manipulated the shift and steering to kick the boat away from the reeds. Then he went back to the crane and pulled the wreck to close the gap he had created. He repeated this procedure twice, and then he was able to lower the crane boom and gently back the boat into the channel with the wreckage in tow. Once they were clear, he left the boat in neutral and dropped the anchor off the bow for the second time this morning.

"Well, that was kinda neat," said the Sergeant, "you're full of surprises, Mr. Anderson."

"Now for the alligators." Anderson reached into another locker and pulled out a heavy duffel bag. "I have a 20-minute bottle of emergency air and a facemask, along with rubber diving gloves and a pair of old sneakers. I also have a wetsuit, but I think I'd rather work around all that sharp aluminum in my jeans. I have a change of clothes in the cabin."

Half an hour passed before Anderson had managed to thread a heavy rope around and through bits of the wreckage and once he was back onboard he had gingerly lifted the twisted boat enough to know he had it securely attached. Then he stopped lifting and called Marjorie and the Sergeant into the wheelhouse.

"Before we finish this, you need to know that this next part is really ugly. One leg of the guy that was probably driving the boat is wedged under some of the wreckage – probably the thwart he had been sitting on. When we pull everything out together, he will be hanging out underneath and will have to be pulled to the side as we lower what's left of the boat onto our deck."

"That's not very nice at all," said the Sergeant. "Don't worry, I'll grab the guy and make sure he's clear. Neither of you should have to do that."

"After looking at that poor twisted and damaged girl draining over the side, this can't be any worse," muttered Marjorie. "That scene will live in my brain for a long time."

Anderson put his arm around her shoulders: "I know, Marj. I know. But you could be forgiven if you wanted to be forward in the cabin for this next part."

"I'll be okay, but there's something else I'm thinking

about: I know John will need to take photos, but I don't think Dave Bradshaw or Mr. Watson should be taking photos of this. They'll be all over the internet by nightfall."

"Good point! John, you're the cop here, so could you call them together and request their cellphones and cameras for ten minutes? Thanks Marjorie."

The Sergeant went out on deck and waved the two smaller boats over. He thanked Bradshaw and Watson for their help this morning, then explained the situation and requested their phones and cameras for the next fifteen minutes. Mr. Watson shrugged and handed over his cellphone. Bradshaw, on the other hand, began to argue about his rights and freedom of information and the police abusing their authority.

Anderson took a few meaningful steps across the deck to where Bradshaw had brought his fancy little runabout alongside, took a firm hold on its gunwale and leaned over the side looking straight down into Bradshaw's eyes: "Dave, I ain't a cop. I think you will be a much happier and healthier man if you just hand over your cellphone and camera to me. Marjorie and I will keep them safe from the police for fifteen minutes and then return them to you in perfect condition. Okay?"

Bradshaw looked back and forth between Anderson and

Marjorie, paused and grunted, "Okay," then handed across his phone and a very expensive camera in its case.

"Thank-you, Dave. Okay folks, this won't be pretty but let's finish this job. I'm soaking wet and I'm getting cold."

***

It was nearly 11:00 hours and the fog had fully burned off by the time *The Beaver,* with her grisly cargo safely under blue tarpaulins, returned from the marsh and pulled in at the commercial dock in Spirit River. The dock was already populated by a half-dozen figures in white coveralls, carrying the tools of the forensics trade in black and gray plastic cases. For the second time in three days, there was a picker crane at the foot of the dock, along with a flatbed trailer, but this time there was also a large ambulance along with an OPS personnel van.

A few onlookers had gathered along the road and around the shoreline. "Anderson, you seem to get more people at your dock than there are in the whole village. You should run for mayor, or prime minister or something," the Sergeant teased.

"Just another peaceful morning, boating on the lake with Sergeant John MacLeod. What could go wrong with that?"

During the 45-minute return trip from the marsh, Marjorie and the two men had tossed around scenarios, theories and the few facts that were already available to them. Anderson was convinced that the small aluminum boat and its two young passengers had been deliberately run over by someone who may not have intended to commit a double homicide but certainly wanted "to scare the crap out of them, and perhaps send a message."

"I expect you are correct in your assessment," the Sergeant had remarked, "but in any case we need to find the boat that did it, whether on purpose or by accident. Any idea what our forensics team should be looking for?"

"Yes, a few things. First, my suspicion is that it was a jetboat, driven by a water jet without a propeller or rudder hanging below the bottom of the boat, so that would mean there would be no scars where the prop or rudder dragged over the boat. Of course, they should be looking for fibreglass or plastic scrapings or paint of course, or even Teflon because that would suggest the layer of Teflon on the bottom of an aluminum jetboat used for river-racing. I'm pretty certain the boat we are looking for is quite big – possibly over 24 feet long, heavy and powerful with a planing hull."

"I guess I'd better let our highway patrol folks know to

check boats on trailers for damage – I expect this collision left some marks!"

"Yes, and maybe even tell Jim at the marina to keep his eyes open."

Marjorie's cellphone went off during the conversation and she stepped down into the tiny forward cabin away from the engine noise to take the call. A few moments later, she had returned to the others and told them that it was Bradshaw who said he needed to talk again to the three of them. "He had some important insight – a call from Horowitz, he said – and he also wanted to apologize to you guys. Admitted he was out of line and that you made the right call."

The Ryerson professor had followed them back from the marsh, and had been making slow wide circles well away from the dock to stay clear of the unloading activities. By now that was all over, and Anderson walked out on the deck and waved him in, indicating he could tie his boat alongside.

After tying up and saying his apologies, he shared the details of the call he had received from Dr. Horowitz a day earlier. "Certainly it seems that not everyone is pleased with Horowitz, which is no surprise – he can certainly be controversial – and if people in high places don't like what's going on here, all the more reason to attack his credibility."

Anderson had been listening, but rather focused on the forensics team cleaning up and leaving the boat and the dock. "Folks, let's go up to the house. I'm going to call Arnold and maybe Marion to come and join us – there are other things we need to talk about and I sense many of them may fit together."

As they were walking up toward Anderson's workshop and house, Marjorie suggested to the Sergeant that she would order some pizza's from the Zoo: "I bet you're all at least as hungry as I am, and I didn't see a huge selection of food at the house; I'll go and pick up the pizzas when they're done."

"Sounds like a plan, but I can go pick them up. I should have my car and radio up at the house anyway," and the Sergeant turned back to the dock to pick up his cruiser.

"Don't worry about the pizza," Anderson called out. "Arnold and Marion will be here in about twenty minutes, after Jamie is back from lunch so there's someone there to serve gas, and they said they'd pick up a couple of big ones on their way. Marjorie and I will make us some fresh coffee and we should be okay for awhile."

Half an hour later, the six of them were settled in at Anderson's massive table, slurping hot coffee and wolfing down slices of pizza. Anderson and the Sergeant filled in

Arnold and Marion on the events of the morning, then
Marion told Dave Bradshaw about the government's
decision to shut down the Protected Shorelines Project.

"Bastards! They have no right to do that. They've used
our PSP at Awan Lake as a BMP – an example of best
management practices – for the last two years, so obviously
we've been doing everything right. What the hell...?"

Anderson explained the feds were using a disgruntled
employee – who quit last week – as the excuse, but that a
government representative, in private conversation, had told
him and Arnold that wasn't the reason. It seems there were
ministry people further up the food chain who wanted to kill
the Awan Lake PSP.

"There's another thing I learned yesterday that may or
may not be related, and certainly isn't for public discussion
at the moment," Anderson continued. "The man who owns
the Spirit River Inn, as well as controlling interest in the
Awan Lake Marina, is apparently a senior Ottawa bureaucrat
at the ADM level in the Ministry of Natural Resources."

"Geez! Who knew!" Arnold turned to his wife:
"Marion, didn't you say that one of the three guys who came
with the mayor to our Board of Trade meeting on Monday
evening is an Ottawa-based government consultant?"

"Yes. Apparently he is the principal in a small

management firm that specializes in mining. I saw the Ministry of Natural Resources on his client list and he is one of two of those guys who own property along the lakeshore – outside the village."

Anderson glanced across the table at the Sergeant, who had his notebook out. "Making notes, Sergeant?"

"Yeah. I'm finding it difficult to sort out speculation from facts. It seems more than somewhat bizarre that there are connections between all these things, but I certainly can't rule out their significance."

"Seems to me that everything, somehow, connects back to Robertson Mines," put in Arnold.

"Maybe so," said Marion, "but everything also seems to connect to the Horowitz event next weekend, and more directly to our Protected Shorelines Project. I am wondering if someone tried to put another scare into the folks working on the Project and it went a little – a lot – too far. After all, our ex-summer student Cyndi may have been a serious wimp but she did tell me last week that she and Adumbi had been pretty terrified, and that was before the events of today."

Anderson had been drawing and writing on some scrap paper. Some would have called it doodling, but for him it was a way of visualizing connections and making plans. "There are a number of things we need to learn, and some things we need to do. One thing has been worrying me particularly: we need to pull Adumbi out of the field, off the lake, and into the office, for his own safety. We don't know for sure if – or why – the young folks who were killed were targeted, but I have a very strong hunch that any conservation research activities at Awan Lake are under potential threat anyway."

"I agree," said the Sergeant. "Those young folks appear to be in the crosshairs at the moment, and for me, that means the people doing the bad stuff are both ignorant and stupid: ignorant of the facts and too stupid to realize they are being played by more powerful people with an agenda they'll never understand. That's pretty typical of how organized crime works, of course. In any case, yes, keep them on shore and in town. Better to be safe."

***

Wendy Webster sat on the deck at the cottage she and her sister shared on what Anderson called "Ship Island". The morning sun had burned off the early morning fog, and she could clearly pick out the rooftops of the village along the green shore five miles to the north west. A light south west wind rippled the clear waters a light blue: *Perfect mornings like this*, she reflected, *are why I love this place so much. The city, and the affairs of men, money and power don't even seem to exist.*

Notwithstanding the peace of her familiar surroundings, however, Wendy's emotions were in turmoil. Curled up on her bed, and fast asleep, lay a very lovely young lady. The two of them had shared a second bottle of wine after Marjorie and Anderson had left last night and had wound up giggling into each others' arms on the sofa, touching, caressing and stroking and soon enough kissing... gently at first then more passionately.

As might be expected, they fumbled their way out of their clothes and into her bed. This morning, sitting on her porch in the sunlight, all that had happened was a blur – a blur of affection and warmth, but this morning, also a blur of bewilderment and apprehension: *My love affairs have always been short and shallow. Dinner and drinks, dancing perhaps and conversation, then sex and – for me, home alone: I never wanted to wake up with my date lying beside me. This time, it's different. Yes, and it's really different, because my date is not some guy I really don't care about... she's a woman, and I really do care.*

I think we need breakfast. Wendy went into the cottage and into the tiny kitchen, where she heated a frying pan, melted some butter, and took a couple of pre-baked English muffins out of the breadbox on the counter. *I even picked up these muffins for her when I saw how much she liked them at the Zoo the other day.* She took four eggs from the tiny solar-powered refrigerator and broke them into a bowl on the counter before tiptoeing into the bedroom. Her gaze softened as she looked at the sleeping Anita, whose bare back, left arm and breast displayed a variety of tastefully-arranged tattoos. She leaned down and brushed some hair off Anita's cheek: "Time for breakfast, sleepyhead!"

Anita went from sleeping beauty to raging tigress in less than an instant. Her left arm thrashed out and caught Wendy across the face and Anita was on her feet, ready to fight, almost all in one motion. Then she stopped, seeing Wendy as if for the first time. She reached out, grabbed her around the shoulders and buried her face in Wendy's neck, beginning to sob deeply as if without end.

"I am so sorry, Wendy. I am so sorry..." was all she could blurt out. They collapsed together on the bed until the sobs had subsided. "I love you and I am so sorry..."

Wendy wiped away Anita's tears and caressed her cheek. "Now, maybe, let's have some breakfast. I've always believed that good breakfasts are the perfect antidote to bad memories."

***

CBC Television News · August 4, 2017 6:00 PM ET
Water Scientist's Opinions Challenged

GCS questions validity of Dr. Sebastian Horowitz'
research
Scientists associated with the Global Conservation
Society (GCS) are questioning the validity of
projections published in *Healthy Water: a Human
Right and a Global Imperative* by Canadian water
protection advocate Dr. Sebastian Horowitz.
According to GCS spokesperson Jeremiah
Lawrence, "any suggestion that the industrial
contamination of global fresh water reserves is on
the verge of becoming terminal has no basis in
science." Lawrence also called attention to the fact
that the title of "Doctor" generally accorded to Mr.
Horowitz stems from his certification as a medical
doctor in pediatrics and not as a PhD in any aquatic-
related science: "Scientists – specifically those who
focus on statistics – on our GCS team have
confirmed to me that their work points out a number
of flaws, both in Horowitz's calculations and his
interpretations of those questionable results."

The Global Conservation Society, with its head
office in Washington, DC, is generally considered as
one of the world's pre-eminent sources of
environmental conservation information. The CBC
was unable to reach Sebastian Horowitz for
comment at either his home or office on Vancouver
Island. He is slated to give a keynote address at *Love
Our Lake*, a public event to be held Sunday August

13 at Spirit River, Ontario, a village on the shores of Awan Lake east of Maple Falls.

***

After the Sergeant, Bradshaw and the Jamiesons had left, Anderson and Marjorie spent the rest of the afternoon cleaning up and servicing the boat, making a shopping list for groceries and supplies, and calling the two lumber yards about doors. That was when Anderson remembered he had promised Sam he would install a working video security system at the Zoo, and Marjorie suggested maybe he should install a similar set-up at his own home and even on the dock. They spent a half-hour looking at video security options on the internet, then agreed that a trip to The Falls for shopping, laundry and dinner might be a nice way to spend the rest of the day. Marjorie was finally able to reach her sister at the island and asked if they, too, needed any groceries, telling her they would also try to get the replacement television and receiver and a computer monitor, a modem, and maybe even a new front door.

"Wendy says hi, and so does Anita. Sounds like they polished off another bottle of wine after we left and had a delightful night with no hangovers, although they did sleep in until after eleven. And... I did get a shopping list!"

"Some day, I expect you'll be wanting your own bed

back!" chuckled Anderson.

"Oh, I expect getting my own bed back is not an issue... they sound pretty cozy out there. Anyway, at the moment I'm pretty happy just to be sharing yours if that's okay, Mr. Anderson."

"No argument here!"

PETER KINGSMILL

08:00 August 5

Marjorie had been awake and up by 07:30, paddling around between the kitchen counter, stove and table in bare feet making coffee, bacon and pancakes. When it was all ready, she kissed Anderson on the left ear and announced that breakfast was served: "This morning, I actually managed to beat our stripy OPS friend to the punch! Let's enjoy breakfast before he calls," she laughed.

And so they did, but not by much. Just after 08:00, Anderson's phone rang and it was indeed the Sergeant. There was no emergency this time... just news: "Mornin', Frank. A couple of things we've found out. First, the forensics folks say that they've only been able to narrow down time of death for those two kids to be between 14:30 and 18:30 on Thursday. She died instantly from the blow to her head and the man died from a broken neck. And, a first look at the wreckage shows no metal-caused scars on the boat – just some white fibreglass scrapings. Obviously enough, I suppose, the 20-horse motor on the wreck had been running at full throttle when it went into the water, and the boat itself appeared to have been struck from the rear on the left-hand side at about a 60-degree angle. We are assuming, from what you suggested yesterday, that the kids were heading east on their way back to the village and the boat launch at the marina. We also acknowledge that is only a 'best guess', based on time of day and end of work. We did sort out some water sampling equipment and sample containers. The guy had a phone in his vest pocket, but we haven't been able to get anything off it yet. We think we have names, and we are trying to contact next of kin. The people at Bradshaw's university have been trying to be useful, but it is a civic holiday weekend, in the summer, and the on-duty admin staff is largely non-existent. Friends of the girl – if it is indeed the right girl – have been trying to make contact since yesterday afternoon because of a wedding she was supposed to be at – not hers, I gather. But, for now, that's all we know about that. There is one other thing – headquarters is hearing noise about the event with that scientist next weekend. Not sure where the noise is coming from, it's just an internal 'heads up' for now."

"Thanks for keeping us in the loop, John! We have nothing to share, really – we were pretty domestic yesterday afternoon and evening, and are planning to go out to the island later this morning to replace the door those clowns broke a couple of weeks ago, and of course replace the television and computer with stuff Marjorie bought last night."

"Yep, my beady-eyed gremlins in the department already flagged your truck in The Falls last night. Sorry about that – you're never alone these days, my friend!"

"That's why I spend so much time on the water," laughed Anderson.

"That brings up another thing I forgot to mention. Super George, as you call him, was in touch with me last night and – because of the new circumstances – he wants me to re-engage your boat under contract. And in the meantime he wants me to give you a satellite phone to keep in your pocket so you can reach us from anywhere. I'll send it over with Andy right away, before you head out to the island. Poor Andy is putting in lots of overtime, what with Marie still off work and recuperating."

"Hmm. Okay, I'm game – again – as long as I don't have to shoot too many more people. Tell Superintendent Daniels hello for me... I was thinking of him last week when I was in BC. I'm sure my old buddy Keith and I must have run into him when we all served on the Coast Guard."

"Will do. I'll call you when I know more."

"I have a feeling Super George thinks there's more to this than a boating accident or perhaps a bunch of idiot thugs. Do you?"

"Yes, I do."

"Yeah, me too. Talk to you later."

Anderson stabbed the end-call button on his phone and turned to Marjorie. "It's not like I'm short of work around here, but it looks like more is piling up. I should have talked to you about it first."

Marjorie put down her coffee cup and took his hands in hers. She looked down, then straight up into his eyes: "We never really talk first, do we? Ever since we met, we just 'do', and then talk later. That's alright with me, Mr. Anderson. I am away too excited about this new life I am living, a lot of which is about falling in love with you. Let's just keep on doing stuff... whatever it is, I'm in."

Anderson gazed at her for quite a long time, then wrapped his big arms around her and whispered, "I love you too, Marjorie Webster. It's a whole new feeling, and I like it."

They sat back down to finish their second cup of coffee while he updated her with what the Sergeant had told him about the early forensics findings, and about his own renewed engagement and contract for the boat. "We should look at the news online while we're waiting for Andy and that satellite phone. I'd like to know what the news is reporting about Horowitz... John and his boss seem to think there's more weird stuff happening than just another murder. Just saying that is pretty weird in itself, I know!"

"I've been meaning to ask: has John ever mentioned Wendy? He seemed to take a shine to her a couple of weeks ago."

"We've hardly talked at all in the last few days about anything unrelated to the criminal stuff, but he did ask after her in a general way, day before yesterday I think. I replied that she was fine, but fixed on sorting out about a bunch of personal stuff. Actually, his response to that made me chuckle. He said 'understanding her is like trying to understand a QR Code – you need some sort of scanner to translate what's going on in that brain'. Although it made me laugh, I sort of realized that Wendy has 'way too much going on upstairs for loyal, pragmatic old Sergeant John. He's one of the finest men I've met, but I hope he likes being a sergeant because he is unlikely to become an inspector, let alone a super, until perhaps the year before he retires so they can jack up his pension and demonstrate to him how deeply he is respected."

Marjorie was chuckling. No, she was laughing out loud: "John nailed Wendy perfectly! I'll never be able to watch her think through anything again without remembering 'QR Code'!"

There are occasions when timing is everything: at that moment Marjorie's phone began playing Gordon Lightfoot's *If You Could Read My Mind* to signal an incoming text from her sister, leaving the two of them breathless with laughter.

Constable Andy Bathgate arrived at about 09:30 and dropped off the satellite phone for Anderson, who asked for some quick instructions on its use. Marjorie offered him coffee but he said they were so busy he was running both ways and meeting himself coming back. He was gone in five minutes, so Anderson and Marjorie locked up the house and took the S-10 with its load of groceries, electronics, a door and some wood-working tools from Anderson's shop to load onto the boat. In half an hour they were headed out of the harbour.

Anderson set the throttle at just over half speed, set the autohelm on course toward Ship Island, and came out on deck to join Marjorie, carrying two coffees and two lit smokes. Together they sat on the cabin top ahead of the wheelhouse and quietly watched the bow wave gently foam by along both sides of the hull. It was an idyllic summer morning, although because it was Saturday on a long weekend they were far from alone on the lake. As usual, there were few boats to the east, but they could see everything from car-toppers to runabouts to small cruisers going back and forth along the north west shore, enroute to and from the island cottages, the village and the river with its channel to Maple Falls. The calm lake was like polished silver, so the sailors were not out yet, waiting for ripples from afternoon breezes to tarnish the silver waters a dark blue.

***

Two men in Saturday shirts and jeans sat by the window at the Zoo, finishing off their brunch and had just asked Sam for a third coffee. "Hey Sam, you got gang-bangers away out here, or just staff problems?"

"You mean that new camera I'm getting installed?" and he motioned to a young technician on a ladder by the till. "Well, staff isn't the problem because I am married to one and the other is my daughter. But there are some kids, you know, older kids, who make me nervous. So, video at the back door and one at the front maybe will discourage them. Or at least my wife will sleep better at night."

"Yeah, what's the world coming to, eh? Can't even have a nice little restaurant in Spirit River without security. Thanks for the coffee – add it to the bill, you can't be giving us free refills all morning!" Charles Morrell turned to his companion: "Actually, Bob, I heard last night that the cops found two kids drowned on the lake yesterday, and they haven't ruled out homicide. One of our guys' wives was at the dock when they brought them in... they unloaded what looked like a crumpled old outboard boat and two body bags. She showed me some photos on her cellphone. From the looks of that boat, there must have been one hell of a collision out there, but there are too many boaters out there to rule out an accident and assume a homicide."

"Well, you know cops: if you're a hammer, the world looks like a nail. I agree, there's no way anyone would target two youngsters out for a summer boat ride." Bob Adamson was the Facility Development Officer attached to Robertson Mines at Awan Lake. "No big deal. Charlie, I need to tell you about a few things that are coming down the pipe."

"Go for it, Bob. I hope those things include some clarification about Maurice Bonner's sudden departure. It's playing out in the plant – and even in the community here – that he was fired, but I haven't received anything from head office except to say I was temporarily Acting Manager. I have no illusions that will be a permanent situation – I don't have the time in or experience to fill that role and frankly, Bob, I don't want any promotion at this point either. I enjoy working with the staff as operations manager."

"I know that is just what head office wants, and I'm almost certain that's what Tom will want. So, Tom – Thomas Manville – will be flying in tonight from Nanaimo, via head office in Washington, and he will start as the new General Manager on Monday morning. I know him a bit – good guy really, but he is essentially a 'fixer' and is being brought in ahead of our expansion here. His style is consistent – everywhere he is sent he likes to make a few big changes very noticeably – to both staff and the general public – to let everyone know he is in charge and that he carries a big stick as far as the board, shareholders and governments are concerned. He was in South America – Brazil, I think – a number of years ago, then southern California, Oregon and Nanaimo, which was his most recent posting."

"Wow, okay. I've heard of him. People seem to either love him or hate him, but mostly they just stay out of his way. Say, Bob, was Bonner let go to make way for Manville, or was there something else?"

"A bit of both, as I hear it. He would have been given a similar posting at some other facility, but he screwed up here. He got too close to some bad guys - some people in government and maybe also some in organized crime, and while he was never accused of any wrongdoing, his overall judgement was seen to be lacking so he was simply fired. I think he got a year's severance, but I also think he'll have a hard time finding a high-level job anywhere."

"Ouch. I have to say I sort of liked him."

"Actually, so did I, but I wouldn't say that to anyone else!"

"My lips are sealed! Where is Tom going to live?"

"For now, probably an executive suite at one of the hotels in Maple Falls. But I wouldn't be surprised if he bought, or more likely built, something in the village here. That would be a public statement of community commitment to go along with the expansion, and in any case the cost won't come out of his pocket, you can bet on that!"

"Must be nice!"

***

It was lunch time at Ship Island and the place was a mess, although now it almost had a new front door. The one space that served as living-room, dining-room, kitchen and office was ankle deep in cardboard, Styrofoam and cables, where Wendy, Anita and Marjorie had been unpacking and assembling computer and television components. Wendy had paused to make some ham sandwiches and take some beers from the cooler, and they now sat under the covered part of the small veranda along with Anderson who had happily downed tools at the sound of the first beer bottle being opened. It was Stella Artois – the favourite among the ladies gathered on Ship Island – but Anderson, who normally preferred something a bit darker, was 'way too polite to squawk. Anyway, it was beer and it was cool and it helped wash down the sawdust from fitting the new door.

"Did you gals get a chance to talk about that CBC news item about our illustrious guest speaker next weekend?"

"Damn. No, I forgot all about it. Anita? Wendy? Have you heard or read about it?"

"Don't be silly, sis – we haven't had any communications out here except maybe-yes-maybe-no cellphone coverage, and no internet. Hopefully we'll have it all running after lunch, but in the meantime, tell us more..."

"Duh. Yeah, that was dumb... of course you haven't had a chance to hear about it. We should be able to find the full story online once we're hooked back up this afternoon, but the short version is that on the evening news yesterday there was a report that scientists from the Global Conservation Society were slamming Dr. Horowitz's opinions about the global impact of industrial activity on water security. As I understood from reading the rather brief report, the society even went so far as to challenge Horowitz's credibility as a scientist."

"Those bastards!" Anita had been leaning forward in her chair, listening to Marjorie with growing intensity. "Why am I not surprised... those pricks at GCS do that kind of crap all the time!"

Anderson chuckled: "Sometime you'll have to tell us how you really feel!"

"Actually, yes please. Sometime is now!" responded Wendy. "We need to find a way to spin this through a media release of our own, to draw attention to the Love Our Lake event next week, and provide our perspective. Tell us why you say that, please!"

"Obviously, I have no use for the so-called 'Global' conservation society. They only started up a few years ago, and have managed to gobble up massive amounts of grant money – from governments, foundations and corporations all over the world – that should have been spent on real projects and issues that need good scientific research, and on real recovery and conservation activities. Some of the grant money they receive goes to their hand-picked stable of scientists and they use the rest to build their empire of communications bureaucrats who filter their so-called science to the public, mostly to generate yet more donations and sell fund-raising T-shirts with their penguin logo and their cuddly penguin toys. They call it public education. I call it bullshit!"

"Okay then," said Anderson as he passed around his pack of Number Sevens. "And here I thought that the GCS was the new church for the tree-hugger sect. Not all is as it appears, apparently, and I can't say I am really that surprised. As an Elder I knew in the Okanagan once told me, 'Sometimes there's just too many damn feathers!' In this case, too many penguins."

"Let's get this damn modem hooked up so I can get out into the world on my laptop. I need to start writing a media release and doing some research. Actually, I'm thinking of two media releases this week: one sent Sunday evening for Monday, and a second one maybe Tuesday. I think we ought to talk about the feds shutting down our PSP project, in tandem with the GCS controversy. Frank, we'll need to establish media contact names for both the board of trade and the PSP."

"Arnold is the board of trade chair, and Marion is the secretary and general everything person. Marjorie, could you maybe talk to them both about that? And I think for the PSP as well. I know I am vice-chair for that, but we probably need a more academic response over the phone than any of us can manage – how about asking Dave Bradshaw to be our contact from the PSP group?"

"How about Arnold for the PSP, Marion for the board of trade, and Dave as specialist for any technical or academic issues?"

"That works for me, Marj. Good suggestion... does that work for you Wendy? Anita?" There were nods all around. "Okay, I'm gonna back out there and get this frickin' door to lock and open properly."

He had just pushed the on-button for his cordless finishing saw when the new OPS satphone started to beep. He clicked off the saw, took the phone out of its belt clip and punched the incoming call button: "Anderson here..."

"Don't panic, Frank! It's just Sergeant MacLeod here. I wanted to test the phone, of course, but there's another thing. Do you remember Monica Winslow, the diver we had with us that river search a few weeks ago? If I can reach her, could you take us back out to that site where the chopper went down? Our forensics folks working on that incident have discovered we are missing one police-issue carbine, and we figure it fell out during the crash or while the chopper was sinking to the bottom of the lake. Or maybe fell out while you were lifting the wreck. In any case, we'd like to make sure we've done a thorough search."

"Sure, we can do that. We'll be okay with just Monica, but bring along a couple of extra tanks and a regulator. Then Marj can skipper the boat, I can be the buddy man, you can be the divemaster and Monica can do all the work! Wanna go Monday morning?"

"That'll work fine. Let's say 0900 at the dock. I'll reach out to Monica and if there's a change I'll call you back."

"One more thing, before I forget. I had promised Sam at the Zoo that I would replace his fake security camera with a real one, and Marjorie suggested maybe I should have one at the house and at the boat. We did some looking around on the internet, then went to that "George The Security Guy" shop in Maple Falls yesterday, and he offered us a really good deal if we got the stuff from him for all three and he would install the equipment and set up the monitoring system. So, that's happening today – I told him to do the Zoo first."

Anderson could hear the Sergeant chuckle on the other end of the line: "Just because you're paranoid doesn't mean they're not out to get you! Joking aside, I think that's a good move. The one at the Zoo may prove useful for investigations, and in your case, you and your boat have bumped up their public profile enough to justify the extra precautions. And if you get bored, you can watch the recordings as the star in your own movie!"

"Thanks John. Only if you bring the popcorn! See you Monday." And he went back to his electric saw.

Half an hour later, he was just tightening up the door handle and lock screws for what felt like the fourteenth and he hoped final time when Wendy joined him: "Nice-looking fix, Frank. Thank you! I got in touch with Marion and she agreed with your contacts list for the media. Then she told me that we were all going to a barbecue at their place tonight. Georgina is off work early so she and Fred are coming, and Willy is in town too. So if that's okay with you and Marjorie, Anita and I will take our boat and stay over with her mum and dad, and maybe head into Walmart in the morning. I need some stuff – including a decent pair of jeans and some thumb-drives to have on hand with our media releases and some photos that Anita has of the PSP project."

"I have learned never to turn down a Marion Jamieson barbecue," grinned Anderson. They're always fun, and it would be nice to see Crazy Willy again! I've just about got this door done... how are things in the computer department?"

"Great! Marjorie has the TV and receiver working properly, and we now have decent internet – at least as good as it's ever been out here. I found the CBC News article from last night and a short follow-up this morning that includes a couple of sentences about two people who drowned in a boating accident on Awan Lake. No more than that."

"Figures. But I have a feeling Awan Lake will be almost famous by the time next Sunday is finished. Not something that will thrill everyone, but I guess we're up on the horse now so we may as well ride it."

PETER KINGSMILL

17:30 August 5

Indeed, the evening at Marion's and Arnold's house was every bit as fun – and tasty – as Anderson had said it would be. A seemingly endless supply of barbecued pork ribs, tender and sweet in the marinade that only Marion knew how to make, stuffed baked potatoes and a variety of roasted veggies fresh from her garden – lots for everyone but prepared with special care for Adumbi whom she had also invited, well aware of not only his devout Moslem faith but also his preference for vegetarian food in any case.

Anderson and Marjorie had picked up a case of beer (not Stella Artois this time!) and a couple of bottles of wine. They thought it would be fun to bring along a bottle of the same Nk'Mip Merlot they had enjoyed a couple of evenings before, to see what Willy thought of it. Nk'Mip is a First Nation-owned winery in the Okanagan, and Willy, of course, is the Indigenous father of Fred Antoine and therefore the grandfather of Anita. Willy expressed the view that – for a Merlot – it was okay, but suggested that maybe those folks in the Okanagan Valley should stick with making beer.

And so the evening went, like a moment of blue sky and

sunshine in an otherwise gray and stormy week. The wisdom of Willy, expressed in quiet smiles instead of words, smoothed the awkward moments when it became obvious to Fred and Georgina that their only daughter was having a rather special affair with that white city girl. Anderson and Arnold tried to figure out how to manage the new video security systems using a cellphone – as it had been promised they could do – and got lost. There were discussions about the Love Our Lake event, of course, and everyone read over early drafts of the two media releases Wendy had been working on. Adumbi and Willy, joined later by Anita and Marjorie, got into a long discussion on spirituality. Perhaps it was like one of those special nights over centuries gone by when prayer, feast and fellowship prepared soldiers and their communities before the battles began.

***

At 22:27 that evening, the lights from three black Chevy Suburbans and one black Silverado crewcab rounded the last curve along the highway west of Spirit River and swept east onto the heavy-haul road that curved to the south toward Robertson Mines' Awan Lake facility. Eight men gave but a passing glance at the tiny community before refocusing on the briefing they had received and the task that lay before them tonight.

***

At 00:35, Gerald Giordano's dog woke him up, barking furiously. He grabbed his shotgun from beside the front porch door of his mobile home and stepped outside into a blaze of four pair of headlights. He could see his dog silhouetted against the first set of headlights, then he distinctly heard the soft 'thrup' of a silenced automatic pistol and the sickening splat as his dog went silent and smacked head-down into the gravel. Then he became aware of four red spots of light playing across the front of his sweat-stained long underwear and he threw down his shotgun without waiting to be told.

"Mr. Giordano?"

"Yes."

"Please step into your office. We have something for you to read."

Two men in black toques and body armour followed him while he staggered to the door.

"I don't have the key."

The first man had the Glock with the silencer. He

walked to the door and fired two shots: one each at the places where the door handle and the deadbolt meet the door frame. He took a step back and kicked the door open. "Go in and turn on the lights."

"Please sit down at your desk, Gerald. Tonight is the last time you will do this. Look over these papers please," and he passed across five documents, one at a time.

"These first two documents are bills of sale for each of the two parcels of land which you own here, and the third document is a transfer of lease of the former provincial park lands, stating that you agree to transfer all rights to the lands as described, including all improvements, vehicles and personal property, to the purchaser, for an amount that totals $450,000. The document also states that the possession date is this morning, and you will notice there is a signed certified cheque attached, for that same amount. Please sign each of the documents, and my colleague here will witness your signature."

Giordano's eyes widened when he saw the cheque, but he started to speak up: "But where will I g..."

There was another smack as the man with the Glock used it to hit the older man across the face. "Shut up and sign, old man, then listen. It's already late on a long night."

Giordano slumped back in his chair and signed and

dated the documents. He pushed the papers back across the desk but kept the cheque: "I'm keeping this, though!"

"Yes Gerald, you are. And I think you'll like the next document even better," and the man flipped a fourth document onto the desk. "This one states that you will receive deposits to the bank account of your choice in the amount of $6000 per month for a period not to exceed five years as severance pay for your services here, and that you agree that you will never contact, or make any statements about, the Robertson Mines Group or any of its related corporations. Please sign that you accept this arrangement."

Giordano was starting to feel a little easier. As he signed, he asked, "do I have a day or two to grab my stuff and load up my truck?"

The man was silent until Giordano had signed the paper and pushed it back. "And this last document won't cost you anything, yet. It simply states that you agree to move from Spirit River to Winnipeg immediately, where you will remain for a period of at least two years. The document also states your agreement that if you choose to reject any of the previous conditions, at any time, all arrangements will terminated. What it doesn't say is that one of those arrangements is our allowing you to live. Please sign the agreement, Gerald.

The man in black scooped up the papers and put them back into a nylon folder he had been carrying. He looked across at Gerald for a moment, then said, "Thank you for your services here, Mr. Giordano. You will now go to your house with three of my colleagues who are waiting outside, and you will put on clean clothes if you have any. Then you will ride in your nice comfortable new truck with one of your new friends driving, all the way to the corner of Portage and Main in Winnipeg. You will be followed by a second truck, so don't even think about trying anything. In Winnipeg, you, your new truck and your cheque will be dropped off at a local bank, where one of our men will vouch for you to open a bank account. It's a 20-hour trip, so you'll have lots of time to sleep. You will also have time to memorize the contents of that fifth and final document. Do you need a copy?

09:05 AUGUST 6

Room 201 at the two-storey Spirit River Inn was a standard-sized corner room with a view of Awan Lake from both windows. It was furnished more elegantly than the regular rooms, with a small fireplace in the corner and some personal touches including recent novels on the bookshelf and an antique roll-top desk. One of the queen-sized beds had been removed to make room for a small sofa, one overstuffed chair and a coffee table in front of the fireplace.

If he had been at his Ottawa residence near the Rideau Canal in Rockliffe, he would have already had breakfast following his normal five-kilometer morning run, but this morning, Leonard Hamilton-Dubois had slept in until 07:30 and opted to spend an hour preparing his antique Dragon-class sailboat which he kept tied up at a private dock just below his window. He was expecting a visitor for a late breakfast followed by a morning sail on the lake, and he wanted to make sure the sleek wooden boat with her polished winches and cleats was rigged and ready for his guest.

At 09:25, Hamilton-Dubois locked his room and went downstairs to the small breakfast room across the hotel lobby from the Spirit River Inn lounge, which would not open until lunchtime. Florence Dubois had been serving the few breakfast customers since 08:00, and had prepared a corner table for two with fresh orange juice in fluted glasses and a gleaming carafe of coffee. She smiled at her brother-in-law and waved him to the corner table: "Morning, Leonard. I see you were just down at the boat. Did you get in your run already?"

"No. When I got in last night, I just had a drink in the lounge and went to bed. I was going to give you a call, but it was late and it had been a long day so I slept in until after seven. You and I will have lots of time to get together after I've done my thing with this Manville guy this morning. I don't plan to leave until about noon tomorrow, in time to get ahead of most of the long-weekend crawl."

"You said on the phone that he is the new GM out at Robertson? Wow, I only just learned that Maurice was gone!"

"Yes, it seemed sort of sudden, but I knew there had been issues with Bonner for awhile. It came to a head over that drug smuggling thing that caused all the fuss a couple of weeks ago. Bonner likely just got too comfortable. This guy

– Thomas Manville – has a strong reputation with the senior Robertson brass in New York and Washington and is known as a 'fixer', so given the planned expansion, they likely made the right call..."

"...and that must be him in the lobby. I'll go and meet him."

His guest was a caricature of a 1960s airline pilot: just over six feet tall, early fifties with ever-so-slightly graying hair at the temples and the physique of a retired quarterback. "Thomas? Good morning! I'm Leonard Hamilton-Dubois, but please just call me Len."

They shook hands with the guarded warmth of men who understand that their relationship will be defined by their senior executive responsibilities to their employers. Hamilton-Dubois introduced Florence as the Manager of the Spirit River Inn and she showed them to their table.

Hamilton-Dubois ordered a poached egg on toast with a fruit cup and Manville opted for bacon and eggs with tomato slices instead of fried potatoes. They talked at length about their mutual passion for sailing – Manville had invested in an extravagant 60-foot catamaran based in the Mediterranean on a time-share agreement, but he fully appreciated Hamilton-Dubois' sleek antique racer with its royal heritage. "Wooden boats fascinate me," he said, "but they take a lot of

TLC and my job requires quite a bit of moving about. Anyway, my wife hates sailing but she enjoys the glamour of the cat, and its location!"

"Are you settled in at the Maple Suites? I hear they are quite nicely fitted out."

"I've only been there two nights now, but it'll be fine, at least until I find a house. I can expect to be here for three or four years, and normally I like to find a good spot and have a house built for us. I've never lost money on that exercise, and it keeps my wife happy, especially now that the two children are off at university. Do you have kids?

"No, we never did. My late wife was dedicated to her career in foreign affairs with the federal government, and sadly she passed away a couple of years go. Monique, incidentally, was Florence's twin sister. Florence – the same lady I introduced to you when you arrived – has worked here as general manager for over 25 years. I brought her in when she lost her husband and was left with a very young son. He grew up here, got an engineering technology certificate in Toronto, and now works in Fort McMurray in Alberta. He's a neat young guy and I've been like a father to him, but he's probably lucky that I was never able to convince him of the charms of being a mandarin in the nation's capital!"

"I get that!" Manville joked, "I have no idea how you

guys – the good ones like you – survive the ass-kissing and still get stuff done while making sure the politicians get all the credit. I mean, of course we all have ass-kissing to do no matter what job, but in the corporate world it is generally assumed that the bosses are, well – the bosses!"

After breakfast, the two men strolled across the cocktail patio and small strip of lawn to the dock where Hamilton-Dubois' boat was cross-tied in a slipway between two wooden docks. He had prepared the sails before breakfast and a light breeze was blowing out of the north west, so he raised and secured the sails, asked his passenger to slip the two port-side mooring lines while he let go the starboard ones, and he gracefully slid the Johan Anker-designed 29-foot sloop away from the docks, around a small breakwall and out onto the open lake.

"Nicely done," said Manville. "I have a captain and deckhand on the cat, and it's a bit like sailing in your living room. The only boat I actually sailed myself was a windsurfer and I like the feel of this, the feel of the breeze and the feel of the boat responding as she moves along. The only thing I don't envy you is all that varnish... do you do all your own work on her?"

"Yes, that's my winter fun. I have an extra-big garage she goes into at home, so on many evenings and weekends I putter away my time on her. I think I enjoy that almost better than sailing... I certainly spend more time in the garage than on the water!"

Manville was checking Google Maps on his cellphone. "Changing the subject for a moment, I should tell you that I haven't been out to our facility yet – it's a few miles south of here along the east shore, over that way," he pointed. "Right?"

"Exactly. Well past that island you can see in the distance, almost straight ahead of us."

"Not only have I not been there yet, I haven't met any of my management team either, although I think I met the fellow who is the facility development officer at a meeting in New York. My first time with the team will be tomorrow morning... I know the plant is shut down for the long weekend but I wanted to get in a full briefing without interruptions so I called in the team for a couple of hours."

"Makes sense, of course."

"And there's one other thing you should know, not that I expect there to be any backlash. There was a fellow out there by the name of Gerald – Gerald Giordano. He worked for us maintaining the crew camp and family residence park. He was a difficult man, I was told, and had been marginally involved with the bad guys who got us into trouble with the

RCMP and customs and immigration folks last week."

"I heard about the goings-on alright. In fact, seems the little jerk who was the gang leader was killed in the lounge of the Inn while trying to shoot a cop. Florence told me a local guy actually got him. The gang leader was an American, I understand, and had a Mexican mother and an Indian – sorry – Indigenous – stepfather from around here somewhere."

"Exactly, and so I wanted to remove Mr. Giordano from our payroll and to eliminate all possibility of future problems, before I even started in here. I used a technique I have employed in other foreign countries – not that we treat Canada as a foreign country, of course – but I brought in a team of contractors to implement the firing and to manage the whole site for awhile until things settle down. Mr. G. is now making a new home for himself in Winnipeg, with all his debts settled and a decent severance package, and the Robertson Group owns his former property. We also concluded an arrangement to purchase the provincial Crown land that was a park and campsite a couple of decades ago. It had been leased by Mr. G. to expand his rental property business. The contractors have been told to keep their presence very low profile, and their trucks will go unnoticed because Robertson's trucks are all black too."

"Thanks for letting me know, Thomas. I, ah... I hope you have informed the local OPS and RCMP folks about this?"

"It's not a need-to-know situation for the police, really. These fellows are, in fact, merely security guards at our facility. But you have my card – if you get asked any leading questions, please contact me immediately. I don't think there will be any problems. These aren't the same contractors the US Government engages in Afghanistan, you know!"

Hamilton-Dubois handed over the tiller to his passenger and went forward into the tiny cabin where he had tucked away a couple of bottles of beer in a small cooler. "As they used to say in the days of naval sailing ships, 'the sun is over the yardarm' so try one of these – Black Forest Dark Lager, not made in Germany but locally in Ontario by Camerons Brewing Company. I'll bring out a couple of glasses."

"Hey, I'm a Yankee, the bottle is good enough for me. Looks good, thank you!" Manville used the bottle opener proffered by his host and handed it back. "I've been meaning to ask you, is that public protest event with that so-called scientist guy – 'Horowitz' maybe? - still going ahead next weekend?"

Hamilton-Dubois took a prolonged sip on his bottle of lager. "That has not been easy to deal with, Thomas. I got my counterpart in Environment to warn off the local proponents with the threat of losing their local project funding if they had anything to do with advocacy, but they managed to sidestep the whole thing by organizing the event through the local board of trade. Last week, Environment received a complaint from one of the local project's summer employees who complained she had been put at risk on the job and was scared, so Environment seized on the opportunity to shut down the project, as they informed me on Friday. But I don't gather that slowed up the locals at all, because they have been engaging with the national media about a scrap between some international environmental scientists and Horowitz. I was hoping to learn more from Florence this weekend, but haven't had a chance."

"Hmm. I think I read about that late last week. I don't know what's going on there either, so let's keep each other in the loop over the next few days. Has Cameron been in touch?"

"No, he seems to have gone silent this last couple of weeks. Has he been in touch with your head-office?"

"Not that I know of, but I have been busy just getting here, and anyway, I expect those discussions are out of my loop until something actually happens. Head Office refers to me as their senior 'fixer' and a 'Senior VP for Development' but I don't get to make corporate decisions at the Cameron level." He paused long enough for another mouthful of beer, then asked: "Hey, Leonard, you actually worked for Garnet Cameron when he was Minister of Natural Resources. How was he?"

"Bah. I know this sounds like sour grapes from a bureaucrat, but frankly he was no different from most politicians during his tenure. For sure he was no genius, and I think the only reason he was in Cabinet is because he had been a Member of Parliament for so long. And I think the only reason he was elected so often is that he spent most of his time buying votes with small projects all across his constituency – like the Protected Shorelines Project here at Awan Lake. Of course, he's still the opposition MP for this riding, and while I am not at all sure how he is able to be such an effective lobbyist for the Robertson Group without being called on it, hey, it works for us all and I get along with him just fine!"

"It would be nice if the folks in our country – particularly the media – were as relaxed about government as you guys," Manville chuckled!

"I've noticed that, Thomas. You folks in the USA get so worked up about everything! We'd be just the same, I expect, but... we have winter!

***

It was noon, and Marjorie had just received a text from Wendy to say she and Anita were almost done with shopping and would return after lunch. Marjorie and Anderson had enjoyed a relaxed Sunday morning, talking about last night's barbecue and figuring out how to work the new video security system. Once they set it up, they could receive alarms on their cellphones as well as retrieve video stored online. All the high-tech security stuff seemed a bit silly on a peaceful summer morning, but they both felt an underlying sense of dread and knew there were still too many unanswered questions to let down their guard.

Anderson suggested they make a couple of ham sandwiches and take them to the boat, where he had to make sure everything would be ready to take the Sergeant and his diver to the chopper crash site in the morning. They sat on a couple of folding chairs on the well-deck finishing their beer-and-sandwich lunch and admiring a varnished-wood sailboat gliding by the harbour with two men onboard. Anderson recognized it as the elegant little yacht that spent the summers docked at the shore in front of the Inn. Florence had told him once that it was her bother-in-law's pride and joy but that he hardly ever took it out on the water. "This must be a special Sunday," he said to Marjorie. "I think it's the first time in two or three years that I've seen that boat away from her dock!"

"Sure is pretty. I've seen it go by the island a couple of times, but you're right... not very often!"

The boat tacked and sailed closer to the shore, and was soon passing by them barely 50 feet away. The tall thin man at the tiller waved: "Can we come alongside for a moment? Got someone here I'd like you to meet."

Anderson shrugged at Marjorie, stood up and waved them in: "Sure! I'll get out some fenders." He pulled three rubber bumpers out of the middle hatch and hooked their lanyards over small cleats along the port-side gunwale. They stood and watched as the helmsman skillfully made a downwind turn to approach his landing into the gentle wind. The passenger had prepared a couple of white nylon lines which he flipped across to Marjorie and Anderson and in just moments the small but luxurious yacht was safely alongside and well-protected from scarring her varnished topsides on the rough oak gunwales of the heavy workboat.

"Someone knows how to sail!" said Anderson with a grin as he stretched out his hand. "Good afternoon. I'm Frank Anderson and this is Marjorie Webster. Welcome onboard – I think we still have a couple of beers that we need help with, or I can make some coffee. That's the good news – the bad news is that we already finished the sandwiches!"

The two men stepped easily across to join them, leaving the sails loose and luffing quietly behind them. "Hello Frank, we've never met but Florence has told me all about you. I'm Leonard, her brother-on-law, and this is Thomas Manville, who just flew in from New York a couple of days to take over as General Manager out at Robertson Mines. Thanks for the compliment on the landing... I even surprised myself. I don't get out sailing nearly as often as I'd like. I actually live in Ottawa, where apparently I am owned by Her Majesty as a loyal servant and she keeps me busy."

"This is a nice little ship, Frank," said Manville. "Can I take a look around?"

"Absolutely. The only thing elegant about her is that she does her job – whatever that is – very well and keeps most of the lake outside the gunwales." He passed around the last four beers.

After the two men had admired *The Beaver*, Manville asked, "There's enough gear on this boat to do a lot of stuff! If you don't mind me asking, just what do you do to use a boat like this?"

"On normal days, she just gets me back and forth to the

island cottages where I fix and build stuff. You know: doing renovations, building docks and boathouses, sometimes recovering boats and motors. I'm basically an all-around handyman, I guess. I also have a small barge and a small trackhoe so I do foundations and septic tank installs too."

"I think he sells himself short, Thomas. Florence told me that he intervened in our lounge at the Inn when that guy tried to shoot a police office two weeks ago. I guess I owe you a beer or two someday... the only damage done was a bullet hole in the wall just below the ceiling!"

"Your bullet?" Manville was giving Anderson a hard look.

"Afraid so. Not my line of work, really!"

"My office tells me you're the president of the local environmental club."

Anderson made a point of chuckling: "Nope, not me. And it's not really an environmental club, it's a shoreline research and wildlife protection organization. And – I have the best committee position ever – just the vice-chairman – which means as long as I can make sure the real chairman stays healthy I don't have to do a damn thing!"

"What do you think, Ms. Webster?"

"My name is Marjorie. Frank undersells himself... his is always the moderate voice at the table when folks get crazy."

"Hmm. As the old saying goes, walk softly and carry a big stick. And apparently in your case, shoot straight. You ever had a captain's ticket in the navy?" Manville's tone was over-polite, Marjorie was thinking, and carried an edge.

"Coast Guard cutter, years ago."

"So with your obvious skills, how come you haven't been able to get the environmentalists around here to stand down? Maybe you agree with them?"

Leonard Hamilton-Dubois was looking increasingly uncomfortable, and appeared to be about to say something – but didn't. He looked unhappily across the deck at Anderson and stayed quiet.

"Well, this is civilian life and a small community at that, so I keep my opinions pretty buttoned up. If someone wanted me to open up in a hurry, they'd learn soon enough that I think the environmentalists are a bunch of wussies, and if they want to get something done to protect the lake they are gonna have to do a lot more than hold love-ins with flaky old scientists. I'd tell them to get real hard-core scientists in here along with a squadron of lawyers and invite a First Nation or two to intervene."

Leonard Hamilton-Dubois was looking around like he was trying to find a hole in the boat to crawl into, and Marjorie had to move away and look into the wheelhouse so they wouldn't see her laughing.

"No worries, though, Thomas. We're a pretty relaxed bunch around here. That Dr. Horowitz will attract a bit of public attention next weekend, the debate will go on for awhile, then winter will come and you can't make waves on a frozen lake. All will be forgotten until spring... sorta like the Circle of Life meets Awan Lake."

"So I gather you don't see any problems with our expansion project and the technology we are proposing?"

"I didn't say that. I think there are many questions people want to ask, and since they live here they deserve to have their questions answered. It's their lake, and their community. Simple as that."

***

A black Suburban and a similar Chevy crewcab, with white "RMG SECURITY" lettering on the front doors, turned into the last driveway of the former provincial park on the east shore of Awan Lake. The driveway was little more than a rough trail that led to a clearing near the shore. In days gone by, the clearing had been the northernmost in a string of nicely-maintained campsites with attractive green picnic tables and steel above-ground fire pit. Now, it was simply a mess: the rotted remnants of the picnic table had long-since been burned for firewood, and replaced by a discarded chrome-legged kitchen table. The table sat between two old slide-in type pickup campers which had been set flat on the ground with the doors facing toward each other in a parody of a two-bedroom suite with a common dining room.

Two armed men in black uniforms got out of each of the vehicles, which they had parked on either side of the beat-up white pickup that sat at the edge of the clearing. One of them – the driver of the Suburban – walked forward to address the lone occupant of the campsite: "Mrs. Mistraika?"

"That's me. What do you want?"

"I'm Mike Smith and we're from the security division of the Robertson Group, which now owns and manages this land." He started to hand her a printed sheet of paper but she slapped it away, so he placed it on the table and weighted it down with a dirty coffee mug. "This is an eviction order. This is not a public campsite and you and your friends are classified as squatters. You must remove yourselves and your personal property by noon tomorrow."

The woman had probably reached the age of sixty, and at least fifty-nine of those years had not treated her well. "I don't give a crap, mister," she spat out, "I've only been here for a couple of weeks and I hate it here so I'll just go back to the farm. You'll have to deal with the two boys, though. They're your problem and not mine."

"So where are these two young men?"

She waved toward a narrow trail that went down to the shore. "They went out fishing after lunch. Dunno when they'll be back. Probably later, near dark."

"Are they part of your family?"

"Nephews, kinda. They brought me here two weeks ago after my old man was killed. They're both little pricks, just like him."

She pitched her empty beer can into a pile of cans and bottles under the side of one of the campers, and opened another one. "Don't know why I came," she muttered to herself as she fished another cigarette from a pack on the table.

The man who called himself Mike Smith had walked back to talk to the other three men who were still standing near their vehicles. He returned to Mrs. Mistraika: "We have a suggestion for you. If you want to go back to your farm, we can take you there, and we'll leave the eviction notice here on the door. That way it won't be your problem at all."

"You'd do that? Works for me – all I have to carry is one bag, my carton of smokes and half a case of beer they owe me. I only live half an hour from here."

"This is all good. Gather your stuff and put it by the SUV... we'll leave in a few minutes." Smith walked back to the others: "Okay. Jim, you and I can drive Mrs. Mistraika to her farm in the Suburban. Tanner, you and Pete go back to the yard and get one of the guys to start walking the Cat back here. No point in loading it onto the trailer – it's only a mile or so. Once they get here they can start digging the pit over there on the other side of the campers. There's nothing here to salvage so it'll all go into the hole before we burn. We'll have to have at least three personnel here until those kids are back, have been given the eviction order, and are on their way out. I was able to get their information... they may be young but they have records and the records include violence, in and out of juvie! One's name is Rodney and the other is David – both are Mistraikas. We can expect they'll take their boat and truck, at least. Take pictures."

"Do you have the eviction notice?"

"Yes, I grabbed it off the table. Give me a couple of minutes while I write up a new one, with the boys' names and I'm backing the time up to 10:00 hours tomorrow when I want them gone."

"What do we tell them if they say they already paid rent?"

"Ask for the receipt. I am sure they don't have one – it

would have been the uncle who paid, if at all. If they do produce a receipt, tell them it's not a legal rental agreement but ask for their address and we'll refund the amount on the receipt. In any case, they are leaving by 10:00 tomorrow. And don't forget to set up three of the guys and two vehicles for the night watch on this place."

06:00 AUGUST 7

The morning was clear and cool, and the sun was just lighting up the trees along the eastern shore. Anderson and Marjorie had woken early and were sitting on the porch, wrapped in sweaters and fondling steaming mugs of coffee. "Remind me, Frank... what time does the Anderson Navy sail this morning?"

"As soon as the troops are boarded, around zero nine hundred hours," Anderson chuckled. "This should be an easy morning. We just have to get the diver out to the crash site, anchor, and turn her loose to look for that rifle. I just hope that marker buoy is still in place."

"You had it marked on the GPS anyway, didn't you?"

"Yes, but hitting exactly the same spot will be quicker if the buoy is still there. Anyway, I'm cheap and I want to recover it and its anchor! The whole exercise shouldn't take too long – a couple of hours travel each way, and if Monica doesn't find anything within an hour, she likely never will. So we should be home by mid afternoon. Sergeant John said he'd bring lunch, but I guess we should have breakfast before we go, and bring lots of coffee."

"I'm still giggling at you and your conversation with Manville-the-Manager yesterday afternoon. And you certainly had Leonard terrified... you say he's Florence's brother-in-law? How did he wind up with her last name?"

"Anita told me after supper last night. Seems that the best way to get ahead in Canada's swivel service is to have a hyphenated last name, one French and the other English. That happens frequently enough when people marry, of course, but I'm not sure how often the man takes his wife's last name. Anyway, in this case that's what happened: Len Hamilton became Leonard Hamilton-Dubois. And, of course, Dubois is Florence's last name."

"I'm just being nosy, but do you suppose there's anything more there than a brother-sister type relationship?

"Really no idea. I do know they are very close. I don't think Leonard – given his job – has many people he can trust, and Florence told me that losing his wife devastated him. She says they talk together a lot... anything beyond that I don't know. As I get older and older, things surprise me less and less. I just hope that he treats her very well, since she has dedicated most of her life to the Inn – which he owns –and to his other investment schemes."

"Do you like Leonard?"

"I don't really know him well enough to say whether I like him or not. He certainly is friendly to me, but I do know that I don't trust him."

"Why so?"

"Well, to start with, he has always had a close relationship with Garnet Cameron, our Member of Parliament and at one time the Minister responsible for his department – Natural Resources. Garnet is a friendly guy too, but again, I don't trust him any farther than I could bounce an anvil in a swamp. And yesterday, Leonard turns up as the personal host of the very newly minted – and evidently very well connected – manager of the biggest mining operation in Garnet's constituency. One might think those concerned with public-service ethics would frown on relationships that close. Add to this that somehow Mr. Hamilton-Dubois, through a few holding companies, owns the Inn and a number of potential development properties outside of the village. And, as I mentioned over dinner the other night, he is also the owner of 51% of the marina."

"How do you know all this stuff?"

Anderson chuckled, and paused. "I'm the new guy in town, I guess, and come across as a bit of a loner, so perhaps I'm not a threat. People just, well, talk!"

It was Marjorie's turn to chuckle. "Every broad in town

– including Mademoiselle Dubois I think – wishes they could take you home and feed you, and guys from cops to crooks all line up to ask for your help and advice. And, you've been here twenty years, so I don't know about the "new kid in town" bit!"

Anderson gave her a big grin and a squeeze on the shoulder. "You're so cute! I think it's my turn to cook the bacon and eggs, which we'd best eat soon or we'll be floating around the lake with only Sergeant John's donuts to eat. I'll bring you more coffee while I go fry stuff."

***

At 09:45, the diving gear, the Sergeant and Monica-the-diver were safely onboard and *The Beaver* was out of the harbour and heading south, leaving Ship Island to starboard "just so they could sound the horn and wake up Wendy and Anita" who had returned to the island after supper last evening. The small detour south of the island had been Marjorie's idea... today she was getting boat-driving lessons while Anderson sipped coffee with the cops. His instructions to the student driver were simple: "choose your own course, keep the boat somewhere around eight knots (with the engine around 2800 rpm), head for the GPS waypoint that marks the crash site, and don't run into anything. If another boat shows up anywhere near, let me know."

Anderson and Sergeant John were going over yesterday's conversations with Hamilton-Dubois and Manning. He also shared with the Sergeant a brief conversation he'd had with Leonard while Manning was walking around the dock: "Leonard told me confidentially that the new Robertson Mines manager had brought in a team of highly-trained security contractors, and that he intended to make some changes, including purging the employee residence campsite and removing its manager."

"Wow, that's a bit over-the-top. We sort of like it when companies consult with us when they engage security personnel, and I've heard nothing about this."

Sometimes, timing is everything, even when it's not on purpose. At that point, Monica came out onto the deck and said Marjorie was curious about some black smoke on the shore and also possibly a boat in the area of the smoke. Anderson jumped up and went into the wheelhouse and grabbed his binoculars off their hook behind the wheel station. "Hey Marj, when did you notice this?"

"Like, less than a minute ago. The smoke went up suddenly and got my attention, then I thought I could see something white moving along the shore. It's straight off to the left – to port I guess."

Anderson crossed to the side window opposite the wheel and rested his arms on the sill to steady the binoculars. "Yeah, that's a lot of smoke, more than just someone burning brush. Sergeant... better have a look at this. And yes, there is a white boat moving fast to the north along the shore. Marj, maybe take the throttle back to about 1200 while we figure out what we need to do, if anything."

The Sergeant took the binoculars from Anderson and scanned the shore. "That smoke is a long way north of Robertson's – maybe a mile or even more. And it's really close to the water. And... the boat appears to have stopped, maybe half a mile from the smoke."

By now they were all gathered in the wheelhouse. Marjorie had cut the speed back, but was still headed toward the original destination – the helicopter crash site, at least 45 minutes away to the south west. "Would you like me to turn in toward shore so we can get a closer look?"

Anderson looked across at the Sergeant and paused for a moment. "Half of me really wants to go take a look, but it worries me that we are not well armed. All I have onboard is an inefficient rifle and a shotgun, and Sergeant – all you have is a sidearm. I'm pretty sure I've seen that boat before, it is a jetboat, and I would bet it's the one that ran over those water-survey interns last week. I also have a feeling it was somehow mixed up in the action two weeks ago. If so, it's really powerful and we'll never catch it, and by the same token we'll never outrun it. And – we know some of the stuff that's happening onshore but we have no details. So I am less than cheerful about getting too close. Is there another way to get eyes on that location?"

"I agree, entirely. Let's keep heading south. I'll call in to get a plane to overfly the east shore and I'll send out a car with a couple of officers. However, I'll need to use your satphone – mine crashed on the weekend."

Anderson took the phone off his belt and handed it to the Sergeant, "Done... Marj, we can resume speed and course to the wreck site. Like me to spell you off?"

She put the throttle back to where it had been and began to step back from the wheel. "Yes, thanks! I had fun though. I think I'm learning."

"One more thing to teach you today." Anderson told her to resume her course according to the GPS, then pointed to the "AUTO" button on the autohelm, and pushed it. "Okay, hands off the wheel... got it! Now you can go for coffee!"

"Jerk!"

"I'm nothing if not lazy! Joking aside, though, the autohelm saves a lot of trouble but it's kinda scary when you realize it could go totally wrong. There are off-course alarms and all kinds of good stuff, but the boat still requires a capable helmsman to keep an eye and ear open – and you, young lady, are just exactly that!"

Fifteen minutes later, after the Sergeant had made arrangements for an immediate overfly of shore as well as a vehicle patrol of the area, the crew had fresh coffee and another dive into the donuts. Monica had been watching the shore and the boat through the binoculars and called out, "Sergeant, I think that boat is now heading our way, and it's moving right along!"

All eyes turned to where she indicated, and the Sergeant took a look through the glasses before handing them to Anderson. "I think she's right. Take a look."

Anderson studied the boat through the glasses. "Sure is. The boat is about three miles back and coming fast – perhaps at about thirty knots. If we hold our course and speed, she'll get to us in seven or eight minutes." He handed back the binoculars and pushed the throttle up to full speed. "That'll give us another couple of minutes, maybe. Now what?"

The Sergeant handed the glasses to Monica and said, "Keep close watch and tell us what you see. Frank, pull out your guns from up front and load up, just in case we need them. Everyone stay in the wheelhouse so they can't clearly see how many of us there are. Is your loud-hailer working?"

"I'll turn it on. They'll have a really loud engine in there so they'll have to be pretty close to hear us. I guess it also might be worth trying them on the marine radio, but I doubt they have one, or even have it on."

"We can give it a try when they are closer. Why don't we change course a bit to see how closely they track us?"

Marjorie jumped over to the wheel and punched the button to turn off the autohelm. She slowly turned the wheel to take them about ten degrees to starboard. "Like that?"

"Yup. Hold that for about a minute and we'll see what they do. Then turn back to where you were. I'm calling that plane and hoping he's in the air."

Anderson dumped the block out of the old Winchester shotgun, loaded in six #12 shot shells and set it on the cabin floor by the steps into the forward cabin. Then he loaded the magazine of the Parker Hale .308 and set it on the floor beside the shotgun, along with both boxes of ammunition. Then he opened the sliding windows on both sides of the wheelhouse.

Marjorie had returned the boat to its original course and Monica, who was using the binoculars through the small rear window behind her, reported that the white boat had roughly followed their course adjustments. "Now I am pretty sure I can see no more than two people on the boat, both of them sitting low behind the windshield. It's throwing up a helluva lot of water behind so yes, I'm pretty sure it's a jetboat – an old one, too."

The Sergeant had clicked off the phone and put it in his pocket. "As it turns out they are sending the old EC135. They were doing a training exercise anyway so there are officers onboard and by now they are probably eight to ten minutes out. He knows where to find us. Now we need to make some decisions: do we let the boat catch up and go by us, in case they just want us to stop and talk for some reason. If not, we risk gunfire. On the other hand, if we turn into them, we are asking for more than gunfire."

"Let's let them get closer and decide which way to pass us. Then maybe we'll see if they are armed, or if they just try to signal us. I'll lie down with both long guns aimed in their general direction, but Sergeant it's up to you to tell me to fire. Marjorie, put the autohelm back on, cut the throttle to less than half and then stay down far enough that they can't really see you."

"I'm in uniform, so I'll fly the flag by standing in the wheelhouse door. They may not suspect a cop onboard... that may change the dynamics a bit. Monica, give me the glasses and get down in the opposite corner."

"Hope you're wearing some Kevlar, John."

"Don't worry, Frank – I never come near you without it these days!"

"I know the feeling, John," Marjorie piped up from her position on the floor. "I really do!"

The white boat was only a hundred yards back by now, turned sharply left to pass and started to slow down. The man at the wheel kept the boat about 50 yards off *The Beaver's* port side, but did not stop. The Sergeant waved at them and motioned for them to slow down and stop, but instead the driver made a sharp turn away to the left, sped up until they were about 300 yards distant, and stopped. The Sergeant could see that the two men were obviously having a heated discussion.

"Looks like we've got them confused. I guess they didn't expect to see a uniform." The Sergeant stepped back into the wheelhouse and asked Marjorie to stay out of sight but to cut their speed back to dead slow. "Let's see what they do next. If we can stall them a bit longer we will have that chopper here to help convince them to behave."

The jetboat snorted a shot of blue smoke and water as it started to move forward. Holding its distance at first, it began a slow circle around the almost-stopped workboat, gradually shortening the distance between them as it passed behind and came back up the port side, perhaps a hundred yards off. The Sergeant used the loud-hailer to call them, and motioned them to stop, but if they got the message there was no sign.

"Frank, could you fire across their bow? That .308 should do the job... and don't worry about chipping some paint..."

"Okay. I'll fire as it passes the port window. Everyone block your ears!"

The report from the old hunting rifle filled the wheelhouse for an instant and the response from the jetboat was almost immediate. The operator turned the boat away and jammed the throttle lever forward, putting a couple of hundred more yards between the two boats before he stopped. The Sergeant could clearly see the two men yelling at one another. One ducked down below the windshield and produced what appeared to be a rifle from under the bow.

Anderson joined the Sergeant at the wheelhouse door: "John, I am willing to bet that if we turn straight at them and goose it, they'll run... and that would be better than having them come back to us!"

"Go for it. Keep your shotgun handy."

Anderson turned back to the wheel, but Marjorie was already there. "Yes?"

"Absolutely. Turn hard, aim straight at them and run the

throttle to the max."

As the larger – but much slower – boat turned and started to speed up, the operator of the jetboat started to turn the boat away. His passenger, however, stepped back to the boat's stern with his rifle and appeared to be preparing to shoot back. Both men were yelling at one another.

"Looks like they're having an argument about what to do. Spray them with some birdshot, Frank!"

Anderson pumped a shell into the chamber, stepped around the outside of the wheelhouse, braced himself against the starboard railing and thumbed off the safety. He aimed about six feet above the stern of the jetboat, and fired.

It took the birdshot just over a second to reach the boat, an instant after the muzzle blast. The jetboat's operator slammed his throttle forward at the same time as his companion felt the sting of the steel pellets hitting his head and arm. When the boat shot forward under power he was already off-balance and after one desperate effort to steady himself against the engine hatch he flipped over the stern and into the water. The jetboat kept going in a straight line – southwest, if anyone cared at this point.

"Okay, let's pick this guy up. He's lost his rifle so he'll be pretty tame."

"Frank, I need you on the wheel for this," shouted

Marjorie, who had already pulled the throttle back. "I don't want to learn rescue maneuvers on a real person, even an idiot!"

Anderson pumped a fresh shell into the chamber and re-set the safety. "Trade you for the shotgun," he told Marjorie as he took over the controls. "Get Monica to help John fish the guy out of the water, while you just stand at the door. Try to look mean!"

As Anderson took the wheel, the marine radio began to squawk: it was one of the officers on the chopper. "Sergeant, you'd better talk to your helicopter. I assume you have a plan for them."

The EC135 was about 500 feet off the water and a half-mile northwest of their position. The Sergeant confirmed that they had arrived at the right location and directed them to intercept the smaller vessel moving away at high speed while his team rescued and arrested one suspect who had fallen overboard. He indicated they would catch up and take the jetboat in tow and arrest the second suspect, and would appreciate having one of the officers transferred to the boat to assist.

They felt – and heard – the downwash from the helicopter as it passed while Anderson was bringing the boat alongside the very scared-looking young man who had seemed so brave six minutes earlier. Monica had set out the boarding ladder and when it became obvious the man was unarmed the Sergeant holstered his sidearm and the two of them helped him up on deck, slapped a set of handcuffs on him and sat him on the floor of the well-deck near the stern.

Once the man was onboard and the ladder was secured, Anderson aimed *The Beaver* southwest to where he could see the helicopter engaging with the jetboat. It took about twenty minutes to reach the scene, and when they arrived, the jetboat was dead in the water with its engine off and its operator sitting forlornly in the cockpit while the chopper hovered nearby with a fully-armoured officer and a carbine tethered at the right-side door.

The Sergeant and the pilot were now communicating by satellite phone, and agreed that they would transfer the officer onboard before arresting the remaining suspect. "Might as well do this dry: just come overhead and cable him down. We'll hold a slow course into the wind – such as it is – our skipper is used to that. Once we're clear and have this guy onside and the boat under tow, you can go ahead and overfly that stretch of shoreline and see what's with the smoke. There should be one of our black-and-whites around there shortly."

Half an hour later, OPP Corporal Jeanette LaFrançois

was safely onboard, the chopper was on its way to the east shore and the jetboat was attached by a short towrope to *The Beaver*. The two suspects had been identified as Rodney and David Mistraika and were handcuffed and shackled together on the workboat. As far as criminals go, they were a bedraggled lot, sitting silent, sullen and scared on the floor of the well-deck.

Anderson had been paying some special attention to the hull of the jetboat. He had pulled the boat alongside, and he motioned the Sergeant over to have a look at some fresh deep scars on the paint and into the aluminum on either side of the bow and well along the chine on either side. After taking a couple of cellphone snapshots, they let the boat go back to the length of the rope and went forward into the wheelhouse where he put *The Beaver* into gear and began to move forward, adjusting her speed to make sure their tow was following comfortably.

"Sergeant, if I were a betting man, I'd say this is the boat that ran over the Ryerson University kids and their little water-sampling boat."

"I agree. Good reason to make sure we have that crane and truck at the dock when we get back. I have enough to go on to hold these dumb kids, but I want enough forensic evidence to lay more serious charges than careless operation of a vessel. Careless operation causing death would be better, and of course I want to nail them with homicide, but I need to find a motive. Who is behind this? I hope they stay really scared for a few hours – they may just spill their guts."

"So, Sergeant John, now that I have this outfit happily underway at about two-thirds throttle, what direction do you want me to travel? Take the boat and the boys back north to the village, or continue south to that crash scene to look for your missing carbine?"

The Sergeant paused for a moment before answering: "Let's go back to the village. I think we've put everyone through enough stress for today... I can't speak for you, but I will speak for Monica and Marjorie, neither of whom are police officers but have been serving as cops for a couple of hours. On top of that, we have suspects onboard and evidence in tow... We'll come back and play underwater another day."

Anderson was already making the slow turn north. "I'm good with that. I want some coffee and... you said you were bringing lunch?"

"Tim Hortons' chicken salad sandwiches and there's even an extra one for Corporal Jeanette. We can give our prisoners donuts and some coffee – we've got lots of that."

"I'll serve them if the Corporal will move the handcuffs

from back to front. But I suggest we don't want to get those two on a sugar-and-caffeine high, so maybe one donut and a cup of water?"

The Sergeant looked across at Marjorie. "Thanks, Marj. And yes, you're right – one donut and no coffee."

***

It was 10:45 and Thomas Manville had checked in with his credentials at the Robertson Mines main gate, a second time with the general office receptionist, and finally – including full introductions – with executive assistant Bonnie Samson at her desk by the door of what would henceforth be his office.

"Ms. Samson, I have asked Charles Morrell and Bob Adamson to meet with me in my office about fifteen minutes from now. Please just show them in as they arrive. Then at 11:20, you can expect to see Keith Austin, our new special security head. Please show him in as well. No other visitors for now."

"Certainly, Sir. Would you like me to have Mariana bring some coffee for about ten minutes after Mr. Morrell and Mr. Adamson arrive?"

"That would be very nice. Thank-you, Ms. Samson."

Manville had brought a briefcase, which he opened at his new desk. He took out some document files which he arranged to the left on his desk and fished out three files labelled 'Morrell', 'Adamson' and 'Austin' then took out a laptop which he connected to the charger and Ethernet cable. He re-set his desk so that his back would be to the window when he sat down, and changed around the chairs at the small boardroom table so that the chair that was obviously where the boss sat had its back to the other window in the corner office. One window looked down onto the company parking lot and its surrounding lawn and gardens; the other looked west across the lake.

Bonnie tapped on the door and showed in his first two visitors. They shook hands and he pointed at the table. "Make yourselves comfortable, gentlemen. Bob, you and I have met before in New York, and Charles, we have not met before today but your reputation precedes you. You've done excellent work here by all accounts, so it is a pleasure to meet you. I want to thank you both for agreeing to meet with me on this long-weekend Monday. We very much appreciate that, and I'll let you go back to your families in time for lunch."

Manville sat down at the head of the table and continued: "The first thing we need to clear up is what I am sure is the elephant in the room this morning – the changes by the gate and accommodations facilities and even further north along the road. Charles, I am sure your superintendent has already told you that the new security division purloined one of the D-8s on Sunday morning and walked it down the road, destroying stuff along the way. And I am sure there is much muttering amongst the staff."

Charles grinned: "Yes, muttering is a good enough word for it... maybe 'WTF' would be better. Word is out that it has something to do with the new boss, and I sort of calmed them down a little by reminding them how much they used to hate Gerald Giordano so having him gone had to be the beginning of better times ahead. I think they bought that!"

Manville chuckled. "Perfect – well handled! I had heard Giordano was a jerk so it sounds like there won't be too many ruffled feathers about his absence. For your confidential information, by now he is in Winnipeg, a much wealthier man than he ever was, but also a very scared one. Certainly too scared to ever come back here."

Bonnie tapped on the door again and ushered in a sweet-faced matronly woman in a white apron bringing a cart with a coffee carafe, cups, and Danish pastries along with some glasses and a jug of ice-water with a slice of lemon. "Thank-you, Mariana, I'm Thomas Manville."

After Mariana had nodded and smiled and the door had closed behind her, Manville continued: "Yes, Keith Austin and his special security team will provide a quick dose of 'shock-and-awe' around here. I have found that no matter where we do business, shock-and-awe is occasionally a good and necessary thing. It also ties in to how we handle the community, some of its key leaders, and the media over the next week or ten days. Keith and the seven guys on his team will be working closely with another group of professionals who will arrive here on Tuesday – tomorrow. They are, essentially, commercial actors... you know, not the famous ones, but the ones who are happy to go on TV and sell you stuff that is bad for you. Politicians use those same types to infiltrate protest marches and over the next few days, they will be moving around in ones and twos in our surrounding community here to get people steamed up against the guest speaker at the Love Our Lake event on Sunday, and to plant some distrust about environmentalists and the media."

There was another tap on the door, and Keith Austin was shown in. Manville stood up and welcomed him: "Keith, this is Bob Adamson, our development officer here, and Charles Morrell, the operations manager for this Robertson Mines location."

Austin wore the same black uniform, body armour and all, that he had worn during his visit to Gerald Giordano two evenings before – except for the toque, which was missing. He was almost a head taller than the other three men, with broad shoulders and closely-cropped gold hair. His eyes were almost white-blue and his face displayed no sign of emotion. He shook hands cordially enough, but wordlessly and without a smile.

"Keith, I was just explaining to Charles and Bob that while we need to stir up some resentment in the community over the next few days, our most important goal is to discredit the media. Of course, you already understand which media to target. We need to remind everybody how scientists collaborate with the United Nations and other foreign-controlled agencies to provide false information."

"Is Marguerite in charge of this team, and is she writing the script?"

"Yes."

"Good." Austin turned to Charles Morrell and handed him a business card. "Here is my 24-7 contact. Call me if you need assistance, or if you are worried about a conflict with any of your operations. For your information, all the residents of the trailer park and accommodations units who are not Robertson staff or direct family have been evacuated from the lands north of the facility and all abandoned assets have been burned and buried. One of my team is walking your bulldozer back to the yard as we are speaking. Our team has set up camp just outside the main gate and we have engaged a sub-contractor to fence off the entire site north of the plant. That will not start until after the public event is over. If that is all, Mr. Manville, I will get back to my team."

"Thank-you Keith."

***

What had begun as a hot and almost calm August day had deteriorated by the time Anderson's workboat with the big jetboat trailing behind arrived at the Spirit River dock. Broken clouds were scattered in the sky and a few short rain-squalls had made it necessary to dig out a small tarpaulin to protect the two Mistraika boys. Swirling wind gusts became more frequent and made landing the workboat and its tow alongside the dock somewhat of a challenge... Anderson was grateful to have good hands on board and a bunch of police and other personnel on dock to grab mooring lines and fasten ropes wherever they were needed. The two prisoners were taken ashore and loaded into a waiting van for transfer to holding cells in Maple Falls, and next came the forensics team to take charge of the jetboat. They took a number of photos throughout the process of placing slings under the hull, looping the slings onto the crane hook and guiding the 28-foot long boat out of the water, across the dock and onto a waiting flatbed trailer with the help of guide-ropes to keep it straight and steady.

The wind was causing trouble so the crane operator kept the boat low as it crossed over. Anderson and the Sergeant watched very closely, looking at the hull for scratches, grooves and dents.

By 16:30, the dock and road were empty and Marjorie and Anderson were left alone on the boat, staring out at what was now a howling wind and beating rain. Waves rolled in from the lake, small, but big enough to gently lift the former lobster boat, pulling at her mooring lines and bumping her against the fenders on the dock. Anderson went into the small forward cabin and came back with a small cooler with a half-dozen GW beer from Saskatchewan.

"Been saving these for the perfect occasion, and this is as close to the perfect occasion as we're gonna get today, my pretty little first mate!"

"Yes, please, absolutely. If someone had told me a month ago that soon I would be driving a small ship and helping to arrest murderers at gunpoint, I'd have said that was crazy. Today, it all just seems normal, so... cheers, my love!"

"Cheers, indeed. And yes, it must be love because I am sharing my GW beer!"

Anderson paused, and rolled his eyes: "Oh crap, I almost forgot. I did forget I guess... Arnold called while we were coming in and said we have to have a Board of Trade – slash – Protected Shorelines meeting tonight. Eight o'clock at the Inn. And here I thought we could drink all of these beers, just you and I, and we could investigate the sleeping quarters in the forward cabin!"

"Keep that thought! Some night, if not this one. Wendy and Anita should be at the meeting too, but they shouldn't be out on the lake in that little boat of ours."

"Arnold texted that they are both at Arnold and Marion's."

"Okay, perfect. Let's try supper at the Inn and see if all four want to come. I assume that's where the meeting will be?"

"Good idea... you call them. Rain's letting up a bit... I'll go grab the truck at the house and pick you up back here."

"Grab the Jeep – it doesn't leak. Here's the keys!"

***

187

Monday nights on long weekends were usually slow times at the Inn, and tonight was no exception. There was no one there when they arrived, and only a half-dozen people came in for a quick drink or to pick up take-out burgers during the time that the six of them ate supper. Florence was serving, and before the hamburgers were done she took Anderson aside for a moment: "Leonard told me he had a really nice visit with you and Marjorie yesterday afternoon. He wanted me to thank you for your hospitality and to apologize for his guest, who was, I gather, the new boss out at Robertson Mines."

"Gee, well, thanks Flo... no big deal really. Marjorie told me I let him get under my skin, and I think she's probably right. I have a tendency to push back when somebody tries to crowd me."

"Well, you're more calm than most people I know, but anyway, Leonard also asked me to tell you not to trust that guy. 'Don't let him tear down what Anderson and his friends have stood up for,' he said."

"I find that very interesting, and thank-you, Florence. Actually, as you know Leonard and I hardly know each other, but I have to say I thought he did not look at all comfortable yesterday."

"I know. I'm really worried about him. Something's going on, maybe at work, or with the endless politics that surround him. Dunno. I hope he's okay. He was on the phone all morning, and said he was going to go back to Ottawa this afternoon, but he told me he had enjoyed his sail so much yesterday that he was going out again this afternoon for a sail around the islands then motor downriver to the Falls for supper and maybe sleep over until tomorrow. Not like him, and the weather has been lousy this afternoon."

"Well, he's a good sailor, and he's got a good boat. Try not to worry too much, Flo. As you say, he must have lots on his mind. I know I couldn't take the pressures of his kind of job."

"Thanks, Frank. I guess I know that. I imagine I'm worried about nothing," and she returned to the kitchen to bring out their suppers.

Anderson returned to the table with alarm bells going off in his head. He sat down and re-joined the conversation, which by now had turned to the big news in town: Arnold patted the arm of Anderson's chair and asked, "Okay, Frank, tell us what's going down. We saw that big white motorboat going by on a flatdeck, along with a crane, a paddy wagon and some cop cars. We've also seen a bunch of black security trucks – Suburbans actually – getting around town today. Don't know about the black trucks, but I am pretty close to a hundred percent sure you had something to do with that boat, crane and flatdeck! Of course we've been trying to drag it out of Marjorie but she keeps saying, 'You'll have to ask Frank.'"

Anderson took a long sip from his wineglass: "Well, we started the day by heading out with Sergeant John and that diver lady Monica to find a rifle that must have fallen out of the chopper we recovered early last week. Along the way, we got chased by that boat but we managed to turn the tables on them and the Sergeant arrested the two men onboard and seized the boat. He wanted forensics to check it out – for drugs perhaps. We never did get anywhere near the rifle – that'll be another day, I guess."

"That's all?"

"For now... until I learn more. For now I'm just happy to see idiot boaters get charged for being idiots! So tell me, what are we doing at the meeting tonight?"

"Well, we have to deal with media calls. Wendy has helped us put off the media by organizing a press-conference here on Wednesday. She and Anita, along with Adumbi, have been getting in touch with a huge variety of news outlets including, of course, the regular print, radio and TV but also special-interest groups and internet media outlets.

Now we need people to talk to the media. Wendy and Anita have agreed to tag-team the introductions and reading the statements from the media release, and we are hoping Dave Bradshaw will represent the academic side... he hasn't confirmed but we hope he'll be here tonight. Wendy? Marion?"

"We need someone from the business community to speak, and we're all hoping you will do that, Frank," chimed in Marion.

"Crap! C'mon guys... you all know perfectly well there's not a microphone I've ever seen that I didn't try to throw overboard, after I smacked it with a hammer and cut the wire! Arnold, you're our chairman, and Marion you're our secretary of everything and you're both highly respected business people, not a loner like me. On the subject of loners, have you thought of asking Willy? In my mind he is kinda like the 'soul' of the lake, and on top of that he represents the Indigenous perspective."

"Don't worry, Frank, he's coming and he's happy to speak up."

"Cool. So Arnold and Marion, why don't we invite Sam and Mathilde from the Zoo to join the two of you, representing the old-and-established and the new-and-growing businesses in the community? That way you split the speaking duty – and the stares. I'll bet that between Wendy and Anita they could write up some short speaking points for all four. Make sense?"

Arnold laughed: "Don't you just hate that, when Anderson closes off with 'Make sense?'... and it does! I'm game if the others are, as long as I don't have to speak for more than about 30 seconds."

Marjorie had been sitting silently beside Anderson, looking deeply concerned. "You know, there is an elephant in the room that is sure to get unleashed this week. The media will treat us folks here at Awan Lake as cutesy locals doing their do-goody thing, but what they will really want to talk about is the political side: scientists calling into question other scientists, the politics of resource extraction and pollution world-wide, and so on. How are we going to hold on to our own narrative in the face of that?"

There was a very long silence before Marion asked, "Isn't Bradshaw able to respond to the issue at that scale?"

"No, I don't think so," said Wendy. "Actually, he's just a convenient target for the reporters, but he won't be seen as anything other than an academic resource from Toronto. And... this is why I should always listen to my big sister. I'm supposed to be the public relations consultant, but Marjorie is the one who just nailed the biggest issue facing us if all this effort is to be worthwhile."

There was another long silence. Anderson picked up the thread: "At the risk of really mixing up the metaphors, I think it falls to us to put Marjorie's elephant squarely on the table, and right up front. Something like: 'We know exactly what you want to talk about, and we will address that right now. There is a toxic blend of politics, greed, and academic and organizational competition that always winds up blurring the lines between environmental oversight and corporate growth. And the first victims are our communities. Our communities are our ecosystem – which includes our people, our land and of course our water – and our challenge to the media is to look beyond the simple heart-warming stories and into the forces behind that toxic blend.'" He paused. "Am I making sense?"

There was a sudden silence around the table. "Yeah, when you put it that way," replied Arnold eventually. "Only thing is, you're the one person we have who can put it that way and make it sound like you mean it. I'm afraid you can't escape this time, my friend; you just wrote the keynote address for the media conference and you have to deliver it."

"I agree." It was Wendy again. "I'll simply get my big sister to beat him about the head and shoulders until he agrees. I suggest Frank's words stay confidential until he speaks them. As planned, I will open the media conference, but before doing any other introductions or reading the full release about Horowitz, I will introduce our vice chair as a man with an intimate working knowledge of our lake."

***

The lounge had been almost empty, and since there were only a couple more people who showed up, they decided to order some more wine and have the meeting in comfort. It was still gusty and raining an hour later, so Wendy and Anita talked Florence out of a hotel room for the night and Marjorie and Anderson drove home, where they were joined by Arnold and Marion. Anderson put some papers and scrap lumber into the big Franklin stove in the corner and lit it, and the four settled at the big table with fresh, strong coffee and brandy chasers.

"You are going to give that short speech, aren't you, Frank? They're all counting on you – me included – although I feel a little badly about putting the pressure on. I'm blaming Marjorie for putting her elephants on the table."

"Hey, I brought the elephant – just one elephant – into the room alright, but it was Frank who put the elephant on the table, not me!"

"You should have kept that critter outside and not led him into the room in the first place. Where else was I gonna put him except on the table! Anyway... yeah, I can do that speech. It won't be the first time I've stuck my neck out... years ago the Coast Guard did not appreciate my opinions very much, and it seems that Manville guy didn't appreciate my point of view yesterday, either."

Marjorie chuckled: "I was so proud of you, although I wondered when the fists were going to fly!"

"Nah... men like that do their bullying with their mouths, not their fists. I just pity his staff."

Marion swivelled around and stared at Anderson: "So... all kinds of stuff going on that I haven't heard yet. Fill us in, you two!"

Anderson explained how they had met with Leonard Hamilton-Dubois and Thomas Manville at the dock, and how Manville had been pushy – and snarky – and Hamilton-Dubois had seemed nervous.

Marjorie was refilling coffee cups. "You three seem to know all about this Leonard guy with the double-barrelled last name, and Frank filled me in a little bit, but I want to know more. Who is he, and how is he connected with Robertson Mines?"

"Yup, he's connected alright," said Arnold. "Probably

better connected than he should be. Frank? Marion? Do you want to fill Marjorie in?"

"No, go ahead Arnold. You know more about his background than I do, for sure."

"Okay. Well, Leonard Hamilton-Dubois used to be just plain old Leonard Hamilton when we played hockey against each other in high school. I lived here, of course, and he lived with his mother in Maple Falls. He was a little older but I was bigger so our meetings in the corners had a habit of being painful for him apparently, because he never wanted to hang out with me after the games. His one big buddy was Garnet Campbell, the same Garnet Campbell who is now our Member of Parliament and has been for four – maybe five – terms. Leonard was the brains in that relationship, and Garnet was the charmer – and Leonard's protector on the ice, so I discovered after many bruises. Garnet was his school's Mr. Hockey, and the girls were all over him, so moving from hometown hero to political candidate was a seamless transition. He worked at his daddy's hardware store and played amateur hockey locally for a few years, but he ran for office and was first elected before he was thirty."

"So what was Leonard doing in that time? Doesn't sound like he followed up with hockey."

"Nah... Leonard was never that good at the best of

times, but he is clever and he was likeable, so when he was nineteen or so, a summer job in Ottawa turned into a stretched-out internship in government while he went to Carlton for his B.Com. then later to Queen's for an MBA. He was already on track for senior management in the Natural Resources bureaucracy by the time Garnet Campbell was first elected. A dozen years later, Garnet was the Minister and Leonard was in the deputy minister's office."

"So where does the hyphenated name come from?"

It was Marion's turn to answer: "Leonard fell in love with Florence's sister (Florence Dubois from the Inn) and when they married they decided they would take her maiden name after his, instead of the other way around. It wasn't entirely about love and devotion. She too was a civil servant, and it had become fashionable for upwardly-mobile bureaucrats to have hyphenated last names, one English and the other French."

"You and Arnold may know this already," said Anderson, "but last week I learned from Jim Russell at the marina that Leonard owns 51% of that business and a number of properties in and around the village, through several numbered companies. And of course he owns all of the Inn and a couple of properties in Rockliffe by the canal in Ottawa, including his house. Pretty big investments on a senior civil servant's salary."

Marjorie had located another elephant, shuffling rather close to the door: "So, has this Garnet fellow been a useful MP? Is there any smell of conflict of interest, or collusion, between them?"

Arnold picked it up: "Not on the surface, anyway. Garnet is, well, Garnet. Lots of smiles and handshakes. He has done us no harm in the village... in fact he was the one who steered us into getting the Protected Shorelines Project funding agreement a few years ago, and he keeps the pressure on his provincial counterparts to help keep our highways and municipal infrastructure in good shape, through shared federal-provincial funding agreements."

Marion looked across at Marjorie and shrugged: "It's hard to know what to think, really. Both men treat their communities well and seem to be loyal to their friends. It wouldn't surprise me that there may be some under-the-table stuff going on, but at that level, find me a place where it doesn't happen. I know that politics shouldn't be dirty, but it always is. Trouble is, of course, that some of the best people choose to stay out of politics when they could actually do some good."

"Totally different subject, but I want to update you both about that boat we pulled in this afternoon and the guys who were in it. In absolute confidence, please." Anderson looked from Arnold to Marion before continuing: "What I described before, that we were going out with a diver to recover a missing rifle from the helicopter crash scene, was absolutely correct. However, when we got about opposite Robertson Mines, things went all to hell. Marjorie noticed some black smoke coming from one or two spots on the shore north of there, and then a white boat moving along just off the shore, headed north. We were heading south, so at first we ignored it although Sergeant John ordered up a plane to go have a look and a couple of officers in a truck to check out the roads."

Anderson took a sip of brandy and continued: "Right after that, the diver was looking through binoculars and saw that the boat had turned and was aimed straight at us, coming fast. By then, I was getting a bit paranoid because in the back of my mind I thought the boat might be the one that ran down the water samplers. To make a long story short, after some gunfire and with the help of an OPS helicopter, we were able to stop the boat and arrest the two men – or boys – onboard. It was the Mistraika boys, and we are almost certain the boat they were driving was the one that killed those two folks from Ryerson. No homicide charges yet, but the forensics people in Maple Falls are spending a long evening checking over the boat while we're having brandy. And of course the Mistraika boys are spending the night deeply engaged in unfriendly discussions with grumpy cops."

"Geesh. You two just can't stay out of trouble, can ya! Marjorie, I should have warned you about Anderson. Maybe I did?"

"Maybe, ages ago, but I never listened, Marion. Now I'm addicted."

"Has to be love, I guess. Which reminds me, how do you think things are going with Wendy and Anita?"

"Must be love, or something very much like it. I've never seen Wendy happier. And it's about 'way more than great sex, which I imagine is sweet enough too. I think it's about two bright souls connecting without pressure from the outside. It's just about the two of them. I've been meaning to ask... how are Anita's mum and dad with all this?"

"Georgina is just thrilled that Anita is more content than she's ever seen her. And, she has settled down and has stopped partying. Fred was a harder sell, but his dad – Crazy Willy – set him on the right path about the honour accorded to two-spirit people in their culture and that he should cherish this as something very special, even if Wendy is white..." Marion chuckled and continued: "Willy has a unique sense of humour, I have learned! And, Fred too could see how his girl was happy and talking openly with him, something he hasn't experienced for several years."

"Thanks, Marion. I'm really happy to hear that!"

Anderson had been making notes and drawings on a sheet of scrap paper. "More different topics – sorry. I'm worried about two things. First, should we talk to Sergeant John about personal security for Horowitz? John could maybe get some information through police networks to learn if Horowitz's public appearances have caused problems anywhere in the past. If so, perhaps his detachment could put some officers on that. And, related topic, do we have enough volunteers lined up to act as hosts, and take care of crowd management? I worry that we may get a pile more people than we expected."

"Yes," replied Arnold, "and yes. Yes, I agree we should talk to John about security, and yes, I think we have enough volunteers to help out with the crowd. Marion and Adumbi have arranged with the fire department, the baseball club and the Golden Age club. It was an easy sell – the ladies from those groups are doing the salads and desserts and a couple of the guys are cooking the pork."

"The other thing, I keep trying to figure out who is behind the Mistraika boys if they are responsible for running over the Ryerson team and their boat. Their uncle was killed – executed really – a couple of weeks ago as part of Juan's drug bust. They all lived out at that park property run by Gerald Giordano... maybe he'd got them involved in something. I don't think they're smart enough to dream up something all on their own, but I think Giordano had dreams of being a mob boss. Almost certainly was involved with the drugs. Maybe he'd been trying to lever support from the anti-environmentalist faction at Robertson Mines. After all, lots of the workers feel threatened by this too. And, that same park land is where that boat came out from."

"I'll bet our Sergeant friend will have a whole lot more ideas by morning. Nothing like some old-fashioned sleep-deprivation to make those kids a bit more cooperative!"

07:30 AUGUST 8

Anderson was sitting on his small porch with his second coffee and his first cigarette. The day had dawned clear, calm and warm, and he was enjoying being alone with his thoughts. Arnold and Marion had left late – just after midnight – and Marjorie was catching up on sleep after several short nights, so he decided to let her sleep awhile longer although he wanted to share with her the conversation he had last evening with Florence, including the part about Leonard being somewhere out on the lake.

So it was a good thing he had brought his phone outside with him because it rang at 07:45. It was the Sergeant, and he had lots of goodies to get the day started: "The Mistraika boys finally caved at about 02:00, and will be arraigned later this morning on two counts of manslaughter each, along with a string of related charges. Of course, they blamed everyone and everything in the world from their parents to the weather, but specifically they blamed Gerald Giordano for telling them to do it."

"That comes as no surprise to me, although I don't think for a minute that the buck stops with him."

"I agree. I'm letting Corporal LaFrançois handle the arraignment and right now I'm taking another officer and heading out to pick up Giordano for questioning. The two officers who drove out there yesterday weren't familiar with the area, but said there were some pretty heavy-duty security guys hanging around. I need to talk with them too. Before I forget, I got a replacement satphone, so I'll drop off yours at the Zoo. If I have time – and no Italian passengers – I'll stop by at your place on the way back."

"What did the forensics team find out about the boat?"

"At the moment they say they are ninety-five percent sure that the damage to the little boat was caused by high-speed contact with the bigger boat. But the boys caved before they even knew those numbers."

"Okay, I'll have the radio on to hear the news. I need to change engine and tranny oils on the boat, so I hope to spend most of the day around here. Be safe!"

"Yes!" he muttered as he clicked the phone off and gave a fist-pump into space."

"Yes what?" said a soft voice behind him.

Anderson turned to see Marjorie with an empty cup and a full coffee pot.

"Yes! Sometimes I get lucky and figure stuff out! That was the Sergeant, and I'll fill you in on the news."

"Do you love me enough to share some closet and dresser space?"

Anderson put down his phone and got to his feet. He took the coffee pot and cup away from Marjorie and enveloped her in a long silent hug before stepping back and taking her hands in his. "I've been afraid of this moment for a while now. Two reasons: first, I was afraid to invite you because I was afraid you'd say no. Second, I was scared you might want a cat."

She grinned at him, kissed her finger and touched his nose, and said, "Cats or kids, one or the other!"

"Actually, I'm quite fond of some cats."

"Thought you'd say that! Well, I also heard you say you had to service the boat engine, and between us we need to do some laundry, so why don't I take a couple of washer loads up to the laundromat and get them started, then come back and pick you up for breakfast at the Zoo? My treat!"

"Almost perfect, except I have to go to the Co-op and get some engine oil anyway, so I'll take my truck and meet you at the Zoo. If we're going to be a family, especially one with a cat, we're going to have to get used to being in a two-truck family like everyone else in town!"

After she had gone uptown with two plastic bags of clothes and bedding, Anderson cleared some heavy outdoor work clothes and coveralls out of the closet and hung them on the inner wall of the workshop. Years ago, he had picked up a huge antique bureau at an auction, so he went to that and re-arranged his rather meager wardrobe so that Marjorie could have the upper two of the big drawers plus the right-hand drawer at the top.

The laundromat was a half-block around the corner from the Zoo, so assuming Marjorie would have already put in the washing and gone to the restaurant, Anderson headed there before he picked up his oil. Marjorie was indeed already there, sitting in his favourite corner with two cups of coffee. "What did you say was the name of that local politician last night?"

"Cameron. Garnet Cameron. Why?"

"About three minutes ago, the radio news reported he was arrested at his home in Ottawa yesterday."

"Holy crap! What in the world has he done?"

"I only caught part of it – don't know."

The door to the restaurant kitchen swung open and Sam joined them. "I heard the full report at seven this morning. Apparently some lady who used to be on his staff years ago has charged him with sexual assault and he is also under investigation for some other matters but they didn't say what."

"No wonder," Anderson muttered as he sat down.

"No wonder what?" Sam asked.

"Huh? Oh, yeah, well, he always thought of himself as a ladies' man. I just thought he was bright enough – and charming enough – to stay out of trouble!

"No wonder what, indeed," said Marjorie after Sam had retreated to the kitchen. You meant something else, didn't you!"

"Yes. No wonder Florence was worried." He proceeded to tell her what Florence had said last night, both that Leonard had been intensely distracted by phone calls all morning and that he had then taken his sailboat out into a cold, wet and windy afternoon, something he had never done before.

"Well, you said last night that Leonard and Garnet were close, but really, would he have been that upset by this?"

"I have often sensed they both might have been involved in financial kick-backs – and maybe more – in the Natural Resources portfolio, where Cameron had been a minister and Leonard was high up in the department. Mutual business connections included management people at Robertson Group International in Toronto and New York, I'm almost certain."

"Do you suppose Leonard may want out?"

"Suicide? Quite possibly. He has really nothing to live for except his investments and his sister-in-law and her son, who is in Alberta and sort of estranged from the two of them. I think I should drive out to the Inn and see if his boat is back at its dock, then check with Flo before calling John and asking for a quick aerial search of the lake. I'd like to think he's anchored behind an island sleeping off a bottle of good scotch, but I'm worried. He may also have had a heart attack – he had trouble with that a few years ago."

"Let's go. We'll take the Jeep so Flo doesn't worry about why you're out looking. She'll recognize your truck."

A quick trip out to the Spirit River Inn and around its driveways showed that Leonard Hamilton-Dubois' elegant wooden sailboat was not at its dock. Anderson and Marjorie stopped in the parking lot and considered whether to talk with Florence first or just go ahead and call for the air search. They agreed that – uncomfortable as it would be – they should first consult with Florence, so they turned off the Jeep and headed inside.

Florence had been cleaning up the breakfast room and planning lunch with the chef. The managerial calm which typically defined her character broke like splinters of glass when she saw Anderson and Marjorie. "Ah, mon Dieu, I am so glad to see you, glad and scared too. Do you have something to tell me? Here, sit down and I'll bring us some coffee. Mon Dieu, what a night. I was going to call you and beg you to go out on the lake and look for Leonard, but I kept putting it off because he might think that would be so silly and he would be so embarrassed!"

"Certainly it would not be silly, Florence. I think we all know he's had a lot to think about – you have already heard about his friend Garnet's arrest, I assume? I wonder if he already knew that might be happening and needed time alone to process it."

"Yes, I heard that on the radio this morning, and yes that could have had something to do with all the telephone calls yesterday morning. Do you think you could go looking on the lake? I know you have been so busy and I hate to ask..."

"Don't you be silly, too! Of course we are going, but we will also ask our friend Sergeant John – MacLeod – to put up an airplane as well. It's a big lake. What is the best telephone number to call you on today? The office number or your cell?" Anderson stood up and wandered into the lobby to put in the call to the OPS office while Marjorie took down both numbers. She took Florence's hand in hers, and told her they would keep her in touch with everything they learned.

Tears welled up in the older woman's eyes: "Thank-you, my new friend. Thank-you."

***

An hour and a half later, Marjorie had dried the laundry and sorted her clothes into the drawers Anderson had cleaned out for her. He was at the dock, had topped up the fuel tanks and was busy changing filters and oil on the two diesels and was sampling the oil in the transmission to be sent to a lab outside Toronto – the transmission oil looked perfectly clean, but he liked to maintain his equipment according to manufacturer's specifications. He had learned over many years that it was always cheaper that way.

Fifteen minutes had passed since the single-engine search plane contracted by the OPS had called in to say it was flying up the river and would start its first pass clockwise around the circumference of the lake in about ten minutes, passing first offshore near the village. In his discussions with the Sergeant, Anderson had suggested that, once that first pass was completed, the plane should next focus its attention on the open water at the west side of the lake, where a skilled sailor might choose to be given that yesterday's wind and rain was coming out of the west.

Anderson called Marjorie at the house, telling her they should plan to leave the dock in about twenty minutes. They would simply aim for the centre-west side of the lake east of the cottage islands and await communication from the pontoon-equipped search plane which was also fitted with a marine radio. He turned on his own radio and turned up the volume, then finished replacing the engine oil filters, refilled the engines with oil, and started them up momentarily to check for leaks and re-check levels. He was just placing a carton of empty oil containers and used filters in his truck when Marjorie arrived with fresh coffee and sandwiches, and soon they were headed south-south-west with the autohelm on, at half throttle, feeling the discomfiting awareness of their purpose but nonetheless enjoying their ham sandwiches and coffee.

Some forty minutes later, the radio crackled to life. Anderson darted across the wheelhouse to the wheel station and picked the microphone off its bracket: "This is the vessel Beaver on Awan Lake. Frank Anderson speaking."

"Beaver, this is OPS-C135. Please move to the designated channel for a transmission."

Anderson had arranged with the Sergeant for a series of channel options to be used progressively. He switched to Channel 28 and spoke: "Calling OPS-C135, this is the vessel Beaver. Please proceed with your transmission."

"Hi Mr. Anderson, this is Constable Bathgate. We have

spotted what looks like wreckage near the south-west shore of the lake, maybe a mile offshore. It's a mess."

Anderson held his course but moved the throttle to full ahead. "Hi Andy – you got roped into this too? You're having a long few weeks, ain'tcha!. How bad a mess?"

"Real bad. The boat has been on fire and is basically just a hulk. The mast is still attached but the decks are pretty much gone. Can't see anyone."

"Thanks Andy. Can we go to the next channel and you can read me the coordinates?"

"Sure thing. I'm out."

Anderson switched to Channel 84 and called for OPS-C135. Cst. Bathgate read out the coordinates, confirmed them and signed off: "'Bye now, Anderson!"

"'Bye Andy. Thanks! We're almost an hour away. I'll call your Sergeant when we get there."

Anderson created a waypoint on the GPS from the numbers the constable had provided, and set the autohelm accordingly. He scanned the lake with binoculars: it was a weekday, and there was no traffic to the south. "Well, this may not be pretty. I can't imagine Leonard would have set a fire on that pretty boat on purpose, but it would have been hard to do accidentally."

Marjorie lit him a cigarette and he shut the wheelhouse

door to block some of the engine noise before settling down with her at the navigation table opposite the wheel. He took the satphone off its belt hook and called the Sergeant.

"Hi John, it's Anderson. I assume you've heard from Andy?"

"Yup. Sounds like you're gonna have a mess out there. You two okay to hook up and tow it back?"

"I hope so. I just hope there's somewhere strong left to attach a rope. It'll be a slow trip back, in any case."

"You may find a body in there, y'know..."

"Yes, I realize that. If so, we won't touch anything we don't have to. And of course I'll keep you informed."

"Thanks, Frank. You will be interested to know that the radio and TV are making a lot of fuss about that MP that was just arrested, and I gather our sailor's name is being mentioned in connection with Cameron's career."

"I was afraid of that. Poor Florence... and there's nothing we can tell her at this point. I don't want her in the loop until we know something."

"Understood. Talk to you soon."

"Poor Florence indeed. This doesn't look good at all, does it, Frank?" Marjorie was topping up their coffee mugs. "I brought along some more ground coffee. Looks like we will need to make some more before we get back."

***

It was almost 14:00 before they reached the charred wreckage. Anderson knew immediately that it had, indeed, been Leonard Hamilton-Dubois' beautifully cared-for wooden yacht, burned almost to the waterline. Strangely, the aluminum mast was still up, with fragments of melted and scorched dacron sails still hanging from it and the boom, lending a somewhat Fellini-esque aspect to the whole scene. Anderson nosed the workboat gently alongside what was left of the yacht and quickly tied a light rope between a winch on the sailboat deck and a mooring cleat on the workboat.

"I'm going onboard, but I'll have to be careful," he said to Marjorie as he strapped on an inflatable lifebelt. "Of course I need to check in what's left of the cabin."

"Take care... don't let your feet go through and get jammed anywhere. That's a mess of burned wood, ropes and cables!"

He stepped carefully across, and spreading his weight between his hands and feet he sort of crab-walked the few steps to the cabin hatch and looked inside. He pulled back quickly: "He's in there. And even without going any further and disturbing things, I can be almost certain it's Leonard. Badly burned of course but I remember he wore a cross around his neck, and it's still there.

"You going to call John?"

"Yup, as soon as I get back onboard."

It didn't take long to pull in some ropes that had been hanging over the side, and to lash the tiller straight so the rudder would help the boat follow as it was towed. Anderson stepped into the wheelhouse and called the Sergeant: "Hi John, we're here, and yes we have a body. And yes, I am almost certain it's Leonard. He's badly burned, but not as badly as I expected – almost as if the fire flashed over him and moved on. We are securing cables and stuff and should be ready to start towing within half an hour. I don't expect we'll be at the dock before 18:00."

"What? No, I think you'll want to get the forensics team working on this before you lift the boat out of the water. Remember she has a very deep solid keel, which means it won't sit properly on a flatbed trailer. We can tie the boat up ahead of The Beaver and the team can do their magic and remove the body and other evidence before it gets all shaken up on a truck. So, ambulance etc. and some extra personnel to tape the area off and guard the dock. I'll call you when we are about 45 minutes out. Are you going to call Florence and at least keep her up to speed? When we get back? Sure, I can go with you."

Someone – likely Leonard – had built-in a stainless steel towing ring on the bow to make it easier to load the boat onto a trailer. The ring was bolted through just above the waterline, so it appeared to have been protected from the fire and was still solid. To this, Anderson attached a medium-sized towrope, and they let the boat float back about twenty feet behind *The Beaver*, then wrapped it on the towing winch and cleated it down. With Marjorie at the controls, they turned north-east toward the village and together they adjusted the length of the towrope and the speed until the sailboat was following smoothly behind at just over three knots (or about 3.5 mph).

"Okay, might as well aim for home and set the autohelm. Time for a smoke break!"

"And we have half a cup of coffee each. Now that we've slowed down I'll make another pot."

"Yeah, there's no wind to speak of and that thing is towing pretty well. I'm glad there's no chop out here... the poor old sailboat doesn't have much freeboard left!"

Anderson took another slurp of now-cold coffee. "This has been the easy part of today, but I'm afraid it's going to get a lot tougher. Whatever are we going to tell Florence? John has asked me to go with him to speak to her, but there's so much we don't know. Including absolute certainty that it is, indeed, Leonard Hamilton-Dubois. Surely there's no way we can ask her to identify what I saw in that cabin."

"I guess we are assuming suicide? Could it have been an accident? And incidentally, I'll go with you and John to see her if you like. One of the sisterhood can be helpful."

"I hated to ask. If you're sure, yes please. And yes, it could have been an accident but I doubt it. I have been giving some thought to murder, too."

"Away out here on a rainy, windy night?"

"What better place, what better time!"

"Okay: Victim, maybe. Cause of death, TBD. Weapon, TBD. Motive...?"

"Shouldn't be too hard for Sergeant John to check off the first three. And I sense there are two possible motives, starting with corruption and influence... and ending with influence and corruption." Anderson took the binoculars outside, scanned the lake ahead for traffic and came back to the table before topping up the coffee cups. "I see some sailboats off to the north-west near the islands, but they're a long way away. Nothing to run into yet." He gave Marjorie a kiss on the cheek before sitting back down, when his satphone rang.

"Hello Sergeant! How are you this fine sunny afternoon? Yes, we're coming along nicely, might even get to the village early, perhaps about 17:30. Really? Holy cow, that's fast. What do I think? We were just talking about that, sort of. Yeah, lots more to discuss. And what? Giordano is gone? And there's more to it? How about late dinner at the Lockmaster's in the Falls – food's good but mostly there's hardly any locals, not even the staff. No, our dime. You're always buying donuts! Okay, I'll call you when we're a bit closer. Bye!"

Anderson reprised the conversation for Marjorie, filling her in about a flood of media reports suggesting corruption in the Ministry of Natural Resources – possibly facilitated by high-level bureaucrats – since Cameron's years in Cabinet. "And yes, we're having dinner in Maple Falls with John, later this evening. We need a quiet place to talk... John, too, thinks that not everything is what it seems."

"What's the thing about Giordano?"

"Oh yeah – really weird! As you know, this morning John went out to Robertson Mines to talk to old man Giordano about the Mistraika boys, and he's gone... moved out! I guess there were some security guards around the area, but they weren't very cooperative... suggested he take it up with the General Manager. John will tell us more later."

"Thinking about murder for a moment, Leonard would have had to take someone along with him – or else it's suicide or an accident. Surely some passerby out boating didn't just cruise over, kill him and burn the boat! And if the person was with him, how did they get back to shore – unless of course they're still in that tiny cabin along with Leonard?"

"Or they could have set up a mid-lake meeting before he left, sort of a secret rendezvous gone wrong..."

And the satphone rang again. "Yes John, what's up now? Tony and Jean Barker? Salt-of-the-earth people, very quiet. Yes, their island is pretty secluded and the small bay where they have a boathouse is almost hidden. Sure, do you have his number? Okay, I'll text it over. Yes, you can mention me, of course. I'll adjust our course and wait until I hear from you. Later!"

He turned to Marjorie: "John wants to ask Barkers if we can take the boat to their island for the initial forensics, body removal and so on." He switched off the autohelm and hunted through the various waypoints on the GPS screen until he found one labelled "Barker". He reset the autohelm and watched as *The Beaver* slowly adjusted its course about 30 degrees to the west. He scanned the lake again for traffic, and went back to the coffee mugs and Marjorie. "This gets weirder by the moment."

"Well, bringing in the third boat this week with either

criminals or bodies onboard does seem a bit much. And this particular dead guy seems to have suddenly earned a pretty high profile, so I can understand John's reasoning. And to top things off, don't forget we have a media conference for Love Our Lake right at the harbour!"

"Yipe, I'd forgotten all about that... good point! John's calling them now for permission and he'll let us know. I can't imagine the Barkers will refuse... hey, Tony writes books! Maybe this will start him on his first novel instead of writing about economics! And Jean is always a good sport, and has a great sense of humour... you met them the other night, didn't you?"

"Sure did! Really liked them." She paused for a short moment. "Y'know, I don't know how John plans to get his team out here but I expect he'll want you to pick them up in the village. I could stay with the Barkers and sort of "guard" the sailboat at the dock until you get back... shouldn't be more than an hour to wait."

"That is a magnificent idea. I'll tell John when he calls back in a few minutes... or right now, apparently."

He clicked the satphone on: "Beaver Boatworks and Towing, how can I direct your call? Okay, they're good to go? Perfect. We should be there in about a half hour. Marjorie suggested that she would stay at Barkers on the dock to sort of guard the wreck while I go into the village to pick up you and your team and equipment. Once the team is settled in we can come back to town and talk to Florence. Oh... you did? Mmm, I see. Is she doing okay? Mmm. Not surprised. I hope Georgina is on this evening, they're pretty close. She is? Okay, that's good. I'll call you when we land the boat at the Barker place... you'll have a half-hour to get your team to the village dock."

He added a few revolutions to the engine to gain some time, and turned to Marjorie: "I guess Florence called him – said she'd been listening to the news, someone had seen us head out onto the lake, and she heard the search plane so she put two and two together. John had no choice but to tell her we had found Leonard's boat, burned, with unidentified human remains onboard. Damn, that's tough... well, you heard the rest. Sounds like Georgina is with her."

***

When they rounded the corner into the small and well-protected bay that formed the private harbour at the Barkers' summer home, Anderson and Marjorie could see Jean and Tony Barker standing on the dock, ready to help. Anderson slowed down and completely stopped the workboat and its tow before inching forward to the dock so they could hand off the tow rope to the Barkers, who pulled the burned-out vessel around the opposite side of the dock and tied it alongside. Marjorie stepped off onto the dock and announced that she would stay on the island "while Frank goes to town and picks up a boat-load of cops!" She was welcomed warmly – they all waved at Anderson as he backed the workboat around and left the harbour.

At 18:15, *The Beaver* pulled in to her home dock at Spirit River, where she was greeted by Sergeant MacLeod, three members of the forensic investigation team, a representative from the coroner's office, and OPS Superintendent George Daniels, who had come out from Toronto a scant three weeks ago when the drug distribution gang was taken down. "We're going to have to stop meeting this way, Frank," Daniels laughed as they shook hands warmly. "Every time I come here you've got my sergeant embroiled in some nasty stuff!"

"It's the only way I get to visit with another Coast Guard guy. Which reminds me, did you know Keith Kirkpatrick out at Campbell River?"

"Sure did, and yes, I know he was killed a couple of weeks ago. I couldn't make the funeral, but I did learn that a certain former officer delivered a particularly fine eulogy. Thank-you for that... he was a helluva good guy!"

"Thanks, George. He was a good friend. Anyway, welcome onboard – I assume you will join the forensics team out at the island?"

"Indeed I will. Headquarters is all over this one. There's a whole bunch of crap coming out of Ottawa that could – does – involve the probable victim. So far, we're one step ahead of the media on this and I'd like to keep it that way until we at least have some preliminary information. I'm willing to bet there will be reporters and TV cameras all over this place by the time we wake up tomorrow!"

Anderson had stepped aside to help one of the team load a couple of pelican cases, but he re-joined the conversation: "Just so you know, there is a media conference – I think at 11:00 – tomorrow, so they'll be here anyway. It has to do with an event here on the weekend, to do with protecting the lake. That might normally attract crickets, but the issue has been attracting some international attention over the last week or so, and now... this! It'll be a busy morning, and I have to remember I got roped in to giving the opening statement."

The Sergeant had shot Anderson a quick glance when he heard this: "Crap, in all the fuss today I had forgotten that. George, the event was organized in response to a large-scale expansion planned for the Robertson Mines facility east of here on the lake. Sorry about that."

"No worries – I'm ahead of you on this one anyway. The brass has had it on their radar for two or three weeks, and there may be some cross-over connections to this victim we're going to learn about now."

"Oh yeah, I'm pretty sure there are," Anderson said quietly. "We can talk on our way out to the island."

***

By the time Anderson blew a short blast on the horn as he rounded the point into the bay, Marjorie and Tony were at the dock to greet them and take their mooring lines, and supper preparations were underway. Anderson told the investigators that the workboat wasn't going anywhere until they were done with their work, and was their's to use as they needed. He would leave the genset running so they had power, and there were good LED lights on the navigation mast that would help light their work if they were still at it after sundown. "Do you guys have food or coffee in one of those boxes?"

"Three cheers for Timmy's," piped up one of the team. "Soup, sandwiches and coffee. Oh yeah... and donuts of course. Enough for five of us, but we didn't anticipate the

Superintendent, or the boat crew, sir. We can probably share."

"No worries," Marjorie chimed in. "Mrs. Barker is preparing supper for the four of us so we'll all be fine." She and Tony headed back up to the well-kept century-old cottage on the crown of the rocky, five-acre island, while Anderson stayed with the investigators until they had been able to have a preliminary look at what they assumed to be a floating crime scene.

The Barkers knew how to do things right. Half an hour later, the three men walked up the dock and along the path to the house. There was a broad veranda with a view of the impending sunset, with a massive stone fireplace which evidently shared its stone chimney with a similar fireplace indoors. The outdoor fireplace was equipped for barbecuing, and a nearby table had platters of salads, bread and a half-dozen rib-eye steaks, all covered with wrap awaiting their time. There were two bottles of red wine on the table, one of which had already been violated: Marjorie, Jean and Tony sat sipping wine and looking out onto the lake.

After introductions all around, George Daniels turned to Tony Barker: "I just finished reading *Corporations and the Environment: an Accountant's Perspective*. I was fascinated, and it should be required reading for anyone involved in forensic accounting and the investigation of environmental crime. It is indeed a pleasure to meet you. And yes, thank-you... a glass of wine would suit me just fine!"

There was a clinking of glasses all around and an easy time of chatter, though it wasn't long before Tony and George were deep in conversation about forensic accounting. Jean and Marjorie eventually had to herd them over to the barbecue to begin cooking the steaks, while Anderson and the Sergeant stood at the veranda railing and traded thoughts about how a murder – which this seemed to be – could have been accomplished without any evidence of a perpetrator. They had just learned from the early stages of the investigation that the victim had been shot, upward through the mouth like a suicide, and there was a Smith & Wesson 686 revolver in the victim's hand with one discharged shell casing in the chamber. Although Marjorie's earlier check-list now had a victim, a weapon, and presumably a cause of death if not a manner of dying, something still seemed "off", There were a lot of unknowns that the busy team down at the dock would hopefully solve, but the issues around motive now loomed larger still: whether homicide or suicide, the questions had become "why" and "who" in no particular order. Each answer would suggest the next question.

Their discussions were interrupted by Jean who

announced that the steaks were just about ready and then said, "Frank, one way or another you are the one who brought us all together tonight. Maybe you could say grace?"

Anderson gulped – he hoped not visibly. Such a thing had not ever been part of his life except at a couple of Navy banquets he had attended years ago. He looked around at the others, and bowed his head: "Thank-you for good food, good wine, and good friends. Amen."

All things were delivered. The wine was good, the food was excellent, and the friendship was extraordinary. The evening could have lasted much longer, but the Sergeant and Anderson walked down to the dock to make sure the forensics folks had what they needed, and discovered they had removed and bagged the body and had done a thorough job on the boat's interior. However, they requested it be held for a few days before being towed away to be scrapped. They would be ready to go back to the village in less than an hour.

The Sergeant remained at the boat while Anderson went back to retrieve Marjorie and Superintendent Daniels. They thanked the Barkers for their stunning hospitality, and Tony found a six-pack of Blue for the team to sip on the way home, if that was okay with Daniels. It was, again with thanks. Anderson said to the Barkers that he would try to get back the next day to remove the charred hulk of a sailboat and find a less intrusive place to keep it and was told he was not to worry about it. Thirty minutes later, everyone was onboard and *The Beaver* motored away from the island with her navigation lights beginning to show clearly in the gathering darkness.

06:10 AUGUST 9

Anderson slithered out of bed away too early as far as he was concerned. He emptied the cold coffee from the pot into a rinsed-out mug, started a new pot brewing, and walked out into the clear, calm dawning of a new day.

Last night had wound up being a late one. On the forty-minute trip back from the Barkers' island, the team of investigators shared some of their initial findings. For starters, all numbers had been filed off the older-model revolver, and a phone call to the office came up empty on any similar models being stolen or used in a crime in recent history, at least in Canada, and USA records would take a bit longer, so on the assumption for the moment that Hamilton-Dubois was unlikely to have owned an unregistered and unlawful firearm, there was going to be no easy trace there.

They had found enough melted red plastic to be pretty sure that a one-gallon gas container had been used to start the fire, and that almost all of it had been splashed on the corpse and around the tiny cabin. They were eager to see if the autopsy showed any sign of gasoline in the victims lungs, an indication that he might have splashed around the gas before he shot himself, possibly suggesting a carefully-planned suicide. Otherwise, it was more likely he was shot in the cabin by someone else and then covered with gas and set on fire. The flames had flashed quickly and then gone to work on the wood much more slowly. The body was actually not burned as badly as they first expected and some of his lower-body clothing and shoes were charred but intact. Although they were yet unable to be at all accurate about the time of death, as Anderson pointed out it was raining very hard at one point last night, which could partly explain the lack of damage to the body and the fact that the wooden hull had not been totally consumed by fire. He had expected to find the wreck burned fully to the waterline and on the verge of sinking, but that had not been the case.

And of course there was the chain and locket around his neck. They had removed that into an evidence bag but had not yet opened the locket.

A black 15-passenger van with an OPS insignia had been waiting in the dark at the wharf to pick up the body and other evidence gathered by the investigators. The van had quickly driven off in the direction of Maple Falls with Superintendent Daniels and the team onboard, leaving one SUV behind for the Sergeant. Anderson and Marjorie had accompanied their friend – and the locket and chain – to visit Florence, who quickly confirmed that it had indeed belonged to Leonard. She said he had never taken it off, and when she opened the locket it revealed a photo of her sister, Leonard's late wife.

Florence was sad, of course, but resigned to her new future – with so many new things to worry about. "The worst thing was not knowing," she had told them, "but now I know I have to take charge of his affairs. I think they are complicated: I have met his lawyer, and I'll be calling him in the morning. Sergeant, I expect you'll be doing an autopsy, of course. Just to let you know, I want to have Leonard cremated and I am not planning a funeral. In time, I guess I'll talk to his colleagues at the Ministry to see if they want a memorial service at some point. Let's go into the lounge," she had said, "and get Georgina to bring us a drink – I could stand a double vodka about now."

Anderson went inside and poured a fresh coffee. Marjorie was still curled up in a ball and fast asleep, so he took his phone from the bedside table and went back outside with his coffee and a cigarette from the pack on the table. *I'm gonna have to cut back on these damn things once the world gets back to normal around here. Or maybe this is, as they say, the "new normal". Crap, I hope not!*

He dialed Arnold's number, which was picked up immediately. "Hey there Frank... was wondering what had happened to ya! It's been busy around here!"

"Nothing much going on here. Spent yesterday, as usual, picking up wrecked boats and dead bodies, but other than that, nothing worth mentioning."

"I figured something like that. You all set for that media thing this morning?"

"Yeah, let's talk about that. Last I had heard we were going to hold that down here at the lake, by the dock. Is that still the plan?"

"Well, sort of, but Marion thought it would be better to stay out of your hair and do it at the marina instead. Jim and Margaret were happy to do that, and they're even supplying the coffee and donut-type stuff."

"Good idea, and much better under the circumstances. You know by now that we retrieved Leonard's body from his burned-out sailboat?"

"Holy crap, no! I knew you were out with Sergeant John again, maybe looking for Leonard's boat, but I didn't know that. What happened?"

"Well, the cops are pretty convinced he was murdered, and I agree but the official word is that 'a burned boat has been recovered from the lake along with human remains' and that'll have to do until the autopsy. John and Marjorie and I visited with Florence last night and she pretty much confirmed it was indeed Leonard because of a neck-chain he was wearing, so hopefully John releases the name this morning. Otherwise that'll be the only thing the media will want to talk about this morning."

"Well, the reporters are already nosing around about Garnet's arrest. For once they are moving quickly by the 'another-politician-takes-the-wrong-lady-to-bed' and are more focused on questions about kickbacks and influence peddling during his term as Minister."

"Yummy. They'll already have the Hamilton-Dubois name linked to Garnet Cameron and when they find out Leonard has died and maybe been murdered on Awan Lake, it's game over. They'll be talking about us for years, not weeks, whether we have Horowitz here on Sunday or not!"

A soft sleepy voice behind him said, "Some are born great, some achieve greatness, and some have greatness thrust upon them." It was Marjorie.

"Hang on... well, good morning! Mrs. Shakespeare I assume?" He stood up and gave her a quick kiss on the nose. "Talking to Arnold on the phone."

"Figured that. Tell him to drop by and we'll feed him a left-over donut and fresh coffee!"

"Did you hear that, Arnold? Okay, sounds good. See you in a couple of minutes."

Anderson put down the phone and gave Marjorie a proper hug. "Says he can't stay long, but you're right, we need to be a bit caught up on stuff – both ways. And I need to get my marching orders straight for my 27-second speech this morning. At least it's been moved to the marina now, and not here. "

Marjorie paddled back inside to upgrade her clothing from a beach towel to jeans and a blouse while he poured her a coffee and one with sugar for Arnold.

His old pickup rattled up the driveway and sputtered to a stop. Anderson met him on the porch: "They say a logger never has firewood and a shoemaker's kids never have shoes. Evidently a mechanic never drives a decent truck!"

"And I've heard that boat captains never learn to swim because they don't believe their own boats ever sink! And your old truck is no better than mine, anyway... coffee? You bet – thanks. Can't stay long... Marion is fretting about the press conference and making sure everything is in order so I'd better make myself available."

"Has she had any more weird telephone calls?"

"Not weird ones, but lots of them, and especially since yesterday's news stories about Cameron. Obviously it didn't take long for the media to connect our story with the fact that we are at the heart of Garnet's constituency."

"Awkward for you, since you grew up with him. That's going to get worse, I fear. And Arnold, I had forgotten that you grew up close to Leonard, too, and I have neglected to say how sorry we are that your old school buddy has been killed, let alone gone missing."

"Thanks, Frank. But that's okay, we were never really close and we seriously drifted apart and went in different directions. And, frankly I'm not too surprised that those different directions might have gotten him into trouble. He always had a kind of "wheeler-dealer" streak about him. I do wonder what Florence is going to do now, though."

Marjorie had joined them on the porch with her coffee and a slightly-crushed box of left-over donuts. "Florence did mention last night that she would have to look after his affairs and would be calling his lawyer this morning. But, if there's anything to the theory that Leonard was mixed up in some influence peddling or kickbacks, I sure hope she is held harmless from all those investments and contracts. I'm pretty sure she has no clue about any weird stuff he might have been doing."

Anderson paused long enough to light his second cigarette of the morning: "I did mention casually to John yesterday, or maybe last night, that links between Leonard and Garnet could well reach into Robertson International somehow. Especially since three days ago Leonard had taken Robertson's new General Manager – Thomas Manville I think – out for a sail. Obviously he knew that company well, and had some influence there."

"What did John think?"

"I actually think my comment sailed right over his head at the time, and I didn't pursue it. He was pretty preoccupied... I should probably nudge him again."

"I would. I think it could be pretty important. And you know, I am pretty sure Garnet and Leonard worked together on getting our Protected Shoreline Project funded here... we always seemed to have a little extra 'consideration' dealing with the bureaucrats on that."

"And a Robertson connection could explain why our project got warned a month ago, then dumped last week!"

"You mentioned that thought when you and Arnold came back from that trip to Ottawa last month," said Marjorie. "I also agree with Arnold that you should nudge John about the sailing thing with Leonard and Manville. I have to say that the new Robertson boss has a sort of nasty edge."

"You mentioned that the other night when Marion and I

were here." Arnold chuckled: "Kinda pushed our friend Anderson's buttons, as I recall!"

"Mmm. And he got walked-on for his troubles. If someone is pushing buttons, Frank somehow finds a hammer. I don't think either man likes being challenged, but my money's on Frank. Manville deserved what he got!

Anderson was thoughtful. "I don't think Thomas has friends... only targets."

***

By now it was almost 09:00. Arnold had returned home to help Marion, so Anderson and Marjorie decided to let Sam feed them breakfast at the Zoo, which would be a good place to listen to the drumbeats of gossip in Spirit River. The café was busy, but there was a back table for two, where they ordered eggs benedict and coffee. Sam's wife Mathilde was evidently doing the cooking duties today, and Sam was bustling about serving tables. When he brought their coffee, he told them he was surprised with the crowd of unknown faces: "Marion reminded me that the press conference was coming up at eleven this morning, but it's been crazy around here since just after seven! Any idea what's going on?"

"I'm betting most of these folks are somehow connected to media – I see two television mini-vans outside.

But I'm willing to bet that most of the interest is in other stuff, like our member of parliament being arrested."

"I caught the tail end of something on the seven o'clock news about a boating accident and one person dead, and I think I heard the word 'homicide'. Perhaps that's why so many reporters?

"Yes Sam, there is that too. I'll tell you about it when you are less busy."

The lone occupant of the next table to Anderson and Marjorie was a woman, small, dressed in expensive outdoor garb such as one would find at Mountain Equipment Co-op or a similar high-end outfitters. She leaned away from her table and tapped Marjorie on the arm: "I couldn't help overhearing part of your conversation with the waiter, and I get a sense that you folks are from here?"

"Yes, we are," Marjorie responded. "Can we help?"

"I flew to Ottawa from Albany yesterday, picked up a rental and drove to Maple Falls, where I stopped overnight. My editor had originally dispatched me to do a story on an environmental controversy brewing at Awan Lake – which Google Maps shows me is close by – but after I checked in, everyone I met has been talking about a political scandal, involving sexual assault accusations. Until this morning, that is, when my editor calls me up and says the story might involve a murder investigation, high-level politics, *and* the environmental controversy."

Anderson smiled at her. "I can see why you might be a bit confused! Don't feel bad... we live here and we're confused too!"

"Especially this morning!" chuckled Marjorie. "What news service are you with?"

"Envirowire. It's a small news service specializing in stories fundamentally related to the environment, including everything from politics through technology to protection. And our editor is particularly passionate about water."

"Well, Ma'm, feel welcome to hang around for a few days," chuckled Anderson. "We've got it all, apparently! My name is Frank, and this is Marjorie."

"Priscilla..." she put out her hand to them both. "...Priscilla Morgenstern. I am very pleased to meet you."

"And here is a couple of people who you really will be pleased to meet," said Marjorie, waving toward Anita and Wendy who had just come into the restaurant and made a beeline for their table. "Wendy, Anita, this is Priscilla from Albany. She was tagged to come up here on behalf of an environmental newswire service, and like many this morning, has more questions than answers!"

Anderson grinned: "Full disclosure, as they say,

Priscilla! These two are the entirety of the public relations committee for the Love Our Lake event this weekend, and are hosting this media conference. They are also passionate about water, perhaps to the point of being considered dangerous!"

They pulled the two tables together and Sam found an extra chair from the kitchen. They had just settled back down when Priscilla's head snapped around to face the door. Sergeant John was a big man, and so was his boss, George Daniels. When either one of them entered a room dressed in full gear, complete with body armour, they had a way of appearing to fill much of the available space. When the two of them entered at the same time, the effect was startling. Anderson waved them over: "Staying for coffee?"

"Yeah, coffee. And bacon. And eggs. Donuts won't cut it – this morning started 'way too long ago for that. You have company..."

"We do. George – Superintendent Daniels, and John – Sergeant MacLeod... this is Priscilla from Albany. She is a reporter for a USA newswire service. Priscilla, unless you got nailed for speeding last night these are likely the first Ontario Police Service members you have met since you got here. And Anita, you know John of course but did you meet George a couple of weeks ago?"

Sam arrived in a bit of a flap and looked around the room somewhat frantically. Then he held up his hand and said "wait a second folks, that centre table is just about to leave. I'm going to move you folks over there."

The patrons of the centre table were just getting up to go, so the move was accomplished almost immediately. Anderson grinned across at Marjorie and winked in the general direction of the cops: they had made it a point to sit on either side of Priscilla, the new girl in town. She was pretty small to start with, and now she seemed particularly tiny. The Sergeant caught the wink and laughed across at the grinning Anderson: "Relax Frank, we just thought our new reporter friend would appreciate sitting with two guys who actually know something!"

Marjorie giggled: "I'm sure she would appreciate that. Where are they?"

Superintendent Daniels joined the laughter which had now afflicted the whole table, but quickly turned serious. "Actually, I think, I really do think, that there is more wisdom about what's going on gathered at this table than anywhere else. That's the good news. The bad news is that none of us knows enough."

***

Over 500 miles west of Awan Lake, along the Trans Canada Highway near Rossport, a battered and burned pickup truck was being retrieved from the north shore of Lake Superior. Earlier in the morning, an elderly gentleman and his young grandson had been trolling for bass near the shore when the old outboard motor on their boat struck something just under the surface, breaking the propeller. The Trans Canada passes close to the shore at that spot, so the man called the boy's father from his cellphone and asked him to drive out with a replacement prop he had hanging on a nail in his garage.

While they waited, the boy and his granddad had paddled their boat around to see if they could find what their propeller had hit. Soon enough they found an object close to the surface which, on closer examination, looked to be the top of a car or truck. They shared that information with the boy's father when he had arrived and parked along the shoulder of the highway. The man immediately telephoned the closest OPS detachment, which quickly responded by sending out a couple of highway patrol officers and calling in the OPS marine unit.

While he waited for the police, the man installed the replacement propeller on the fishing boat and sent his dad and his son in the general direction of home, figuring that his nine-year-old didn't need to hang around to see what might be in that submerged vehicle. That was likely a good decision: when the marine unit arrived, a police diver confirmed that the vehicle was, indeed, a badly-burned truck with a corpse inside. A flatbed tow truck was already on standby on the shoulder of the highway, and (two extra lengths of cable later) the truck and its grisly contents were soon chained onto the truck's deck and covered with a tarpaulin, ready for transport to the OPS forensics yard and laboratory in Sudbury.

***

Anita and Wendy had finished a very quick cup of coffee at the centre table in the Zoo before saying they had to go and set up the public address system at the Spirit River Marina. They drove down Marina Drive and up to the marina store and office. Leaving the Accord running, they went in to ask Jim or his wife Margaret where they wanted to set up.

"We're 'way ahead of you, sweetie," Margaret said to Anita. "Right over there on the lawn beside the ice cream shop," pointing to a grassed area beside the ramp to the gas dock."

"Thanks so much – you guys are wonderful. One last favour – do you have an extension cord that'll reach there from a plug-in? The little P.A. system doesn't draw a whole lot of power."

"I'm sure we do, but I'm also sure I have no idea where. Jim will know... go through that door into the main boathouse. A couple of guys came in this morning with a boat that needs some fixing, so he's in there greasing up his T-shirt again!"

"You go talk to Jim and I'll go move the car," said Anita. "You likely know Jim better than I do, 'specially since you're a regular customer!"

Wendy walked through into the boat house. Oddly for a city girl, she particularly loved the smells in here, a blend of water, the faint fishy odour of what people call seaweed, fresh gasoline and lubricating oil, and wood. Those smells were her introduction to Awan Lake on the day she and Marjorie first got to see their island cottage, and that excitement always stayed with her.

Two big men in black slacks and buttoned shirts were kneeling beside a big inboard-driven ski-boat tied into one of the slips. It had a white hull and deck with broad red stripes, and it's engine hatch cover was raised while Jim hovered over the engine with a small screwdriver in his mouth and small tester and electrodes in his hands. The two men looked up as Wendy walked down the dockway between the slips. The looks were appreciative: Wendy was a pretty blonde wearing tight jeans and a tank-top. "Jim," one of them said. "Someone here to see you."

Jim stood up and banged his head on the engine hatch. That caused him to lose the screwdriver which disappeared into the bilge. "Damn. Oh, hi Wendy! Getting things ready for this morning? Hope you get a good turn out... how can I help?"

"Hey Jim, you've been doing lots to help already. Margaret showed us where to set up and Anita is fiddling with wires for the P.A. system but... and that's why I'm here – of course I forgot an extension cord. I could maybe run up to the Co-op and buy one, but perhaps you have one here that we could use."

"You bet! See that white cupboard door on the wall over there, at the head of the second slip? That's where I keep extension cords and stuff. You'll probably need two fifty-footers to reach... grab what you need!"

Wendy stepped over to the cupboard and found the two cords she needed. "Thanks Jim! I owe you a beer for banging your head on that hatch cover!"

"Shut-up, pretty lady! But I'll take it!

Wendy jogged over to where Anita was setting up the microphone cord and stand. "Jim's so nice! Here are some cords."

"He is nice, but he's kind of an old guy and so flirty. He sorta scares me!"

"Jim? Hell no, wouldn't hurt a fly. He flirts because he admires, not because he's horny. He's just fine!"

"Really? Well, perhaps you're right. He certainly is friendly and helpful. Now, just plug this in here and... pop! Yeah, we are live from radio C.R.A.P. in Spirit River. It's sunny and bright and we have two hours of perfect programming for you!"

Wendy leaned over and kissed her on the neck. "You're a riot! But good grief, let's hope we can get this done in one hour, not two!"

"Well, the Love Our Lake part might only take an hour, but I have a feeling a lot of those folks hanging around the Zoo this morning have other things to ask about, like politicians and dead bodies. But, I will say it was nice to meet Priscilla... she's a real catch for us, because Envirowire is a heavy hitter. As Rolling Stone is to music, so Envirowire is to environmental issues. Let's hope we can spend some quality time with her talking about what we are trying to do!"

"We have no more than half an hour before we should be back here, but I need to go to the Co-op and pick up some smokes. All this cutting back on smoking shit has gone all to hell this past week!"

As they turned the Accord around and headed up the broad driveway, they both noticed one of the guys in black slacks and shirts standing by the boathouse door watching them leave. "He's kinda weird."

"Yeah, him and his buddy, dressed just like him. I'll give you 'weird' and add 'creepy'!"

***

By the time they got back, the locals involved with the event had started to arrive. Anderson and Marjorie were already there, along with Priscilla the reporter. Sergeant John and his boss had pulled in near the entrance and parked, facing their well-marked SUV out the driveway. They were both deeply engaged in conversations, which included each other, a cellphone, and the OPS radio system. Dave Bradshaw had arrived in his little speedboat and was tying up at the dock beside the boat launch, and Marion and

Arnold had set up a garden table to distribute Protected Shoreline Project pamphlets and to collect business cards and take notes. And Margaret had begun to put out an urn of coffee, a tray of juice boxes and ice-cream pails of donuts, of which she was vey proud.

By 10:45, there were four TV network vans parked near the OPS vehicle and four camera tripods were arrayed in front of the microphone. Anderson whispered to Marjorie: "This is going to be a real success, at least as far as turn-out is concerned. I hadn't dared to hope for half this number... if I wasn't nervous before about speaking, I sure as hell am now!"

At 11:00, there was a good-sized crowd at the foot of the marina dock, overlooking the water. Anita had arranged the podium and microphone so the TV cameras could not help but film the lake. Wendy and Anita were at the podium making a few introductions, and now it was up to Frank Anderson to provide the opening remarks. Here is what the Journal quoted the next morning:

Good morning.

We welcome all representatives of the media, including reporters from our neighbours to the south. You were invited here today for a specific reason, but we also know there are other things on your mind this morning, as there are on ours.

All along, though, we have known that many of you would want to talk about the toxic blend of politics, greed, and academic and organizational competition that always winds up blurring the lines between environmental oversight and corporate growth. As usual, however – and especially today – the first victims are our communities, and that is why we called this media conference before our event on Sunday. Our communities are our ecosystem – which includes our people, our land and of course our water – and our challenge to the media is to look beyond the simple heart-warming stories of locals doing their best to save what they love. We want you to look into the forces driving that toxic blend... here, at Awan Lake, as elsewhere. Thank you for attending!

There was applause. Anderson returned to Marjorie's side: "Wow, that was pretty impressive, Mr. Anderson. You're gonna be a hard act to follow!"

"The others will build the story far better than I could, but I thought I might as well lay down some concrete for them to build on!"

"You certainly did that. Didn't know you had it in you!" It was Superintendent Daniels, who had come up from behind. "Your friend Wendy, the MC, just asked John and I if we would consider releasing some information about the homicide charges etc., and John – lovely fellow that he is – tagged me with the job. I hate to be a spoiler, but you did open the door to 'other things' on our minds this morning, so

I hope I can make it fit."

"No worries, George. And anyway, I am pretty sure (as I think you are) that there are big-time connections between all of these things... things we can't say yet, but soon."

"Yeah, yesterday I would have called you paranoid. This morning, I'm not at all sure."

Anderson made a quick "just a moment" gesture and walked around behind the audience to the Ice Cream shop, bypassing the two black-suited men standing at the boathouse door. "Hi Margaret, is Jim out in the shop?"

She nodded, and he walked on through the back door and out along the slip where he was still fiddling with the speedboat's engine. "Hi Jim, getting her fixed for those guys?"

"Hi Frank! Yup, fuel problems, just making sure it's not an EFI problem."

"You know these guys?"

"Yes and no. The boat's from Robertson Mines. They keep it in a boathouse over there and have an account here for maintenance. Never seen the guys though. Kind of a strange pair, seems like. Not their usual bunch of technicians."

"Security types, maybe?"

"Yeah, smells that way."

"Okay, thanks. I'd better get going before they see us talking." He went back into the shop, bought a maple-walnut cone, and walked back outside, where the questions had begun. The focus was on Dave Bradshaw and university research, but quickly turned to Willy Antoine for the First Nation perspective. He was a superb speaker, talking with a strong gentle voice about the importance of the waters – and the fish – of Awan Lake and the Spirit River system that had sustained his people for centuries. He also made reference to "our new settler neighbours who have also been a welcome part of our community for a couple of hundred years, and who have given my people new and different opportunities." He went on to say that "Awan Lake, its people and its industries, must not allow industrial growth to become so great than it destroys everything we share as a community."

Anderson had strolled back to Sergeant John's side. "See those two Johnny Cash imitators over there by the boathouse?"

"The men in black? Yup, they look like first cousins of the gentlemen I talked to at Robertson's front gate yesterday. Security contractors. Why?"

"Thought you might like to know that they came here from the boathouse on Robertson's property, in a fast boat that Jim says they've had out there, probably for years. He's checking their fuel system. And the boat doesn't look like it ever had a registration number."

"Do you suppose I should get one of our new constables out here to check that out?"

"Yup. If we can hang onto it long enough to get a hard look at the inside, and the starboard outside in particular, that'd be even better. But if not, at least photos."

"Mmm." The Sergeant stepped back to the SUV and started a radio call.

***

The official part of the media conference was over by just after 12:00, but a number of reporters hung around afterward, munching on Margaret's donuts, sipping coffee and trying to engage anyone they could in more conversations. Wendy had prepared the committee and speakers for this, and had asked them to hang around as well, mixing with the media and being friendly but staying on message, answering questions with facts, not suspicions.

Anderson kept a low profile. He found the Sergeant again and suggested they find somewhere else to store the burnt-out wreckage from yesterday: "I really don't want the Barkers to have to put up with it any longer than today sometime. They won't even want to have guests over until it's gone!"

"Good point. Any suggestions?"

"Well, I can drag it back to my dock, of course, but you may want to keep a guard on it there. Or we could maybe ask Florence if we can put the boat in its own slip, which would be maybe a bit more private, but... geez, I dunno about that..."

"Nah, we can't do that to her... that would be just cruel. Let's just put it at your wharf, along with all the other bits and pieces you collect from time to time. I'm sure the forensics folks will clear it for disposal in a few days, or at least let us lift it out and take it back to our yard in The Falls. They can send guards out there if they want."

"Okay, Marj and I will get at it after lunch. Y'know, it might be fun to let the men in black see what we're doing, and see what kind of reaction we get... if Marjorie and I hustle out there we could be back in about an hour and a half from now... could your registration-checkers keep them around that long?"

"You are really crazy, you know that? But it's worth a shot. Go for it, and keep in touch."

"No worries, I have my genuine magical police satellite phone on my belt!"

Anderson pried Marjorie away from the donuts and a long conversation with Margaret, and they headed home to his dock with enough left-over donuts and buns to feed a small army. They stopped at his house long enough to pick up part of a case of beer and their jackets, fired up the main engine after checking oil and fuel, and left the harbour with more haste than usual. The Barkers had been at the media conference but were home already. Anderson called Tony to let him know they were coming and would be removing the unlovely wreck in less than an hour, thanking him again for letting it stay there overnight. "That was a really-well-run event," Tony said, "and your opening remarks were right on the money. I guess I'm not surprised, but Jean and I really were impressed."

"Thanks Tony. I hope we left the right impression. I expect we'll know more tonight after the evening news! In the meantime, we are going to parade the wreck by some people we think should worry about what we know already. See you soon!"

"Yes, I get that. Good for you!"

Anderson had no sooner clicked off when the Sergeant rang. "Okay, Marie Beauchemin is out of hospital and back at work on light duty, so they sent her out with a cruiser to check out the boat registration, with strict orders not to engage. She's just pulled in. I'll get her to take as long as she can with hassling them for paperwork, then she's to radio me to step in for a look and to determine what to do about the boat. By the time we screw around with that, you should be getting close. Unless I call you with something different, maybe you could just parade by the marina with the boat in tow, turn slowly near the dock at the Inn, and then take her back to your place. I'll keep you informed."

"Perfect. We're well on our way, as fast as this little tub can go. It was built to chase lobsters, not sharks!"

After they settled into the trip, Marjorie and Anderson were feeling giggly and light-headed enough without the beer, but they each had one anyway. Less than forty minutes later, they were headed back to the village with the burned-out hulk in tow. Anderson pushed the throttle as far as he dared, thankful for the elegant design of the classic old sailboat's hull that kept it steady at close to its hull speed – the design speed for a boat of its class – despite the damage done to everything above the waterline.

Half an hour, two beers and what seemed like several pounds of donuts later, Anderson called the Sergeant: "Hey John, we're probably fifteen minutes out. How's it going?"

"The men in black are well-schooled at not letting their emotions show, but they are some pissed, just seething inside. They want to take their boat and get the hell out of here, and they're pissed at the little chick with a limp and her boss. Marie has them filling out forms on the workbench, and I'm just standing around. I'll take one of them out on the dock and start asking some questions left over from my visit there yesterday, when they didn't want to talk to me very much."

"Cool. I'll give a short blast on the horn when we pass my dock, then two blasts when I turn at the Inn and head back." Anderson clicked off and turned to Marjorie: "Tonight, I think you and I want to try out that v-berth in the bow. I'll pick up a pizza and bring some Cognac, since I see you like brandy! And we'll make sure the security cameras are set on the dock properly!"

"All your weapons loaded?"

"Absolutely. All of 'em!"

***

The timing worked out well. *The Beaver* and her battered tag-along cruised by the end of the marina docks while the Sergeant was talking to the two men before they boarded their boat to go home. Ten minutes later *The Beaver* and its tow came back the other way and pulled slowly into the commercial dock where Anderson kept his boat.

Anderson landed the workboat carefully while Marjorie walked the tow-rope around in front and together they pulled the sailboat around the end of the wharf and tied it up securely at least two boat-lengths ahead of *The Beaver* and on the opposite side of the dock, as far away from each other as they could get. The men in black went by slowly, keeping their distance, then turned south and sped off toward Robertson Mines on the east shore.

It didn't take the Sergeant long to drive over from the marina. "That's a two-minute walk or a three-minute drive, but I guess a guy has to keep his squad car in reach," teased Anderson.

"Wise ass! Well, that worked: if the goal was to worry the crap out of those guys, we got 'er done!"

"So they went home with things to think about?"

"Yeah, that they did. They're not dummies at all and I bet they know that we think their boat had something to do with the fire – and the murder, which it now officially is."

"If it's them, they made some serious misjudgements. For starters, I think they expected that a gallon or two of gasoline would burn the boat right to the waterline and she would sink. As I recall the Dragon class boats have over a ton of ballast and keel, which would have taken the whole outfit, corpse, revolver and all, straight to the bottom. In that general location the lake is over 300 feet deep. But... they didn't count on that downpour two nights ago. Just can't keep a fire going when you need to!"

"The victim was wearing an inflatable lifejacket. That explains why someone cut the bottom out of it... they didn't want the body to float to the surface."

"Right. And I expect the killers brought their own gasoline... there is no auxiliary engine on that boat, although as I recall from last weekend he had a small trolling motor and a battery stuffed in the cabin."

"Yes. We wondered about that."

By now the Sergeant was sitting in the house with Marjorie and Anderson, drinking fresh coffee and trying to finish Margaret's donuts. It was Marjorie's turn for some questions: "So, gentlemen, I agree with you that we've discovered the how, and probably the who, but it's really the motive and the rest of the connections we're missing. First, I can hardly believe the same Leonard we met on Sunday would go off sailing that elegant boat deliberately into a storm. The only thing harder to believe than that is that nobody, unless they have Frank's skills and equipment, could have hunted down that sailboat unless they had made plans to meet at a specific location beforehand. So, who, and why? The 'who' may indeed give us the 'why', but this girl doesn't think those men in black – dangerous as they look – would have originated the whole thing. I think there is a guy somewhere who pays those guys, and who set up a secret meeting with Leonard and hired them to kill him."

"You're suggesting that Robertson Group International is entirely behind this?"

"Walks like a duck."

It was Anderson's turn: "So Leonard Hamilton-Dubois was the key. He manipulated all the political connections and was the conduit for all the pay-offs, and Garnet Cameron was his shield and protector. With Cameron now in legal trouble, Hamilton-Dubois became a liability because he knew every transaction, every piece of legislation and regulation that got subverted. He knew where all the bodies were buried and exactly where the money came from and where it went. In short, Garnet gets to go down in disgrace as the hockey goon he always was, but Leonard, well, he just couldn't stay alive.

The Sergeant's normally friendly face was like stone. For a long time he just sat still. Marjorie opened beers for each of them, lit herself and Anderson a cigarette, and placed the pack in front of the policeman. "As clever as we have been to string this together, I'm afraid we've only just scratched the surface."

Anderson had been doing his usual scribbles and lines on blank paper while he had talked. He flipped a sheet of paper over and began again: "Over the next few days, most people – reporters included – will pounce on Garnet for tripping over his own dink and getting mixed up with the wrong woman. For awhile, any focus on Leonard will be on the tragedy of it all, a hard-working and loyal civil servant who possibly committed suicide but might have been murdered by an out-of-control rent-a-cop from the states who argued with him in the middle of a lake. So, two low-level people have made serious mistakes: Garnet, by, well, being Garnet, and the rent-a-cop by assuming he had completed the job he was sent to do and neglecting to make sure the damn boat sank. Two men may go to jail eventually, and the folks who write the big checks in New York, Washington, and São Paulo won't even miss one martini."

Anderson paused, listening for a moment then glancing out the window. He sat back down and continued: "We can be pretty sure that Thomas Manville, the new GM out at the plant, is the person who directed the killing. He has a reputation as being a fixer, a fixer at a very high level, but I believe he's well-distant from the bosses. They just tell him they want all the trouble stopped and the mess cleaned up and they give him a regional vice-president title to keep him happy. The senior management at Robertson Group International are not miners or geologists any more... they play their management game in the very public world of the stock market, and a murder at Awan Lake or a few out-of-control employees are not nearly as damaging to the share price as a well-planned and very public assault on things like their management of the environment and their running roughshod over democratic governments. I think – weird as it sounds – that is how we get to them. After today, we have some very skilled opinion-leaders on our side, thanks to the experience and skills of Wendy and Anita. I think we need to carefully feed the right information to the media, focused on bottom-level government corruption thanks to the Garnet and Leonard show, while we keep the lowest profile possible, not letting anyone know that we have a clue about what's going on."

The Sergeant had remained quiet, staring at the table and occasionally glancing at Anderson's scribbles, but now he looked up: "Unfortunately, Frank, you're making sense again, and I have learned to find that somewhere between extremely helpful and somewhat terrifying. This line of thought I find extremely terrifying, but I suspect you are correct. We need to make a plan that is both highly detailed and very flexible, because your goal is basically to force the

Robertson Group to panic. It's setting a trap and not getting ourselves caught in it, right?"

"Yup." Anderson turned to Marjorie, who was deep in thought. "Marj, you have way more experience with senior government and high-end corporate behaviour than we have. John and I obtained most of our wisdom in quasi-military surroundings. And without any doubt at all, your thinking is more subtle. Certainly more subtle than mine. So... don't be a stranger. Let us have it!"

"You're scary," she laughed. "I'm just glad you're not off somewhere planning a revolution or something! Seriously, though, I think you're onto something..."

"Onto something, or just 'on' something?"

"Well, maybe that too. But nonetheless, I think John kinda put it perfectly when he talked about setting a trap and not getting caught in it. That's going to be tough."

The Sergeant had been staring out the window when he suddenly jumped up: "What the hell, the dock's on fire!" He pulled his sidearm and ran out the door and down toward the dock.

Anderson was right behind him, as was Marjorie except she stopped in the doorway and dialled 911. She figured they already had a cop, but what they needed was a fire truck.

Leonard's sailboat was a fireball. Someone had emptied

at least five gallons of what seemed like a mix of gasoline and diesel into the cabin, then evidently poured a trail of the mix from the boat down the dock past *The Beaver*. Anderson grabbed a fire bucket from the deck of his boat and handed it to the Sergeant, shouting at him to throw water on the dock while he started up the fire-pump he carried onboard.

It took less than five minutes for the village's fire truck and four volunteers – including Arnold – to arrive. Anderson and the Sergeant had already put out the trail of fire on the dock and were trying to keep the side of the dock wet beside the burning sailboat. The volunteers laid a single hose line from the fire truck and were able to completely extinguish the fire in short order.

Which was a good thing because no sooner had they shut down their single nozzle than a 911-dispatch call came in on the fire truck radio, saying there was a pickup truck on fire on the highway outside of town. The firemen took their nozzle, dropped the hundred-foot section of hose on the dock, and were gone up the road and out of town in less than a minute, leaving Anderson, Marjorie and the Sergeant standing together on the dock in mild bewilderment. "Kind of a peaceful evening, really," said Anderson as he stepped into *The Beaver* to shut down the pump.

"Well, what do you expect? Nothing exciting ever

happens in this town anyway," added the Sergeant.

"Actually, not quite so. While I was at the door of the house calling in the fire, I heard – and caught a glimpse of – an old rattletrap of a truck taking off from behind the trees. Over there," she pointed. "Something tells me that same truck is now on fire, and the people who lit up the dock are long-gone in another vehicle."

"You're probably right, Marjorie. This wasn't the work of a couple of bored kids. I'm going back up to my car to get on the radio, and maybe I'd better get out to that truck and have a look-see. If it's okay with you guys, I want to grab Arnold and bring him back with me. And I want you guys to think about how much we should tell our Superintendent – Super George as you call him. I'm not telling him anything just yet."

The Sergeant jogged up the road to his vehicle, and Marjorie turned to Anderson: "You okay?"

"Yes, I'm fine. How are you doing?" and he leaned over to give her a kiss.

"Bored silly, of course, but I'll be okay."

"Since you're bored, do you wanna go up to the computer and check out the video recording of the last half hour while I drain and roll up these hoses?"

"Perfect!" She grabbed his hand, pressed it against her

left breast, kissed his nose, and headed and up the road.

07:15 AUGUST 10

Marjorie had been up since just after six, and had spent the last hour quietly cleaning up around the house and getting ready to make breakfast. Unusually, she had the television on, tuned to the CBC Network News channel, and occasionally stopped to watch and listen – with the sound away down. Awan Lake, Spirit River and Maple Falls were, in one way or another, mentioned in over half of the news items this morning. The big item was still the philandering MP from Maple Falls and speculation about who the wronged intern might be (ignoring, Marjorie noticed, the fact that Mrs. Cameron was a victim too). A suspicious death in a possible boating accident on Awan Lake – the second accident with fatalities on the lake in less than a week – was causing an uproar in Toronto about boating safety on Canada's lakes. And finally, the tiny village of Spirit River was raising red flags about industrial pollution of their water, and expected to have several hundred people turn out on

Sunday for an address to be delivered by controversial climate scientist Dr. Sebastian Horowitz from British Columbia.

Marjorie sighed. *I wonder why the networks even bother to send out their staff to events like yesterday. If they cared at all about accuracy, they would have been better to keep that bunch at home nailed to a desk and working the telephones.* She remembered, though, that in their conversations last night they all understood that misinformation would probably serve their own investigation better than good in-depth coverage, at least until they started to unearth some senior players and their motives. Sergeant John would be coming at nine o'clock – "zero-nine-hundred" as Frank and the Sergeant called it – and he would be bringing the Superintendent with him. John wanted to set it up so Anderson would introduce his theories from last night: "My boss has a very high regard for Frank, and that old Coast Guard connection will make this go much easier," he had said.

And now I should wake him up with the smell of bacon frying. Twenty minutes later, a soft nose nuzzling his ear and the irresistible aroma of bacon did, indeed, bring Anderson to the surface. He took a quick shower, towelled off and dressed in clean jeans and an old but clean Coast Guard shirt. "Well, aren't we shiny this morning, Mr. Anderson," Marjorie chuckled.

"Might as well play the Coast Guard hand for all it's worth," he said as he eyed the progress of the frying eggs over her shoulder. "I've been wondering if we should have asked Wendy to come – she's the one who knows best how to play the media."

"Yes, but we can always involve her later. She is barely known to Super George, and there's always the lingering shadow of Wendy and John eyeing up each other a few weeks ago. And Frank – I love and respect Anita all to pieces but she might unnerve people in high places. Best to involve them after this first strategy session."

"Strategy session? Really?"

"Yes, really. All conspiracy theorists need to have good working strategies."

"Thanks a lot, lady!"

***

OPS Superintendent George Daniels had a lot on his mind this morning. The Sergeant had already informed him of the arson event last evening, and Daniels wanted a look at the dock and the security tape Marjorie has saved. There wasn't much to see in either case. The sailboat had finally succumbed to the second attempt to sink it and was sitting half-upright on its cast-iron keel seven feet down on the bottom of the harbour, its mast leaning against the dock at about a thirty-degree angle. The dock itself had been charred in a few places, but the flames had not had a chance to penetrate very far.

And the infrared video, as might be expected, showed two figures in dark clothing carrying what appeared to be jerry cans stepping onto the dock from the side near the shore, emptying the cans into the boat and along the dock where they lit the gasoline and ran back off the dock, disappearing out of the camera's field of view. The rest of the video was all about orange flames and flashes of silhouettes of Anderson's workboat.

John had attended at the burned-out truck on the road near the dock, and basically only learned that it had been an older white crew-cab with an unreadable VIN. Of course there was nobody near, and the firemen had pretty much obliterated any tracks in the gravel from the vehicle that must have picked up the truck's occupants.

As the four of them sat at Anderson's table slurping coffee, the Sergeant explained to his boss that "Last night, Frank had what I think is a pretty clear-headed analysis of where this case is at, and how it fits into a much larger picture that he is well aware of. He also came up with a strategy – or at least the beginning of a strategy – for how we could successfully use information, and connections that we already have, to manipulate the real bad guys to reveal themselves so we can nail 'em. Sounds complicated, I know, but I think if I let Frank explain it as he did last night, it will all make sense.

The Superintendent had been sitting quietly with his head turned to one side, listening carefully. He lifted his head toward Anderson: "Frank, by all means, please..."

Anderson explained the relationships between the various players, local and otherwise, as well as his suspicion that Manville, the new boss at Robertson Mines, directed the killing of Hamilton-Dubois after realizing that MP Garnet Cameron's arrest and impending investigations would open up the long-standing relationships – including a money-trail – between Robertson Group International and Hamilton-Dubois. It was generally well-known that Hamilton-Dubois had built up a pretty sizeable investment portfolio, mostly in real estate.

The Sergeant asked, "Last night, Frank, you were figuring that the media would only cover the easy targets for the moment, like the MP's arrest for having an affair and

Hamilton-Dubois' unfortunate death from undetermined causes, but missing the natural resources and Robertson Mines connection."

"Exactly, and Frank was bang-on with that," chimed in Marjorie. "I've been listening to the CBC news network since just after seven, and it would be hilarious if it wasn't so disgusting. There were three stories coming out of the Awan Lake and Maple Falls area: the passing of Hamilton-Dubois in a boating accident, the various love affairs of Garnet Cameron, and the impending visit of Sebastian Horowitz, a controversial scientist from BC. Absolutely nothing about Robertson, and the story involving the death of Hamilton-Dubois had morphed into a story about the tragic issue of boating safety regulations on Canadian lakes. And absolutely nothing whatsoever connecting the stories, despite the fact that the reporters and their cameras were all in the same place yesterday!

"You're kidding!" blurted out Anderson.

"No I'm not! It's crazy – stupid crazy!"

Even the Superintendent was laughing: "Now you know why we cops hate being grilled by reporters at media conferences. It kinda destroys your faith in humanity!"

The Sergeant, though, was silent. When the laughter had settled down, he said, "Frank – and Marjorie too – know we have a resource in our toolkit that no one else has, and that's Marjorie's sister Wendy, who you have met. Until a month ago, Wendy was embedded at the heart of Robinson Group International as the company's contracted Public Relations Consultant of record at their Toronto office. Frank, with that fact in mind, is this where your strategy to nail the real perpetrators comes in?"

"Yes. As you can understand from Marjorie's news-watching this morning, the media is – at the moment anyway – everywhere but the right place. This means that for a little while, clever people with a plan could manipulate the media. If our goal is to force RGI – Robertson Group International – to panic, and if we feed enough stuff to escalate that panic, we may be able to drag all the dirt out into the open while solving at least three murders and bringing attention to the criminality of their lobbying efforts to suppress scientific assessments. I don't think we have long to put a strategy in place before they find a way to bury everything, but I do think we can get it done."

"See Superintendent? That's what I was talking about. I admit that it stretches the 'normal' for police work, but I figure we have a rare opportunity."

"Thank you, John, and thank you Frank and Marjorie." The Superintendent paused at length. "Our job as police officers is to investigate crime and as you know we have solid evidence that two crimes have occurred and they are indeed under investigation. We have suspects in one double homicide and we may have persons of interest in a separate single homicide. Frank, you are suggesting that there is a common perpetrator behind these homicides, although we don't have enough evidence yet to even tie the crimes together, let alone identify common perps." The Superintendent paused again.

"Three weeks ago I appointed you to serve as an Auxiliary Sergeant during a particular event. If I reinstate that appointment, you will ultimately be bound by the same regulations as other OPS officers, and I am not altogether sure that will serve any of our purposes at this time. We all have a high regard for your abilities and those of your friends and colleagues, and we would like you to continue collaborating with us as ordinary citizens, with all the responsibilities and freedoms that involves. Your boat and her crew remain on the clock in these matters, under the verbal contract we already have in place. Try to stay out of trouble." Another pause.

"Off the record – and you didn't hear this from me or John – let's get at it!

***

The rest of Thursday morning was devoted to a lot of grunt work. The OPS forensics team had already arranged to tow away the burned pickup truck, but they also wanted the sunken and charred sailing yacht taken to the OPS compound in Maple Falls. The boat was too far out on the dock to be lifted with a small picker crane, so Anderson, assisted by Arnold and Marjorie, managed to loop some chain slings under the bow and stern and lift what was left of the boat clear of the lake bottom with the workboat's gear. They manoeuvred the hulk back along the dock until it was close enough for the truck-mounted crane to grab, then secured it upright until they had cut the wire stays that held the mast and lifted it clear. The picker crane operator set the mast on the trailer, then loaded the boat itself, making sure it was chained down securely.

As the crane and trailer moved carefully up the road on its way to Maple Falls, Marjorie stood on the dock, watching. *Sunday, when that beautiful varnished boat with her white sails came by the dock, she seemed so alive. Tuesday, drifting charred and helpless far out on the lake, she looked full of mystery – haunted, perhaps. Today, she has been reduced to a pile of dead garbage. I find that very sad.*

***

Marjorie had earlier texted Wendy to say that she and Frank would be coming out to the cottage for a "scheme-and-slurp" (as Wendy liked to call luncheon meetings) and that she and Frank would bring the slurp part with them. As soon as they had watched the truck with what was left of Leonard's sailboat drive up the road and go out of sight on its way to The Falls, they cast off from the dock and headed south-east to Ship Island. Marjorie had driven up to the Zoo and purchased four "Emmett's Chicken Neptune Croissants" and four big cinnamon rolls for lunch, and she had also gone to the beer store and picked up a six-pack of Black Forest Dark Lager, two for the trip and four to share at lunch.

The first hour at the island cottage was spent over lunch and updating each other about yesterday's media conference, the fire at the dock, and the discussions with John last night and the two cops this morning. If Marjorie had been attentive to the news channel this morning, that had nothing on the attention Wendy and Anita had paid to media reports last night and today.

"We got all kinds of coverage," said Anita. "Even that

chick – Priscilla – from Envirowire was interviewed by Global, just because she was here from the almighty U.S.A. I guess!"

"She also posted a story on her wire service," said Wendy. "It was a good one and perhaps the only one that reflected why we held the news briefing in the first place. She covered Robertson's proposed expansion, the potential hazard to the lake, the dedicated efforts of the community, and the upcoming address by Dr. Horowitz on Sunday. She's a believer."

"Did anyone address the scientific controversy surrounding Dr. Horowitz's credibility?" Anderson wanted to know.

"That's where Global was most useful, although a free-lancer for the National Post had a lot to say as well. Both – especially the National Post article – were looking to pick holes in the theory that the expansion project might be harmful to the lake. The Post reporter characterized Horowitz as a "pediatrician and well known left-wing advocate" and an "anti-development conspirator with a global anti-development agenda."

"And the others?"

"Pretty much like what Marjorie described from the CBC. Tragic boating accidents, warm fuzzy home-town activism, and the former hometown of disgraced Tory MP and cabinet minister Garnet Cameron."

"That stuff drives me crazy!" Anderson mumbled. He finished off his beer, lit a smoke, and continued: "Looking on the bright side, we now know what's out there and it leaves things open for us to manipulate lazy and incurious reporters to change the news cycle to our advantage. Wendy, am I wrong to assume that the Robertson Group works to control the public relations agenda (including politicians) primarily to ensure the company's shares maintain or grow their value?"

Wendy nodded.

"So what do your instincts (and ten years or more of insider knowledge) tell you about where they are most vulnerable, and how to prick a hole in their carefully-crafted bubble? For one thing, I am pretty sure their chief executive, board of directors and major shareholders don't have a clue that there are senior managers directing black-ops on Canadian soil and that people are dying."

"How about seeing if we can co-opt Priscilla?" responded Wendy. "She – and her news service – have an established reputation, and one that is firmly on the side of the angels in this case. Anita and I were going in to see her this afternoon, and maybe have supper together."

"You're kidding me! She's still here in Spirit River?"

"You bet, Marj! She is sticking around until the event on Sunday and staying at the Inn. For people like her, a laptop and cellphone are all she needs for an office!"

"Wow, that's incredible. She could be our pipeline, and get herself a hell of a story while she's at it. I liked her, and have a lot of respect for her dedication!" In her enthusiasm, Marjorie hadn't noticed that Anderson's face had clouded up. "Problems with this, Frank? Seems ideal!"

"Yeah, I'm worried... better late than never, I hope. I have been pushing the bad stuff – the dangerous stuff – to the back of my mind. I have been assuming the Webster sisters and Anita and I are all in this together and that nothing bad can happen anyway. But I worry that we are all in danger because those 'men in black' have each of us in their sights, mostly because of me. I know that Manville – Robertson's new manager – was highly suspicious of me even before we recovered a murdered Leonard and his sailboat. I think dragging yet another talented and totally innocent person into the spotlight is a step too far, especially if we plan to use her to turn up the heat under the Robertson Group. I apologize for not thinking this through earlier. So starting right now we have to take steps to ensure you three ladies are safe."

An uneasy silence permeated the room. Except for the ever-practical Marjorie, who walked into the cottage from the porch where they had been sitting and returned with four bottles of Corona. "This is the ideal beverage for a Mexican Standoff," she chirped as she opened and passed around the bottles. "Let's hope we don't wind up in one!"

Anita had been scribbling nervously on her scratch-pad: "I'm not about to move away or go into hiding. This has long been 'way too important for me, and as you all know, I did my hiding bit a few weeks ago. And, one of my friends was killed, partly because of me. So, Mr. A., do you have a plan? You're good at that."

Wendy and Marjorie nodded back at Anita, and Wendy spoke up: "Yes, Frank. I think we all want in, and if we want to engage Priscilla in any way, we have to have full disclosure, to somewhat misuse a public relations phrase. Any ideas?"

"I was going to suggest we keep all of you here at the island, but in fact that's too obvious and access is too hard to control. We might be better off to put you all up at the Inn, in plain sight along with Priscilla, until the event is over. Then you can come and go in ones and twos, and we would probably only need a plainclothes guard at night. I'm sure John will go for that when I explain."

"What about you?"

"I'll talk to John and the Superintendent, and work out a plan that involves some increased protection. I'll talk it over with him. More importantly, though, what do you think about heading into town, as soon as possible?"

"I like it," said Marjorie. "That way we're closer to you and our support people like Arnold and Marion and Sergeant John. And we would attract a lot less suspicion, just staying in town until the event is over so we can be of more help to the committee. It seems less mysterious, and we'd have good cell coverage all the time so we can reach out for help."

"I'm calling Flo to see what she can arrange. If it works out for her, I can drop by and do some explaining." Anderson took the satphone from his belt, looked up the number for the Inn on his own cellphone, and dialled.

***

Half an hour later, the cottage was locked up and Wendy and Anita were headed into the village marina in their little skiff. Marjorie and Anderson were following in *The Beaver*, keeping a good distance between them. Anderson had explained to Flo that the ladies had office-type work to do, and she had been pleased to welcome them. She would put Anita and Wendy in the room she had always kept for visits from Leonard, giving them a desk and workspace at a larger table. Rooms 201 and 203 were adjoined, with a connecting door between them, where Marjorie could share space if necessary. Journalist Priscilla Morgenstern was in 205, a single room, and by 16:30, the ladies were all settled in and having a quiet conversation with a delighted Priscilla.

Anderson had caught up with the Sergeant by phone and explained the need for a night-time plainclothes guard. He assigned Corporal Marie Beauchemin, saying, "She'll love that, better than stuck behind a desk while she finishes recuperating from her injuries!" She would stay at the Inn, where Flo had saved her a separate room on the same floor as the others.

Anderson had stopped into the Co-op for more diesel and headed down to the dock to spend some time attending to his boat, checking fluids, re-fuelling and generally cleaning up. He had only just started re-fueling when his satphone started beeping.

It was the Sergeant again: "You'll never guess what I just learned! A late-model crew-cab truck leased to Robertson Group International with a Gerald Giordano as the named principal driver was just pulled from Lake Superior near Nipigon. It had been torched, and there was a body inside... they tell me it will be awhile before they can provide positive identification."

Anderson was silent for a few seconds.

"Frank, are you still there?"

"Yeah. Still here. I'm trying to connect the dots – too many damn dots. How many unexplained violent deaths have happened around here in the last couple of weeks? Four? Four apparent murders in two weeks... that's 'way too many for a small community. Like we went through a month ago, it was outside forces at work and even if all the murders seem to revolve around Robertson Mines and have little or nothing to do with our community or the lake, they don't seem to have much to do with mining copper for that matter. Last month it turned out to be drug smuggling – poorly run, clumsy, dangerous and totally unrelated to local realities. Good God, man, you couldn't make $25 a week selling drugs around here!"

"So what are you saying, Frank?"

"Well, this is sort of the same, don't you think? These last four murders have all been poorly executed, so to speak, and seem to be – I say 'seem to be' for good reason – seem to be happening in the shadow of a low-level showdown between environmentalists and miners... with a bit of typical Canadian politics thrown in just for fun. It just doesn't make sense on the surface. Even Giordano's murder near Nipigon seems out of synch, although I don't think his untimely passing will cause many tears around here!"

"So you're not seeing the connections?"

"Oh yeah, John, I'm seeing them all connected... just don't know why!"

"You think the murders are clumsy?"

"Of course! The two research kids – the dummies actually confessed... duh! Leonard Hamilton-Dubois? Boat didn't sink – rushed job. Trying again to set the boat on fire? Panicky, and just plain stupid. The murder of the fabulous Mr. G.? It took less than twenty-four hours from finding the truck to identifying who and where from. Yeah, all clumsy, stuff done by thugs with poor training, under poor leadership, and with all the subtlety of throwing a lead brick through a stained-glass window."

"Geez, some day let me buy you a beer so you can tell me what you really think," laughed the Sergeant. "While we're talking, let's talk about security for the event on Sunday. My bosses are having a fit."

"How about you and George and I having dinner somewhere... maybe in Maple Falls? But only if you'll put extra security on my bevy of ladies at the Inn while we're away."

"Yeah, you certainly have assembled a bunch of beauties with brains, haven't you! Can do... tonight at 19:00 at The Lockmaster's?"

"Works for me. I'll have one seriously jealous lady on my hands but, yes."

"I was going to suggest you bring her with you. Some days I think Marjorie has more on the ball than all three of us."

"That really works for me. Make the reservation... we'll be there."

***

Anderson had phoned Marjorie and asked her to pick him up at about 18:15. They took her Jeep, leaving his truck at the dock, and were settled in over a glass of house red at The Lockmaster's House restaurant by the time Super George and the Sergeant arrived. It was a lovely warm summer evening, which was a good thing because the restaurant was full inside and they wound up seated outside on the wide veranda.

"Seems busy for a Thursday," the Superintendent remarked as they took their seats.

"See all those little yachts tied upstream of the lock?" Anderson replied. "Looks like nobody wanted to cook onboard tonight!"

"Well, perfect for us... nobody knows enough to be nosy!"

Wine was the chosen drink of the evening, and they ordered their appetizers and entrées. "Let's talk about security this Sunday." Marjorie had brought a couple of pages of handwritten notes from her discussions with her roommates at the Inn, but little of the material concerned security. "None of us have felt that security for the event itself is a big issue, although Wendy says that the guest speaker had requested – and been granted – an RCMP plainclothes officer while he was in Spirit River. I imagine you know about this, John?"

"Yes, with their usual Curt Courtesy Communication – the three Cs – nothing more. I think they are sending two officers actually – plainclothes and uniformed. We had been planning four uniformed officers in two vehicles, but considering the recent... er... activities, George and I have been wondering if we should have a bigger presence. What are your thoughts?"

"We've been talking about it, lots, but the more we talk, the less we think security will be a problem. Certainly some uniformed police attendance would be appreciated, so thank-you for that – four sounds about perfect. Thing is, this event is going to be pretty local, despite the international implications. We're a long way from Ottawa and from those hundred or so people who always turn up in the city to protest almost anything. And Wendy says her old buddies in Toronto haven't heard any back-chatter. Her friend and former colleague says the Robertson Group International will be doing most of their media work in Toronto and New York – and of course Washington where she understands they are holding a media conference of their own tomorrow morning. Wendy says that RGI will be following the procedures she had established over the several years she had served as their Toronto public relations boss: be polite but avoid engaging locally and focus advocacy on the state, provincial and national politicians although this time they'll avoid Ottawa – too close to their facility and the source of the controversy and they'll want to downplay that."

"I imagine they'll also want to stay a long way clear of the political controversy about Garnet Cameron – and the death of Hamilton-Dubois, in case anyone connects the dots," Anderson interjected.

"Indeed they will, and that's where we will be busy. Priscilla put an article on Envirowire late this afternoon with a subtle focus on cosy relationships at high levels of government, including of course certain elected officials being 'way too cosy with female staff, and very cosy corporate relationships between former cabinet members and senior government officials. She made sure to point out the connections between government agencies and permits for RGI's proposed expansion. Her article also questioned whether the current government might be trying to discredit former cabinet members and all those same cosy relationships."

"Geez, you said 'subtle' focus? I can hardly wait to see what happens when she gets intense. It'll be fun to see how all that unfolds!"

Marjorie laughed: "Priscilla is pretty clever. The article manages to lay out all those possibilities and connect them without it reading like the writer was biased. There may be some reporting on the late evening news tonight, but I expect the fur won't really start to fly until after RGI's media conference tomorrow."

The appetizers had arrived and been hastily consumed. While they waited for the evening special – Steak Oscar – Marjorie filled in the two police officers about the program for Sunday, including the barbecue and short beer garden following the presentations and discussions.

The Superintendent had not added much to the chatter, but during a steak-filled lull in the conversation he observed,

"I agree with something John said earlier today: you folks seem to have this event under pretty good control, and it's well-planned with lots of local involvement, so as far as the village is concerned, security during the event should hardly be an issue. But while we four have this opportunity to talk privately, I'd like to consider the other apparent local threats. We have already had three apparent homicides within the last ten days, and just today we find out there is likely another one with local ties, even though the victim was found five hundred miles away. Those stats would be high for Toronto, so for a town of under 500, they seem more than a little extreme! What are all your thoughts on the common thread that links them all?"

A long silence was spoiled only by the clicking of steak knives. "These guys sure know how to serve up a nice meal," said Anderson.

"Well, George," he continued after another pause, "we all know there's some weird stuff that has been going on out at Robertson Mines, and we all know that the parent company, Robertson Group International, is less than pleased with our conservation efforts here and even less pleased that we are bringing their proposed development to the public's attention through the Love Our Lake event. But – just like we talked about a few minutes ago with regard to local event security – it seems that Robertson tends to stay out of local fights, preferring to manage things from the top through manipulating media and senior politicians. But... and this is a big 'but'... a month ago we witnessed what happens when local Robertson management goes rogue and allows – or even encourages – getting involved with international drug smuggling."

"But Frank, we've been all over that this last few weeks, and that whole nest seems to be cleared out. The last two punks who might have been involved with that are now sitting in remand, and they seem to be totally clueless anyway. They just keep bleating that Gerald told them to do it, and it appears Gerald was just pulled out of Lake Superior and won't be available for comment."

Anderson chuckled: "I know, George, but I really don't think what's happening now – including the death of the water research kids – has anything to do with drug smuggling like last time. They were such a badly-organized bunch of yahoos anyway, and Robertson's local manager who let it happen on his watch is likely sitting on a beach with his trophy wife, living off his severance pay. What's going on now is different, though. For starters, six weeks ago the folks involved were all local, or at least had local roots. Now we have a small police force out there at the mine...

how many did you figure John?"

"That Manville guy wasn't very forthcoming when we visited out there the other day, but my guess is that there are at least eight of them – the 'men-in-black' as you call them."

"So eight men-in-black, military-trained but loyal only to whoever pays them. They are there because Manville imported them, I'm almost certain, but I'm certain that RGI head-office knows they are out here. I expect their being here has little to do with Sunday's event, and a lot more to do with cleaning up after the last manager – Bonner. For me, the big question is all about Manville. Are all Robertson managers prone to going off-book, running local scenarios to their own benefit, or is Manville – a more senior "fixer" – here entirely on a corporate-directed mission?"

"We know – from what the late Leonard said to Frank – the men-in-black were engineering the clean-up out there. According to the Mistraika boys, they were kicked out just before we arrested them, and Leonard himself said they banished Gerald and sent him out west. You don't suppose, do you, that they also engineered his post-barbecue swim in Lake Superior? And if so, were they freelancing or following Manville's orders?"

"Well, John, you also know that I think the same guys tried to dispose of Leonard." Anderson paused a moment:

"But again, whose orders? Not just the men-in-black on their own initiative, I'm pretty sure... they may be bored out here at Awan Lake, but even so..."

"I think the only thing that would have made Leonard seem a possible threat must have come down from much higher up the RGI food-chain," ventured Marjorie. "After all, just on Sunday Manville and Leonard were sailing buddies drinking beer together. I'll bet the bosses suddenly became aware of the mess that MP Cameron was likely to cause, so they called early Monday morning and told their 'fixer' Manville to 'fixit' somehow. Manville would then have set up the secret meeting out on the lake, although of course we don't know whether he pulled the trigger or not, whether that matters much."

The Superintendent had been silent through this whole conversation and so had finished his steak and crabmeat early. He asked the waiter for coffee and sat back in his chair, gazing along the canal at the foot of the lawn and upstream toward the lake some twenty-five miles distant. "I think we need to put some pressure on the folks out at Robertson's facilities. I can get a warrant to search their fleet records, since that burned out truck near Nipigon came from here. I'd like to go through their entire fleet, on the grounds that two similar trucks were spotted getting gas in Sudbury.

And while we're at it, let's get a warrant to go over their boat and get details about their security personnel – names, training, addresses, everything we can. John – can we get a half-dozen officers from your division tomorrow morning, or should I get on the phone and order up a few more, to report here in the morning?"

"The detachment can only spare a couple – they've been burning the clock pretty good this week."

"Okay, I'll get on the blower. We'll take four vehicles – trucks if possible. I'd like to get this happening by 08:00 tomorrow, with John and I in the lead. Frank, if you could arrange to be sitting in your boat about a quarter-mile offshore in front of the Robertson office (north end of the main building) at the same time we arrive, that would be great. Just cruise back and forth until we call you. I assume you'll take Marjorie with you, but Marj, if you could get your gang of communications folks to just lay low at the Inn, and monitor all the communications and media stuff they can, that would be great. Call, radio or text Frank and Marjorie with anything remotely relevant. Between the OPS presence and the media reports that are likely to happen anyway, we should be able to shake something up before tomorrow is done!"

Anderson looked around the table at the others, nodded,

and said, "Sounds like a plan. Let's have a brandy and a smoke and get back to Spirit River. John, maybe make sure Marie is on-deck out at the Inn while we're gone, daytime or not."

"Good idea. And Frank, stop off at the detachment before you leave town... you need to become an armed auxiliary sergeant again, certainly while you're out there on the boat tomorrow."

07:30 August 11

Anderson slipped the forward spring line and watched with a happy grin as Marjorie quietly nudged the workboat's stern away from the dock, turned the wheel to let the bow follow, then edged out into open water. Once they were clear of the harbour, he attached the OPS flag George had given him to the port flag halyard, hoisted it to the cross-arm and tied it off, opposite the Canadian flag he always flew off the starboard cross-arm.

He went into the wheelhouse and gave Marjorie a kiss. "I guess if we're going to the party we might as well be dressed." He busied around the control station, turning everything on including both radar units. "There, now we look really official! So, set a course for your island, put the throttle at about three-quarters and let's have some coffee and get into the donuts we picked up on our way out of The Falls last night!"

"Heading for the island? Thought we were meant to go to Robertson Mines!"

"Well, the island is pretty much on our way there... I just want to slide by and make sure everything looks alright."

"Jeepers, are we both getting paranoid? We just left there yesterday after lunch, but I confess I had the same thought!"

"These days, on a foggy morning at Awan Lake, paranoia feels like wisdom."

It was going to be a beautiful day when the fog lifted off the east shore. Offshore, visibility was likely two miles but the fog thickened over the land and there was no wind. Anderson intended to stay well offshore until they were within two miles of Robertson Mines, then move in close as they approached the buildings, as the Superintendent had requested. After passing close to Marjorie's and Wendy's little island, and affirming that everything appeared in order, he re-adjusted their course and telephoned the Sergeant.

"Hi John, Anderson here. We're about thirty-five minutes out, heading south along the shore. Where are you guys?"

"Just left Spirit River ten minutes ago – we got away a bit late. Four vehicles in the convoy; we should be there in just over a half hour. Can you speed up a bit?"

"I'll push her a little harder – maybe you take your foot off the gas a bit. Call me when you are at the north end of the old park land. If we are both there at roughly the same time we should be good. We don't want them trying to get the boat away from their dock and making us track them down."

"Roger that."

As *The Beaver* moved south, ever closer to the shore, the fog thickened somewhat so Anderson switched off the autohelm and took control of the wheel. The Sergeant called again at 08:47 to report the police vehicles were just passing the north end of the park. Anderson could just see the shore appearing and disappearing off the port side; the radar and GPS showed they were about half a mile offshore, so he opened the throttle up full and edged closer. Some five minutes later he and Marjorie could see the outline of the large mine building looming out of the mist, so he began to slow down and move even closer to the shore.

At 08:58, with two minutes to go before their targeted time of arrival, he brought the workboat to a full stop in front of the buildings. His sonar showed 32 feet of water under the keel, and they could clearly see boathouse, launching ramp and short dock that all appeared to be attached to the main building. There was no activity along the shore, but up on the road behind they could see flashing blue and red lights moving along. "John and George must really want to get those guys upset," Marjorie remarked.

"Yeah, I heard them talking about 'lights-and-sirens on approach'. Sure as hell that'll spook everyone. Sitting out here is like having nosebleed tickets to a Grey Cup game... great view of everything but it's all happening too far away to be sure who's carrying the ball. I'd love to be hearing the radio conversations right about now!"

"Couple of guys just appeared on the dock by the boathouse."

"Okay then, time to look mean!" Anderson put the transmission in gear and swung the workboat's nose toward the boathouse, switched on his two mast-mounted spotlights and aimed them straight forward. He watched the sonar as he closed the distance to the dock. When they were about 100 yards offshore they still had about 20 feet of water: "Think I'll just stay here, so I still have some wiggle room in case they decide to do something weird. They can certainly tell we mean business."

Marjorie chuckled: "All fluffed up and nowhere to go, kinda like a tomcat... we'll just scare them into staying inside their house?"

"Exactly! We don't have very much in the way of claws and teeth, so we'll have to hope the intimidation game works!"

"Too bad we don't have a police scanner so we could

hear the radio chatter."

"Crap. Where's my head at... I'm so used to being alone out here on the water that I forgot John gave me that hand-held unit last night, which I cleverly hung behind the seat and forgot it was there." He reached around behind the helmsman's seat where the set of binoculars were kept and produced a bulky radio with a microphone on a curly cord. "Now, if I can just figure out how to make it work..."

It didn't take any figuring. Anderson clicked the radio on and it immediately began to squawk. There was certainly lots of activity on the radio, but it was difficult to tell exactly what was going on, so Anderson picked up the microphone, keyed the talk button, identified himself as 'Anderson' and reported he was holding his position about a hundred yards offshore of the boathouse.

"Roger that, Sergeant Anderson. This is Superintendent Daniels, and we can see you. Is there any action on the shore. Over."

"Superintendent, this is Anderson. There were two guys on the dock a few minutes ago, but when they became aware we were here they seem to have gone into the boathouse through a side door and disappeared. Over."

"Roger that, Anderson. Hold your position and keep an eye on the boathouse. We'll send a couple of officers down to check out the inside of the building. Out."

***

Room 201 at the Spirit River Inn was a hive of activity this morning. The evening before, Wendy and Anita had talked Florence out of a couple of TV sets from nearby rooms along with some extra cable, a knife, screwdriver and pliers so they managed to get three TVs set on different news channels. Priscilla, Anita, and Wendy had set up their laptops on the larger table, and Florence had brought up coffee and fresh breakfast biscuits for "the ABC girls at Awan Broad Casting" as she had named them. Corporal Marie Beauchemin had checked in at about 08:30 to make sure everything was alright before she went to bed, armed with several biscuits and a lot of thank-yous.

Things were unfolding well on the news front, considering the ongoing reality in the USA that the first-term president of that country had a knack for sucking the life out of the news cycle on a daily basis. This morning was no exception, although his latest social media outburst had fallen short of outrageous and was mostly just noisy. Happily, one of the American "big three" networks had picked up on Priscilla's Envirowire piece about "Chaos in

Canada's Commons" where a former minister of natural resources, possibly with ties to an international mining group, was being charged with sexual assault, and that an associate of his within the ministry had been found dead from a boating incident. The boating incident had taken place in the former minister's constituency, where a protest against a proposed mining expansion was planned for the weekend.

And, of course, one Canadian network had picked up the "Chaos in Canada's Commons" article, crediting the article to 'Envirowire, an American environmental news service'. The newscast said there was an investigation underway "to determine the circumstances surrounding the death of Leonard Hamilton-Dubois, a senior federal bureaucrat with ties to former natural resources minister Garnet Cameron, himself facing charges of sexual assault." The news item closed with a reference to the environmental protest against the proposed expansion of Robertson Group International's mineral processing facility at Awan Lake, where international water expert Dr. Sebastian Horowitz would be the keynote speaker this weekend.

"Not bad for a couple of days' work, ladies!" said Wendy. "Priscilla, you managed to touch all the right sore spots... can't wait to see what happens at the RGI media conference – that's at ten o'clock, isn't it?"

"Yes, ten eastern time (same as ours). The media release said they would be talking about their operations in Africa and how they were fulfilling cooperative environmental agreements with local governments. After this morning's news, they'll have a hard time keeping the focus where they want it. And don't forget, I made that call yesterday to Samuel Brighton in our office to make sure he is at RGI's media conference to set up questions in support of my article, particularly in light of what they are claiming for their African operation."

Anita had spent the past two days seemingly without sleep, hammering away on her Friends of Awan Lake Facebook page. Yesterday she had started with just under four thousand followers; now she was reaching close to six thousand, and had also begun a Twitter account which already had over a thousand followers. At about six this morning, she had first posted Priscilla's article direct from Envirowire, and then followed its tracks as it progressed through the other media, tweeting and posting and responding as fast as she could keep up. "Gotta make this thing go viral!" she muttered from time to time.

Wendy's cellphone rang, and it was Marion, calling from the Zoo where she and Arnold were having coffee: "Hi

Marion, how's it going? Oh, yes, she and Frank are out on the lake – something to do with the cops and some activity over at Robertson Mines. RCMP? Okay, maybe I should meet you all at the Zoo... we should keep our profile out here as low as possible. Yup, give me ten."

She hung up and turned to Anita: "Have to go and meet with Marion and some RCMP guy – something to do with Horowitz and his security detail I think."

"Shit. I don't like that at all... could be dangerous out there with Frank and Marjorie and half the police detachment gone."

Wendy went over and cupped her chin gently in her hand, planting a tender kiss on her lips. "Don't worry, my love, it's early in the day, and it'll be with Arnold and Marion. And anyway, there's an extra cop out here doing day duty... I'll let him or her know where I'm going!"

"Okay, if you're sure. Text me when you get there, and when you leave to come back."

"Will do." She gave Anita a little kiss on her right ear, grabbed her purse from the bureau by the door and went out to her car, stopping along the way to talk briefly to the young OPS auxiliary officer sitting on a bench outside the Inn's front door.

Marion gave her a hug when she got to the Zoo and

introduced her to RCMP Sergeant Marianna Mankowski, based out of RCMP Headquarters in Ottawa. Arnold explained that there were some uncertainties in Dr. Horowitz's travel plans that had everyone worried: "They got in touch with me as the event organizing committee chair, not understanding the depth of my ignorance, but at least I know that you have been back and forth on the phone with Horowitz. We're hoping you can be of some help."

"Thanks for coming to meet with us so quickly, Ms. Webster. I gather you live on an island out on the lake, but are staying in town helping with planning the event... glad I didn't have to swim out to meet you!"

"Well, you'd likely have enjoyed the water-taxi ride to the island," Wendy laughed.

"Budget cuts, y'know. They'd never have sprung for it – I'd have had to swim!"

The four shared the laughter, fresh coffee was brought, and the sergeant began the conversation by asking, "When did you last talk or text with Dr. Horowitz?"

"Hmm, this is Friday." She paused: "It was probably Tuesday morning. Could have been Monday... but no: Tuesday."

"Not since?"

"No, definitely not. We just briefly confirmed that he

would be flying into Ottawa on Saturday – late morning flight from Calgary – then driving from Ottawa to here and staying overnight at the Inn. We were to have dinner together out at one of the island cottages."

"Well, that coincides exactly with the information we have – except that we've lost him! We wouldn't even have known about it except that the doctor was expected to drive from North Vancouver to Lake Louise on Wednesday for an international water conference planning meeting, and he never showed up. His car drove off the ferry at Horseshoe Bay alright, but he never arrived at Lake Louise that evening. His colleagues there didn't think anything much about it until later in the day Thursday – yesterday – when they thought they'd better call the RCMP. So, now we're working backwards along his planned itinerary."

"Silly question, but... telephone?"

"Goes to voicemail, and has since early Wednesday morning when he called home from the ferry. And no, no sign of his car either, although we've only been looking for it since late yesterday."

"I really don't know him at all, but I have a sense from Dave Bradshaw from Ryerson that he has a reputation as the consummate absent-minded professor."

Sergeant Mankowski laughed: "I have to say that even

his wife admitted that to us, but she seemed to think that wasn't an issue this time."

"Actually, I've read some stuff about him and this conference he's planning..."

"Arnold? You? Have been reading?" interjected Marion.

"I do that, Mother, from time to time!" laughed Arnold. "I read that he considers this upcoming conference the pinnacle of his career. He is helping with the organizing, of course, but he is also the conference chair and... it's even named after him: 'The Sebastian Horowitz International Fresh Water Symposium' I think it's called. He surely wouldn't go all absent-minded over that, one would think!"

"Highly unlikely," said the sergeant.

Wendy was silent for a moment, then: "Well, apparently a lot of people suddenly have a big problem. The good doctor himself, of course, and you folks at the RCMP. And Mrs. Horowitz. Soon enough, perhaps, the conference organizers, but immediately we here at Awan Lake have a huge and urgent problem. Arnold, how are you at public speaking?"

"Not even the slightest chance," chuckled Arnold. "Not even close, but I am willing to bet that Tony Barker... who is a well-known technical author with a passion for environmental accounting, and who has followed Horowitz's career for a long time, could fill in very credibly. Wendy, didn't you say he was going to introduce Horowitz?"

"Yes, and from a listener's point of view I'd bet that he's a more interesting speaker. That could work."

"Sergeant Mankowski, you are more than welcome to stay and chat with us, but I am sure you will want to get back on the trail of our missing professor. Let's hope and pray you can find him well, and that he can get here for Sunday, but we will be making alternate plans just in case."

"Thanks Mrs. Jamieson – Marion – and Arnold and Wendy. Here is my card, Wendy... I have Marion and Arnold's contacts now but I would appreciate yours too, so we can update each other."

Wendy fished in her purse and came up with her old corporate card. "Here Marianna... don't hesitate to call, and thanks for your help!"

After Sergeant Mankowski had left the Zoo, Arnold, Marion and Wendy stared at each other for a few moments. Eventually, Marion shrugged and said, "Well, let's get at it and make new plans in case we have to."

"I wonder when Frank and Marjorie will be back. Arnold, I think you're dead-on to suggest Tony Barker, but I think Frank knows him best of all of us, and I'd sure like to have him along when we go and explain the situation and beg Tony's help."

Arnold tried Anderson's number but it went to voicemail. "He's still out of range. He has that satellite phone Sergeant John gave him, but I never did get the number, and John's out there too. We could go through the detachment, but I think this can wait until they're all home safely."

"I'll go back to the Inn and tell the girls the news. There will be shrieks."

"Yup," said Marion, "I bet there will be shrieks! Got a few of my own, but we will get this done! Keep in touch Wendy, and give a hug to Anita!"

"I've got the coffees," Wendy called as she walked toward the till. She was waiting for her change when they heard the siren: an OPS van was headed east along the highway, followed by two flatdeck tow trucks with their flashers on.

"Seems like they're having fun out there," called Arnold.

"Hope they're okay."

"My money says they're just fine!"

***

And they were, in fact, just fine. It had been a slow morning for Anderson and Marjorie on the boat. They had held their position for an hour or so after the OPS officers had gone to the boathouse, then the Sergeant had called Arnold on the satphone and requested that they nudge into the dock and take the boat from the boathouse in tow and haul it back to the village.

The boathouse had a wet slip inside, where the speedboat could be hauled out of the water on slings. Marjorie and Anderson landed the Beaver along the off-side of the dock, tied up, then with one OPS officer assisting they lowered the speedboat into the water, straightened and lashed the wheel, and fastened a towrope to the bow. They backed gently away from the dock into open water, turned and began the trip to the village. It was a slow trip... the speedboat went fast enough under its own power, but when under tow it behaved like an angry steer on the end of a lariat.

On the return trip, they learned that at least two black trucks had been impounded and that nine people – all men – had been arrested or taken in for questioning. Apparently there had been no physical resistance to the investigation, but a lot of grumpiness and many calls to lawyers, on both sides. And, significantly, the new general manager had been one of the men taken in for questioning.

The Sergeant promised to fill them in on some of the details later in the day. In the meantime he had arranged with Jim at the marina to put the boat back into the indoor slip where it had been on Thursday morning, and sling it up out of the water. Anderson and Marjorie took the boat there, handed it off to the somewhat puzzled marina owner, then returned to Anderson's dock around the corner of the bay and tied up.

Arnold had telephoned while they were delivering the speedboat, and Anderson told him he would be at his dock in fifteen minutes. Arnold arrived there about two minutes after they docked, and he looked worried.

"Hey, man, what's up? You look like your dog just died, and you don't even have a dog!"

Arnold told the two of them the details of the morning's visit with the RCMP, and of course with Wendy. "I haven't spoken with any of the others in town yet, because I think maybe we have an emergency solution, and Wendy and Marion agree. I know that's not any comfort for Mrs. Horowitz, but we have to play the hand we've been dealt. How about asking Tony Barker to take on the role of keynote speaker?"

The three of them had been walking up the access road from the dock to the workshop and house, where Anderson unlocked the house door and motioned to the table: "Wow, that's not what we needed to hear, with only a day left to fix it."

He took three GW Pilsners from a case beside the fridge and set them on the table. "We definitely need beer," he muttered as he popped open the cans and passed them out. "But, on the bright side, I actually think Tony would be a better speaker than Horowitz, and maybe bring something extra to the table. He told us weeks ago – just after he agreed to sponsor the event – that he was looking forward to talking with Horowitz because they had already made contact and shared some of the same perspectives, particularly the inclusion of accurate and complete environmental assessments on corporate and – above all perhaps – government balance sheets."

"I know you like this Saskatchewan beer at the bar, but where the hell did you find a case of it here?"

"Florence special-orders it for the bar, so she saves out a case for me from time to time."

"I expect, then, that you're her best customer for it?"

"I expect he's her only customer for it," Marjorie chirped. "She spoils him rotten! But back to the issue at hand, two things are churning in my head. First, we need to go out and talk to Tony and Jean and make sure he'll do this, as soon as possible. And second, I have this awful feeling that the disappearance of Horowitz may not be a coincidence, considering all the other stuff that's going on around here. Should we mention that thought to our friendly Sergeant, or will the RCMP do that?"

"I don't think the RCMP will say anything at all to our provincial police. They perform the role of provincial police from Manitoba to British Columbia, and at the moment there is no reason to think he may have gone missing in Ontario. But yes, John should definitely be told. I'll try him now... then we should go out to Tony's as soon as we can get away."

Anderson called the Sergeant on his cellphone, assuming he was back within range either on the road or back at the office in Maple Falls, and he answered immediately. "You're where?" Anderson glanced out the window overlooking the lake. "So you are. We're not. Coming up to the house? Cool."

Anderson looked up at the others. "He's down at the dock wondering where we are, since two trucks and a boat are there. He's on his way up."

The Sergeant was there in moments, greeted Marjorie

and Arnold, took the beer offered by Anderson and said, "Shouldn't, but gonna. It's been quite a morning, and the day is still far from over. Arnold, I stopped by your garage on our way through town and Marion said you were here and had something to tell me. So, the talking stick is in your hands... what's up?"

Arnold gave a quick description of the meeting with the RCMP officer, and said that the three of them had wondered if there was any possibility of a connection to the rather more local issues involving the Robertson bunch.

"So, did you or Marion, or Wendy, mention to Sergeant Mankowski about any of the stuff going on here, except obviously Sunday's event?"

"Hell no... if she didn't know already, then we wanted you to know first. She gave no sign of knowing anything at all except Horowitz's speaking engagement."

"Perfect, that's a good thing. I'll have to call her, of course, and I'll tell her you filled me in, but things will go much better if I open the subject with her, because then the RCMP owes us and they can't make us ride in the back seat." The Sergeant paused, then went on: "I suppose that really screws up your Love Our Lake thing on Sunday. Do you plan on cancelling?"

"No, not at all," responded Anderson. "Arnold has just

been telling us that Wendy and Marion figure we should ask Tony Barker to take it over and I think that's a brilliant idea. He has the credibility, if not the profile."

Arnold joined in: "Of course, we are still assuming that Horowitz is on his way here and got distracted somehow. He still has a ticket for the flight from Calgary to Ottawa tomorrow, so unless we get word through Horowitz himself, or his family, or the RCMP, he's still expected to show up by tomorrow night or even Sunday noon – although that's probably stretching things a bit."

"I gotta go... we have a lot to sort out in The Falls before today is done. Once we've done some interviews, a bit of forensic stuff and some phone calls, I should have lots to tell you – probably tonight. Thanks for your input and Frank, Marjorie – for your work on the lake this morning. I'll let you know if I hear anything about Horowitz that you don't already know."

***

The ABC ladies had been having a very busy day. After Wendy had returned from her meeting with the RCMP sergeant at the Zoo, she updated Anita and Priscilla with the Horowitz problem, and their thoughts on getting Tony

Barker to fill in. Priscilla immediately put on her investigative journalist hat and went to work on getting some professional profile material about Barker as well as more information about the planning meeting Horowitz was supposed to have attended. Wendy urged her not to release anything to her news service yet, and she agreed, albeit somewhat reluctantly. She felt there was certainly some juicy stuff there, even though it was mostly speculation. They all agreed there would soon be an appropriate time to throw another rock in the pond and watch where the ripples went, but now wasn't quite the time.

Priscilla had talked with her colleague who attended the Robertson Group's media conference in Washington just a few hours ago, and he confirmed that his questions – and some from a CBC reporter – had thrown the RGI spokesperson thoroughly off-message. The event – complete with African ethnic foods for a light lunch and two supposedly high-profile government speakers in colourful tribal regalia – had been designed to show off all the initiatives RGI was undertaking in Africa to ensure cultural and environmental sustainability, including especially source water protection, and the RGI speakers were totally unprepared to answer questions about source water protection in Canada, let alone collusion with crooked government officials.

Priscilla was particularly gleeful that the other media outlets in attendance had immediately pounced on the Canadian issue, once the first couple of questions were posed by her colleague. She gave her new Awan Lake friends high-fives and hugs: "This is the kind of stuff reporters can only dream of, and the fun isn't over: expect lots of telephone interview requests over the next few days, from columnists wanting information to spin the story and keep it alive! My inbox is already filling up, because my byline was on the first article."

Wendy was smiling... but thoughtful: "Did your colleague say anything at all to you about Sebastian Horowitz?"

"Geez, I'm sorry. If he did, I missed it. I was too excited!"

"Could you reach back out to him and ask? Could he maybe call the RGI media contact for a point of clarification about whether they were aware of him, and if they know whether he will be here Sunday, and maybe if they know about the international conference in his name next year in Lake Louise?"

Wendy paused again, then: "We probably need to know what RGI knows, anyway. But I have to say I am a bit worried about Dr. Horowitz and it might be useful to get all the immediate information we can. In any case, it won't hurt to annoy them a little, just by asking!"

"I'll get on it now. I have Samuel on speed dial, so it shouldn't take long."

***

People travelling east along the Trans-Canada Highway between Canada's west coast city of Vancouver and the prairie city of Calgary cross two mountain ranges: the Coast Mountain Range and the Rocky Mountains. The shortest route is just over 600 miles, the highways are excellent, if busy, and the scenery ranges from magnificent to spectacular.

In fact, the Trans-Canada Highway – or Highway Number 1 – does not entirely take the shortest route. The original Trans-Canada, and a much newer Highway 5, part company near the town of Hope at the bottom of the west slope of the Coast Range, and don't catch up with each other until near the small city of Kamloops. The 340 mile stretch of Highway 5, known as the Coquihalla, was built in the mid-1980s, providing a less daunting stretch of highway than the steep and circuitous Highway 1 which follows the Fraser

River Canyon north through the mountains between Hope and Cache Creek (then on to Kamloops to the east).

The Fraser Canyon route has often been featured in country and western truck driving songs, with its epic ice and snow storms and resultant semi-trailer wrecks. Nonetheless, the scenery is spectacular and on a nice sunny summer afternoon, a careful driver is rewarded with a safe and relaxing drive. On Friday, August 11, 2017, however, department of highways workers, the RCMP, and a tow-truck driver from Hope were busy recovering a car that had recently finished its drive some 800 feet below the highway on the bottom of the Fraser River east of Hell's Gate.

The light blue five-year-old Toyota Camry Hybrid had definitely not been improved by the 800-foot plunge down the steep canyon wall, but there was no evidence there had been anyone onboard. There was no blood, and the seatbelts were all unfastened. The RCMP constable on scene had recovered a still-closed suitcase containing toiletries and men's semi-casual clothing, wedged in the backseat area. One of the highway workers found a leather briefcase which had apparently fallen from the car during its descent. The case had sprung open and landed along the edge of the river, and was empty except for a small leather notebook which held an Air Canada ticket folder containing a sodden mass of muddy wet paper.

"I'll take the suitcase and the folder back to the detachment," said the constable, "and before you load up to take the car back to our compound I'll get the VIN and a couple of photos." He called in the VIN, and was asked by the sergeant on duty how in the hell that car wound up going over the edge with no driver. "There's a turnout along the side here with a little trail to the edge. Looks like maybe he drove in there and forgot to put it in park when he got out to take a leak or something. It does look as if the driver door may have been open – the others all stayed shut but the driver door had broken right off its hinges."

Thirty minutes later, Sergeant Marianna Mankowski received a call on her cellphone to tell her that Sebastian Horowitz's 2012 Toyota had been found in the river along the Transcanada north-east of Hope, but there was no sign of Mr. Horowitz nor any indication he had been onboard when it went off the road.

The sergeant had left work a little early to do some weekend shopping before heading to her home in Kanata, west of the RCMP headquarters where she worked. *Damn, I guess there's a chance the guy is still alive, but it's still not real good news for those folks at Spirit River. I'd better give Ms. Webster or Ms. Jamieson a heads-up so they can work on their plans for Sunday... whatever happens it seems unlikely that Horowitz will get there in time to make his speech.*

"Ms. Webster – Wendy?" This is Sergeant Mankowski calling – you will remember we talked this morning about Mr. Horowitz? Well, I have some news. His car has been found, wrecked, off the road, in between Vancouver and Lake Louise, but he was not in it and there is no sign at this point that he was injured or abducted. We are not releasing any news yet, so please keep this confidential. I am sharing it with you because I know you may need to work on your plans for Sunday, and you'll be the first person I call when I get more news... how's that? Oh, you're welcome, Wendy. I'll be in touch."

***

The Beaver, with Marjorie and Anderson onboard, was rumbling along at half throttle enroute to the island cottage of Jean and Tony Barker, when Wendy called on Marjorie's phone. They were far enough out from the village tower that the reception was terrible. Marjorie told her to text, which she did, with the message "Call ASAP from Barker's... Horowitz."

Twenty minutes later, having given a single blast on the horn, Anderson pulled into the bay at the Barker's cottage and tied up at his wharf. Tony was there with a big grin to meet them, and as they stepped off the boat Anderson presented him with a brown paper bag that looked suspiciously like it might contain a bottle: "Hi Tony, we're not here for long but I thought we could all share a glass or two of this single-malt. I was given this a couple of years ago, and it's been waiting at home for you to drop by, but today I thought we'd better bring it right to you!"

"There's an old saying: 'beware the Greeks bearing gifts'... are you Greek?"

"Today, yup. We need to talk, and I need to call back to town... can I use your booster?"

"Absolutely – although the easiest way is for you just to use my phone. Unless you're calling Greece. Come on up to the house and I'll get us some glasses!"

"It's about Sunday, and Horowitz, and I'll know more after I phone Wendy. We've been having quite a day."

The three of them walked up the rocky path to the cottage, where an enthusiastic Jean greeted them both with hugs and laughter. Anderson took Tony's phone and handed it to Marjorie: "You're the one Wendy needs to talk to."

It was a short call. "Okay," Marjorie said after she

clicked off. "Thank you. Here's the scoop. Wendy got a visit from the RCMP this morning to say they had lost track of Dr. Horowitz, somewhere between Vancouver and Lake Louise where he was headed for a meeting two days ago. Just now, she got a call from the same RCMP officer to say that Horowitz's car had been found at the bottom of the Fraser Canyon. He was not in it, and there was no sign that he had gone over the side of the highway with the car – no trace at all, but his luggage was still in the wreck."

"My God, that's terrible." Jean was aghast. "I mean, it's good that he wasn't in the car but it still doesn't sound very promising."

"No, it doesn't, Jean. Before we left to come here this evening, all we knew was that he was over a day late at the meeting he was supposed to attend in Lake Louise, but this latest news seems to indicate that we can be pretty sure he won't be able to deliver his speech on Sunday, even if he is found alive between now and then."

"That's not at all good. If nothing else, I was really looking forward to meeting him, especially when you folks and he were coming to dinner Saturday evening and I could pick his brain a little. What are we going to do?"

"We – Marj and I, on behalf of the others – weren't going to do anything. Except ask Tony Barker if he would give the Keynote Address on Sunday."

"Ah ha, and hence the bottle of single-malt, right?"

"Something like that. But I will add this: Ever since we started to line up this Love Our Lake event a couple of months ago, it has been in the back of my mind that I would much rather hear Tony Barker give that speech than Dr. Horowitz. And the reasons are, well, really real: First, you really do love our lake, so you bring that perspective. But second – and from a more professional perspective – your work and published papers on the importance – imperative – of accounting for environmental costs and liabilities in corporate and government accounts is of such fundamental importance that it needs to be heard – very publicly. The business case for environmental, and of course water, protection needs to be top-of-mind for Canada – the world, in fact – and even here at little Spirit River. Wouldn't it be nice if we could be the community that helped make that very public... beyond conserving ducks and otters and fish and frogs."

Tony was looking across at his spouse, who was grinning broadly and laughing. "What are you laughing about, Mrs. Barker?"

"I've been thinking exactly the same thing for weeks! Truly, I think you have a lot to say and a lot to bring to the table, nationally and beyond. And at least you know for sure that your wife and your friend Frank will listen to you. Anyway, remember I'm your publisher and I want to sell books!"

"I pity the audience, is one good reason not to. Remember, as much as I love to charm my good wife and tease the grandkids, at the end of the day I am an accountant, not a rock star. As a class, we are not known for our wit!"

"Nonsense – how about that presentation you made a couple of years ago to the national convention?"

"That was the height of dry, PowerPoint and all. Very technical."

"Not that one, silly – the next year, when you gave the keynote address. You got people laughing, and really engaged. And half your audience was spouses, not technical people, and they really loved it too. They all heard and understood your passion about the subject... and you even managed to really annoy some of your stuffy old colleagues!

"Oh, yes. That one... I'd still have to spiffy it up somewhat. You're all going to have to help me though, at least review a draft and tell me if I'm too dry. Or worse, all wet."

"No sweat at all, Tony," said Anderson. "After all, you've got thirty-six hours, as long as you don't need sleep!"

"Okay folks, I will give it my best. It could be fun to do. We'll have some explaining to do for the crowd... Frank, will you do the introduction? I heard you speak at the media conference and I was very impressed with how you did it."

"Yipe." He paused. "Sure, it would only be fair. If we can't come up with anyone better, I'll do that."

"Frank, just do it, please," responded Jean. "For many reasons, there's no one better. Bradshaw will have his twenty minutes, but he is 'way too academic. Give him twenty-five minutes and he'd dry up half the lake!"

"Wendy has been a professional speech-writer for politicians," said Marjorie. "We don't want politician stuff, but I'm sure she'd review your final draft with you if you wanted."

"Okay guys, you got me. Let's open that bottle!"

"Thank you so much Tony! Marj, could you use Tony's phone again to let Wendy and them know... all of them, Marion and Arnold too? They'll all be sweating about this."

Half an hour later, they were sitting on the veranda of the Barker cottage, drinking down their second scotch and munching on some marvellous finger-foods Jean had produced, seemingly out of nowhere. Night-time was settling on the eastern skyline, and the colour behind their backs in the south-west was draining from the sky.

"Time for us to slither on home," Anderson said. "Sergeant John called me on the satellite phone just after Marjorie talked to Wendy, and he's supposed to be at our house at around nine. He said he has lots of stuff... damn, here he is again." He unclipped the satphone and clicked it on: "John? Frank here... yup, right away... you're kidding! Crap! At the dock? Okay."

He stood up. "All he said was get your ass home and be careful, and take a look at the sky over the village." He ran to the island shore, followed by the others, and looked north: where the village was supposed to be was a ball of orange fire. "He said the fucking marina was on fire and I guess he was right... sorry Jean, thank-you folks! We're gone!" and he and Marjorie ran down the pathway to the dock, where they cast off and were headed full throttle out of the bay within a minute and a half.

***

As they pulled the workboat into the dock, he could see four local volunteer firefighters waving flashlights at him. They were carrying two gasoline-driven forestry pumps, suction hoses and a couple of lengths of hose with nozzles. He got the implied message, landed hard and held while they quickly loaded their gear into the boat and joined them on board as he backed away from the dock. "Arnold wants us around the far side of the marina to see if we can save the last two docks and some of the boats that are on moorings. This sucker got hotter than the hubs of hell within five minutes... some kind of explosion in the main boathouse."

He knew exactly where Arnold wanted him and turned toward the east-side marina docks, both of which were on fire at the shoreline and about twenty feet out onto the harbour. He turned on all the boat's spot and flood lights, including the LED working flood over the deck. The fire crew had their pumps going and the inch-and-a-half lines fully charged as he poked in toward the shore. When they were about fifty feet from the flames they opened up their nozzles and began to wet down the burning docks and the boats closest to them, which were already on fire.

Anderson called to the firefighter closest to him. "Are Jim and Margaret safe?"

"We don't know," she called back. "The house was totally involved when we got here, and we were pretty quick. I don't like the looks of this, though... his truck is here and burned up beside the boathouse, and her car is in the garage."

"Shit. Damn it." He focused on straightening the

workboat against the kickback from the two hoses. "There's going to be nothing left of that boathouse... was that where the fire started?" he called again.

"So it seems. Already one explosion inside, then it heated up and exploded that big above-ground fuel tank inshore of the boathouse and then got into a couple of fuel drums and two 100-lb propane bottles beside the house, and now you see what we've got. All we've been able to do with the truck pump is keep the fire from spreading over to your place and up the driveway to the next houses!"

Anderson grabbed the satphone again and called the Sergeant, steering with one hand and holding the phone with the other. Marjorie came into the wheelhouse from the deck and said, "I'll try to hold her in place. Don't go anywhere!"

He got out of her way and crossed the wheelhouse by the time the sergeant had picked up. "John, I'm not at the dock, I'm over on the east side of the marina with two pumps and some firefighters. I think we're making headway, but crap it's hot. If we lose it here, it will take off through the bush and up the slope to the Inn. Would you quickly make sure to secure the girls at the Inn – including Florence and especially get her out of sight. Or better yet, get all of them away from town or into a safely guarded location but not the Inn. I'll tell you why as soon as things settle down, but it's important." He clicked off, went back to Marjorie and took the wheel.

Some twenty minutes later the crew and the pumps had managed to beat the flames back off the dock to the shore and Anderson had nosed the boat into the dock so they could spend some time with one nozzle putting out hot spots on the dock and on the two boats that had started to burn. The other nozzle they directed across the slip-way to the neighbouring docks. They had already been badly damaged, and the best they could do was try to cool down the flames.

Arnold came along the shore from the roadway and was able to walk out on the dock to where they were working: "Nice job guys, you really managed to quiet things down here. Way to go folks!" Marjorie was moving hoses around on the deck for the crew, who were using one of Anderson's axes to open holes into burning decks so they could put out fires inside. Arnold stepped onto *The Beaver* and joined Anderson in the wheelhouse, where he was still focused on keeping the boat where it was needed. He did not want to tie up to something that was still on fire!

"We've never had a fire anything like this in the village, and I am worried shitless that we've lost Jim and Margaret."

Anderson leaned away from the wheel and gave Arnold a long squeeze on the shoulder. "I know," he said. "But I am very sure this fire was deliberately lit, with the goal of doing maximum damage, probably including killing the owners. Whatever, there was absolutely nothing you or the crews could have done to change the outcome, except keep it from eating up more buildings in the village."

"But why, Frank? Who the hell would do something like this? Such a good business for the village and such nice people."

"Not sure. Not certain at all. I may be crazy, but I think it's not over. More is going to happen, and very soon – maybe even tonight."

"You're kidding, right?"

"Nope. I want to hear from Sergeant John... he may have more information. I have just asked him to remove the ABC girls – and Florence – from the Inn and hide them somewhere. He's doing that, but I do owe him an explanation. He probably thinks I'm as crazy as you do right now!"

"Well, back to the moment. Can we leave two of the crew and one pump on the dock here, then see if there's anything you can do around the fuel dock and the long dock beside the launch?"

"I think so – just make sure the folks you leave here aren't abandoned in case things flare up, and those forestry pumps burn gasoline like an elephant sucks up water, so both pumps will soon need fuel."

"I'll phone old Jeremy to bring a jerry-can to your dock, and then walk one along the shore to the other guys."

"Two-gallon cans would likely be enough, and make it a little easier for the old fart to carry!"

"Good point. I'll call."

Anderson motioned to Marjorie to take over the wheel, then helped the crew make the necessary changes. Once the second pump and two firefighters were on the dock with the pump primed and re-started, he went to Marjorie and gave her a long warm hug and a short kiss, then took over the wheel and backed away from the charred wharf before turning for their home dock to pick up gasoline.

They got to the dock to find the Sergeant standing waiting. Anderson saw that his face was stone, and that he looked small for a man who stood six-foot-two-inches. "Not a very good night, John?"

"About as bad as it gets, but it keeps getting worse. A neighbour just found Garnet Cameron at his house in Maple Falls with a bullet hole in his forehead and an old Colt .45 on the floor. We're saying possible suicide, but that's very preliminary. I think not."

07:45 August 12

Anderson never slept on his back. *Except last night anyway,* he mused, waking up in the same position as when he must have fallen asleep, well after midnight last night. Marjorie hadn't moved much either. Her head was still on his shoulder with one hand on his chest. *Didn't know she snored. That's kinda cute!*

He tried to wriggle free without waking her, but that didn't work. The two of them rolled over to their respective sides of the bed, then he reached across and took her hand: "I for one will be very glad when this week – and this weekend – are over."

"I know. I have to confess that I sometimes enjoy the adrenaline rush, but this has become... so sad!"

***

Last night, Sergeant John had accompanied them while they spent another half-hour dousing what was left of the two long docks on the west side of the marina, before returning to their own dock and unloading the firefighters and their equipment. Anderson had suggested that Marjorie and the Sergeant head up to the house and make some coffee while he spent a full fifteen minutes cleaning up, checking the workboat's engines, and filling in the log book.

Twenty minutes later, over coffee, the Sergeant assured them that he wound up reinforcing security at the Inn to protect the ABC girls and Florence, with uniformed and armed officers on both floors and one patrolling the grounds. He then filled them in on the outcome of yesterday morning's "invasion" at Robertson Mines and the arrests. "Four of the men arrested – all members of that so-called "security team" – were found to be Americans working illegally in Canada. They were ordered to report to the Canada Border Services Agency office east of Kingston by 09:00 Monday where they would be returned to the U.S.A. A fifth illegal American was identified as the driver of one of those black trucks when it gassed up at Sudbury last Sunday. We have charged him with homicide in the death of Gerald Giordano and he is locked up awaiting a bail hearing next week. Two others had work visas – a guy named Keith Austin who was apparently head of the security team, and the new General Manager Thomas Manville, whom you have met already. They were interviewed, charged with the unlicensed operation of a private security business and released. The eighth man – you likely know him – is a Canadian citizen, Bob Adamson. He has been the project development officer at Robertson Mines for the last three years and he lives near the village. He was interviewed and released, without charges at this point."

"Wow, that'll be spooking the folks at RGI's head office. How about the trucks? I know that boat we picked up is now a chunk of melted plastic and scrap metal mixed up with whatever is left of the marina boat house."

"Well, we're holding on to both trucks. One is definitely the truck that had been seen in Sudbury. The other one we are pretty certain picked up the torch guy who tried to burn up the sailboat – and your dock. Now, I know you wanted protection for the ABC girls, but why Florence?"

"Ah, yes. Linkages: Hamilton-Dubois was closely associated with the head-office types at Robertson Mines, and almost certainly made a pile of money from there. He invested in the marina and the Inn. I think – and I expect you agree – that the marina had been deliberately set on fire, partly maybe to destroy that boat, but also a convenient way to get rid of the 49% owner of the property and force a sale. Same with Florence – Leonard owned the Inn outright, I gather, but I am sure he protected his sister-in-law's interests there. With her gone, more capital to control. And Garnet Cameron is the other leg of the triangle. With him gone, the chain of corruption would be almost impossible to prove and the investments would be easy to liquidate and recover. There – is that enough of a conspiracy theory for you?"

The Sergeant was silent for a moment, then: "As you are fond of saying, 'Walks like a duck, swims like a duck, quacks like a duck... likely it's a duck.'"

"Quack."

"One more thing," said the Sergeant. "The folks in the lab tell me that the revolver that killed Cameron was a real old-timer, last registered to a collector in Virginia many years ago. It had never been registered in Canada, and we now have to wait for the ballistics people to see if it was ever used in another crime. Preliminary investigation shows it had been wiped clean of prints before being fired last night, so whoever fired it last wore gloves – mechanic's gloves, they think. Didn't even try to make it look like suicide. Only two rounds in the cylinder, one fired, and no prints on the casings either. Almost certainly a professional hit."

"When will you be able to find out if Jim and Margaret were at home?"

"When the scene cools off enough to work in there – hopefully tonight. The coroner is standing by, and we have a couple of fire investigators on the way. They'll let me know as soon as they know anything. Did they have kids?"

"I don't think so. They had an old house on a rural property near Ottawa where they were hoping to retire – inherited from Margaret's late mother, according to Jim when we talked the other day. I know they wanted out of the rat race... seems like the rats got them before they could leave."

There was a knock on Anderson's door at 23:00. An exhausted-looking Arnold poked his head in and said, "John, I'm pulling the truck and most of the crew back, but I'm leaving two onsite with one portable and a couple of hundred feet of hose to take care of any flare-ups. I think we have it pretty well secured, and we need to get the truck back into service and let some of the crew go home. As you know, the coroner is standing by, but the fire investigators still haven't arrived."

"Coffee, Arnold?"

"Love one, but I need to get my firehouse in order and help the crew. Tell you what, though... could you make us some coffee – maybe ten cups?"

"Coming right up Arnold," said Marjorie. You go on ahead, and when it's ready I'll bring it to the firehouse. I think we even have some donuts in the freezer – I'll nuke 'em and bring them too."

"This is 2017 and I'm no longer allowed to say this, but... you're a doll! Thanks Marj..." and he was gone.

***

Now, of course, it was a new day – Saturday morning – and it seemed like their whole world was upside down. Marjorie was a city girl by breeding and experience, and her experiences had been almost entirely friendly and safe. Stress was a traffic jam on Highway 401 trying to leave the city for the cottage.

Anderson had travelled around more and had been involved in the Coast Guard, a cross between the military and the police with a search and rescue focus. In his twelve years of service, he had never had to fire a weapon while fighting crime, and while he had regularly been involved with the recovery of drowning victims from boating incidents, the corpses seemed mostly sad, and not sinister.

Marjorie and Anderson knew there was lots to be done today, but they took a half-hour to have a leisurely breakfast and that all-important second cup of coffee on the porch, where they shared that assessment of their individual experience and the trauma of their current shared reality.

Seven people they knew had died a violent death in the last week, each of the deaths almost certainly being homicide. They – and some of their close friends and relatives – were under threat, and some were under 24-hour guard. And the peace of their lakeside community was being shattered by mistrust, fear, and now – fire.

"Frank, I have been plagued by self-doubt since I was a little girl, but now I feel almost overwhelmed. Do you think there is anything – anything at all – that we could have done differently that would have made none of this happen?"

Anderson reached across the small table and took her hand. "I'm a lousy guy to ask, frankly, because I'm an arrogant prick and have never experienced self-doubt. Oh, I've been wrong lots of times, but I just fix it, shake it off and carry on. I've also had a troubled relationship with God, being more inclined to accept coincidence than he would probably like. So, deprived of his insight, I don't see the future – I can only guess, and try to guess intelligently."

He paused for a time, and smiled sheepishly: "That was the long answer. The short answer is 'no'. We have been caught up in the lives of people with agendas about which we knew almost nothing, and we have been doing our best to reduce harm and stop things from getting worse. Welcome to the Summer of Seventeen!"

Marjorie gave his big hand a squeeze and smiled. With her other hand she rubbed away a couple of tears and said, "One more coffee? I guess, then, we need to figure out what's next."

"We do. First I think I should call Tony and bring him up to speed. We haven't heard anything about Dr. Horowitz, one way or the other, so I guess Tony is still on for the speech tomorrow. And he'll be wondering about the fire, too."

"Are you going to wing-it for the introduction?"

"Kinda. Might make some notes."

"You could do worse than use parts of that little introduction you gave at the media conference last Thursday."

"Was thinking along that line." Anderson found Tony Barker's number on his cellphone and pushed the call button.

"While you're calling him, I'll call Wendy. She must really be wondering what the hell's going on, and I'm itching to know what the media are saying this morning."

The conversation with Tony Barker didn't take long. He reported that he was happily fine-tuning his conference speech from last year for the Love Our Lake event. "Kind of like putting lipstick on a pig," he said, "but I think I've found a really pretty shade of lipstick! I'll be just fine, and thanks for asking!" Anderson asked him to send along a short biography so he could introduce him correctly, and they hung up the call.

Marjorie was still on the phone with Wendy, so Anderson busied himself with cleaning up after breakfast, changing his shirt from last night, and starting a second pot of coffee. He took a couple of cigarettes from the pack on the table and went back out on the porch just as Marjorie was finishing her call. "Well, what's new over at ABC media consultants?"

Marjorie grinned and chuckled: "They're having a ball, although they were a little worried last night. They could see the marina fire from the hotel room but they got enough information from Corporal Marie to know that we were okay. In fact, she said at one point they could see *The Beaver* with all her lights on making like a fireboat on that last dock. Anyway, some news on the Horowitz front. That RCMP gal called first thing this morning to say that they had found badly-smudged fingerprints all over his car, but all the recent ones – overlapping, so to speak – were probably not his. Or he could have been wearing gloves, or maybe someone else was wearing gloves. So now they are trying to trace back to the last time anyone confirmed seeing Horowitz near his car.

It appears they confirmed him – and his car – when he bought his ferry ticket at the Departure Bay terminal near Nanaimo but had no reported sightings after that. Just evidence that his car had driven off the ferry at Horseshoe Bay."

"Well, that's just getting more weird as we learn more. I assume they're trying to figure out whose fingerprints?"

"One would assume. You're right... it's just weird! Anyway, Wendy doesn't expect he's going to make it here for Sunday and she is delighted that Tony is already prepping for that."

"Had they heard about Garnet Cameron?"

"No, she hadn't heard a word. I should..." and Anderson's satphone started to beep.

"Anderson here. John? Crap, just as we feared. What? Son of a bitch. Okay, thanks. I've got one for you... Horowitz apparently never drove his car off that ferry in West Van. That's right... they have him confirmed getting on, but not off, and there are strange fingerprints all over his car... more like smudges on top of his prints. Yes, the event will proceed with Tony... he's set to go. Yup, I'll let you know. Bye," and he clicked off.

"Jim and Margaret were in the house, and John is pretty convinced they were shot first."

"My God, this just gets worse and worse. I guess you suspected that, but it feels worse when it goes from suspicion to fact! I'd better call Wendy back."

"Hmm. Let's talk about this. Maybe not."

"Maybe not?"

"No. I think you need to drive over there and bring her back here. It's not that I don't trust Priscilla, but remember her profession. We have a lot of important, but unconfirmed, information and I don't think it needs to be spread around yet. The OPS – and even the RCMP – have shared a lot of confidential stuff with us and I don't think we want that trust to be broken."

"You're absolutely right. I'll go pick her up and tell the others I need to take my sis out to breakfast."

"Cool – want me to come, and we can go to the Zoo?"

"Still hungry, aren't you! Yes, good idea."

They had some explaining to do, ID to share, and a phone call to make before the OPS officers on watch would let them take Wendy away. "Good for them," Wendy said. "I am impressed, and very grateful!"

On the way uptown to the Zoo, Marjorie suggested a change of destination: "The Zoo is going to be in tragedy mode this morning, and they'll be all over Frank in particular, since we were fighting last night's fire. We'll never be able to talk confidentially. Let's go back to the house, and I'll put in a breakfast order and go pick it up."

"Good point. Going there will just confuse everyone. But we'd better go back to that Constable at the Inn and tell him the change of plans, or they'll have a fit."

The Saturday morning and lunch special at the Zoo was traditionally ham quiche, and Sam had wisely decided not to change that this morning... it was sort of "comfort food" for the folks at Spirit River. And, of course, Anderson and the Webster sisters followed the tradition happily. Forty-five minutes later they had polished off the brunch Marjorie had ordered, but they ate it at Anderson's big table.

"Wendy, you probably saw through my plan to get you out of the clutches of the ABC girls, and yes, you're right, we do have things we need to share with you in confidence. I'll let Frank fill you in... he's not only our resident conspiracy theorist, he's also part detective."

"You did say 'part detective', not 'part defective', right? Cool! Well, it's pretty straightforward really. We have information in strictest confidence that Jim and Margaret at the marina were murdered last night, before the fire, which was set to cover up – or at least confuse – the evidence. And, we have similar information that MP Garnet Cameron did not take his own life – he too was murdered, with no real attempt to hide the evidence of homicide."

"Over at the Inn we heard speculation that they had been trapped in the fire, but not murdered. Oh my God!"

"I know. It's horrifying. And don't forget that those three people were directly connected through Leonard Hamilton-Dubois and his criminally accumulated wealth and investments, which in turn is almost certainly connected to lobbying activities for the Robertson Group."

"Makes sense."

"There's more. In case you are wondering why Florence has joined the ABC girls under police protection, the Inn was entirely owned by Leonard. Unless there's someone we don't yet know about, taking out Florence, Jim, Margaret and Garnet closes the loop, and unless the OPS can find and document the linkages, RGI and any other bad guys get away scot-free. And there's one more thing – maybe related to RGI but with much less certainty – Dr. Horowitz is no longer just a befuddled old man who went missing on a road trip – there is growing evidence that he was kidnapped or killed on the ferry and his car was sent over the edge of the Fraser Canyon as a distraction. That evidence – or even the suspicion – has not yet been released and there are no other connecting threads at the moment."

"So now what?"

"Not sure," said Marjorie. "I guess we should keep our eyes open and try to help make tomorrow a happy, safe and useful day for everyone. I noticed when I went to pick up the quiche that a corner of the sports grounds is filling up with camper trailers and tents. I wonder if one of us – or someone from the committee – should wander through there periodically and 'read' the crowd to see if there are any obvious agendas – people wanting to demonstrate instead of listen."

"Wow, there's a Marion job if ever there was one," laughed Anderson.

At that point, Anderson's cellphone started beeping again: "Hey John, what's up? I have Wendy here with us, can I put you on speakerphone? Huh – secrecy? Yeah, I'll threaten her with having to drink GW beer all night if she tells anyone. Here goes..."

"Hi Wendy, Hi Marj. Just wanted you to know that more weird stuff seems to be happening. We put a tail on Manville, Austin and the others last night, and now we've lost some of them. Bob Adamson went straight home to Spirit River after questioning and he's still there. Most of the others, including the ones who are to be returned to the U.S., had gone back to their accommodation at Robertson Mines. We had Manville at his suite in The Falls until two hours ago, then at Tim Hortons where he met up with Keith Austin, who had stayed overnight in the motel on the west side of The Falls. Amazingly, after they left – together – our folks lost them. I'm pissed off, obviously, but our staff is getting tired and I understand that. We have an alert out for them... they are in Manville's gray Subaru SUV, with New York plates."

"How long have they been gone? Maybe they're on their way out to the RGI facility where the others are."

"They left about ten minutes ago. If you're right, they should go down the highway in about fifteen minutes."

"I'll call Arnold and ask him to keep his eyes open."

"Okay, thanks. I'll keep in touch."

Anderson clicked off. "Well, if we were worrying about what to worry about today, our problem is solved, apparently."

He reached Arnold on the second ring. "How are you doing this morning, my friend? Got some sleep? Good. I'll be up to visit shortly, but could you keep your eyes out on the highway for an east-bound gray SUV – a Subaru. John thinks it may be headed to Robertson Mines – it's carrying Manville and his security chief – Keith Austin. Thanks!"

After he clicked off again, he shrugged and said to Marjorie, "I sorta hope he doesn't see that SUV – after last night he'd probably like to shoot Manville himself!" Anderson went over to the counter and started to run through another pot of coffee. As he flipped the switch he looked out the window toward the docks... and there was a gray SUV with funny-looking plates driving past his house.

"Damn. There he is! Girls – hit the floor and stay down!" He moved across to a different window so he could watch what the SUV was doing, and ducked down to keep a low profile. Manville slowed down to a crawl, then turned left and headed down the lane that connected along the shore to the marina and was soon around the corner out of sight.

"Okay ladies, stay down for now – he's out of sight around the corner. Marj – here's my satphone – please call John and tell him, then Arnold. I'm going to get out that old service revolver I keep in the cupboard for awkward moments just like this!"

"I hope he doesn't come back any time soon," said Marjorie. "An old service revolver is a poor match for what those guys play with, even for sure-shot Frank!"

"No kidding. Just call!"

As she was finishing a brief conversation with the Sergeant, Anderson's cellphone rang and it was Arnold. "That car just came up Main Street, turned left and headed east toward the mine. Did he drive by your place?"

" Sure as hell did... scared the crap out of us. He went out by the marina - must have been looking over his handiwork! Yup, Marj just called John. They already have someone out there and he'll send out another car to keep an eye on them. Yup, we're taking Wendy back to the Inn and we'll come by the Zoo for coffee." He clicked off.

"Okay you two. It's not even coffee time and we've already had our full adrenaline rush for the day. Let's take you back to ABC headquarters, then Marjorie and I will go to the Zoo and observe the animals."

As they drove the four blocks to the Spirit River Inn, Anderson asked Wendy, "I've been wondering how the media wars are coming along...?"

"For starters, of course, this morning's news carried a report about the sudden death of MP Garnet Cameron, which is under investigation by the OPS as a probable suicide."

"Do you have either RGI or the Government of Canada back on their heels yet?"

"Looks that way. Of course we can't always know what is going on inside, but we've been able to read – and influence – the chatter. RGI has gone absolutely silent for the moment, but I don't expect they'll stay that way. I think Priscilla – along with her colleague Samuel – threw a rock into the well-oiled gears of the RGI media machine, which has tended to portray the company as loving father who knows, and will take care of, everything. So, suddenly one of the kids came home from school and challenged father's mantra. Father is now bewildered, and pissed off."

"How about the feds?"

"On the government side, we've heard nothing, although a Calgary television reporter went after the current Minister of Natural Resources at a constituency function yesterday afternoon. The Minister obviously didn't have a clue what she was talking about, and – being an oil and gas guy from Alberta – didn't even know where Awan Lake was or if they had a mine and if they did, what they were mining. Not surprising, I guess, but you can bet the telephones and emails were flying back and forth with department officials this morning!"

"Do you think there will be much media presence tomorrow?"

Wendy chuckled: "Frank, it's a small-town event on a Sunday afternoon in the summer. What do you think?"

"I guess we should have offered free Mai Tais at the beach?"

"That might have done it – but at least we're offering a free pork-rib barbeque and a beer garden! Actually, I do expect the CBC to turn up, possibly Global 'cause they've been phoning a lot. And perhaps some free-lancers like Priscilla."

"Let's not forget to talk to Marion about doing a walk-through out at the sports grounds. Marj – would you go with her?"

"You bet. It'd be fun, and you never know what we might learn!"

***

It was close to lunchtime and the Zoo was filling up. Sometimes, on particularly nice weekend days, Sam would put some garden tables and chairs out in front of the restaurant, and indeed, that's where they found Arnold and Marion.

"Hi you two. Thought we'd sit out here and have an early lunch. You eating?"

Marjorie grinned. "We haven't had lunch, but we did have two breakfasts. Bacon and eggs the first time, and ham quiche the second time to feed Wendy, so, well, maybe we'll just have coffee. Actually, I'm going to go crazy and have a lemonade."

"Worries me when she goes off-book like that. Okay, I'll have a lemonade too."

"Actually," Marion chuckled, "he makes his lemonade from scratch, and it's really good!"

"Arnold," Anderson asked, "where does that Bob Adamson live?"

"About a mile and a half out of town on the way to Robertson's. He and his wife built a nice little house on an acreage. It's one of those 'low impact' houses with thick insulated walls, solar panels on the roof, that kind of stuff. And she keeps a really big garden. Why?"

"Just wondering if Manville and his enforcer drove out there this morning. Adamson was one of the guys the cops picked up – and released – late yesterday."

"Don't ever go fishing with an OPS cop unless you take sandwiches. They always do catch-and- release."

"Just ignore him," laughed Marion. "He's grumpy this morning!"

"I can hardly blame him after last night," Marjorie chimed in. "Long night, people trying to burn down the village, people dying. I'd get grumpy too!"

"I'm just glad I'm not a cop. Well, a real cop. Even in the Coast Guard, usually if we apprehended people we didn't have to manage the court cases – we were just witnesses. Cops – RCMP or OPS, whoever – have to deal every day with legislation that seems to favour the criminals and endanger the victims. For small-town fix-it guys like us, that seems somehow illogical. For the cops – really frustrating!"

"Marion, what do you think about you and I doing a walk-through of the sports grounds? When I drove by this morning there seems to be a little encampment of tents and trailers, people presumably here for the shindig tomorrow. Might be interesting to check them out, very informally and friendly-like."

"Say, Marjorie, that's a really good idea. The village doesn't have anyone formally managing campers on that site, because it's not used all that often – just the occasional passers-by on their way to somewhere else. After we're done lunch? Jaimie can look after the front-end of the garage for a bit longer."

"Maybe take Marion's car," said Arnold. "That shiny black jeep of yours with the tinted windows might look a bit too official!"

"That'll work. I'll take the Black Beast home and do some work on my, ah, introduction to Tony for tomorrow. He said he'd send me his résumé this morning. I know I won't sound very professional, but at least I don't want to insult the poor guy!"

"Great! I'll drop Marjorie off after we've lined up all the best-looking guys for ourselves! And by the way, have you talked to Dave Bradshaw about what's going down? Not, of course, that he's one of those best-looking guys..."

"No, I haven't. Deliberately... I'll call him later this afternoon and fill him in, but I don't want him trying to change the arrangements we've made. He will already get his time in the sun behind a microphone tomorrow, long enough to put that he co-hosted the event on his own résumé. Whether Dave likes it or not, Tony's the star."

"I think, in the end, Dave will be thrilled, because I think Tony is going to blow everyone away."

"Really?" asked Arnold.

"Yes, really. Haven't had time to finish his book, but I read quite a bit of it while I was waiting in Toronto for Frank to get back from the coast. It's brilliant, and he's actually quite funny."

"Okay then. Now I want to hear it too! Let's go for a stroll, Ms. Webster... my car's across at the garage and Frank can take your Jeep home, if in fact you give him your keys."

***

Anderson drove the Black Beast back to the house, took a walk around the dock, tidied up some ropes on *The Beaver* and returned to his porch grabbing a clipboard, some cold coffee and his cigarettes. He had no sooner sat down than he remembered to check his email for Tony's résumé.

It had arrived. He quickly read it through and highlighted the points he would want to include in his introduction, and went back to his clipboard, coffee, and a smoke. The cigarette tasted good, and covered the smell of the lingering smoke from the burned-out marina that drifted across to his home. The little road and the marina driveway was crowded with vehicles, and the place was crawling with boat-owners and insurance adjusters trying to get a measure of the damages from last night's fire.

The village-owned commercial dock where he kept his workboat, otherwise normally empty, was now crowded with boats of pretty well every kind, tied up two-deep in some places as well as smaller boats pulled up along the beach. Anderson knew he would have to address all of that very soon, and indeed he expected a visit from the mayor and the administrator at any moment. But the Love Our Lake event was just hours away, so everything else was going to have to wait until Monday. *One nightmare at a time!* he had told Marjorie earlier in the morning.

After half an hour of thinking, scribbling, thinking again and re-scribbling, he took his clipboard into the house to his computer and hammered out some notes for a short speech to introduce the new keynote speaker. Wendy and Anita had agreed to split the Emcee duties, so at least he didn't have to worry about that.

He had just finished when he got a phone call from Sam at the Zoo: "Frank, can you come by the restaurant, right away? I have a recording here that I think you need to hear, and some video to go along with it. Come to the kitchen door."

"I'll be right there, Sam." Anderson went out and jumped back into the Black Beast and drove quickly up the street. *Sam never calls... something must be up.*

When he pulled up beside the restaurant's back door, Sam was waiting and waved him in. The kitchen was still busy, but mostly doing clean-up from lunch and serving coffee. Beside the cooler door there was a tiny room, in fact a broom closet, that doubled as Sam's office. His computer was on and the screen showed a paused video-feed from his security system. The picture showed the east half of the restaurant, with a close-up view of the edge of a table where one man was obviously in conversation with at least one other across the table but out of the frame. The video was clear, and the man was Thomas Manville.

"Frank, I never told you this because I thought you'd be mad, but when those guys from Maple Falls hooked up the video system, I got them to hook up microphones as well, one at each camera. I've seen one of these guys before, often, and the guy in the video I've seen once before. I was serving the neighbouring table and heard something that made me think 'not good' so I came into the office and listened to the recording just before I called you. Listen:"

They're going for Project X, as discussed, zero one thirty Sunday. Make sure there's lots of fuel and make sure it spreads to the office. I'll have the boat I brought to Bob's place last week ready to pick up the two of you at the boathouse so we're clear of any road traffic.

"Holy crap. That's pretty wild! Run it again..."

They're going for Project X, as discussed, zero one thirty Sunday. Make sure there's lots of fuel and make sure it spreads to the office. I'll have the boat I brought to Bob's place last week ready to pick up the two of you at the boathouse so we're clear of any road traffic.

"Can you make a copy of that – maybe a minute or two on either side – and put it on a thumb-drive or a disk?"

Sam foraged around in a desk drawer and came up with a thumb-drive. "Here, we can erase this and use it..."

"Whoa, man, I don't want to erase something you were keeping!"

"No worry, Frank." He laughed: "It was some

instructions for my old cooler and I threw it out and replaced it anyway! I'll make a copy."

"Were there three men or just two at the table?"

"Three. The guy who is speaking, and I think also the guy who has come in here often – maybe 'Bob' is his name? And another man who looks like an angry football player. They left about two minutes before you got here. They drove a pickup truck. It was green, and it wasn't a new truck."

Sam checked that the recording had copied properly and handed Anderson the drive. "There, I hope it helps."

"Big time, it helps. Thank-you Sam, I'll be able to tell you why soon enough!" Anderson drove home as quickly as he could and went into the house. He was just going to call the Sergeant when the phone started to ring. The caller name was R. Klassen, so he diverted the call to voicemail and dialed the Sergeant. *Figured the mayor would call. He's definitely gonna have to wait!*

The Sergeant's phone rang five times before he answered: "Frank, what's up?"

"Bad stuff. Seriously bad stuff. The video security system at Sam's place – the Zoo – picked up a conversation between Manville and two other guys – one of them probably Adamson and the other one may be that Austin guy – is he big and mean? It's about going with Project X at

01:30 Sunday – tomorrow after midnight – and it's about fire – almost certainly out at Robertson Mines. You have to hear this."

"I'm on my way – you at home?"

"Yup."

"See you in twenty. And the big and mean guy would be Keith Austin, Manville's head of security."

Anderson clicked off and dialed Marjorie. "Marj? Can you guys get back here in about 20 minutes, and bring Arnold with you? Big bad stuff happening, and we all need to talk. John's on his way. Love you!"

He chuckled: *Well, that'll spook them all. I'm never in a hurry!* He started a pot of coffee, then loaded the contents of the thumb-drive into his computer and found the right software to play back the audio-video recording.

The Sergeant was the first to arrive, driving an unmarked bronze-coloured SUV and wearing jeans, a gray T-shirt and an Ottawa Red Blacks jacket which effectively covered his sidearm.

"All dressed up and nowhere to go, Sergeant?"

"Well, I thought this poor little village has enough going on this weekend without yet another cop hanging around! What's with all the boats? It looks like Toronto Harbour out there!"

"That's what happens when you burn down the only marina on the lake. Those folks are all pretty traumatized, I think, along with a herd of bewildered insurance adjusters. This lake may be pretty remote from the cities, but it's a boaters' paradise and the reason most of our summer residents are here. Me too, for that matter! Help yourself to coffee – I believe you know where it is. Marjorie, Arnold and Marion are on their way. In my judgement they need to know. Ah... here they are..."

"Hi John!" called Marjorie. "You're in hiding, today?

"I'm gonna hear about this all afternoon, aren't I! Believe it or not, I wasn't born wearing a uniform. My mother wouldn't even let me play with guns until I was old enough to date girls. Then she thought the guns looked less dangerous!"

"Okay folks, gather around Uncle Frank's computer screen and see why we're all here this afternoon." Anderson started the video and turned up the sound which, considering the source microphone was about the size of a match-head, was amazingly clear.

The video showed Manville talking on his cellphone, but the sound was muffled until he said "Okay" and hung up. He put down the phone and looked across the table:

They're going for Project X, as discussed, zero one

thirty Sunday. Make sure there's lots of fuel and make sure it spreads to the office. I'll have the boat I brought to Bob's place last week ready to pick up the two of you at the boathouse so we're clear of any road traffic.

He – and apparently the others – pushed back from the table and could be seen walking to the door. Manville paid the waitress at the till, and the three men left the building. That was the end of the clip.

"Can I hear that again?"

"Sure thing, John." Anderson fished around with the mouse to find the beginning, and hit the "Play" arrow again.

They're going for Project X, as discussed, zero one thirty Sunday. Make sure there's lots of fuel and make sure it spreads to the office. I'll have the boat I brought to Bob's place last week ready to pick up the two of you at the boathouse so we're clear of any road traffic.

"Wow." They're gonna set fire to the mine and smelter buildings, or part of them anyway," said the Sergeant. "I'm guessing they aim to start the fire in the machine shop, which we learned the other day is adjacent to the office. Manville is a senior VP from Robertson's head office in the U.S... what the hell is he thinking? They'll be shut down for months!"

Arnold was looking equally stunned. "That's an

amazing piece of footage. We're lucky Sam was alert enough to put two and two together and go looking in the playback so quickly. He must have overheard part of the conversation while he was out front serving."

Anderson nodded.

"Thing is," asked Marion, "can we even stop them from doing this?"

"Thing is," said Arnold, "if we don't stop them, that fire will be massive, and maybe even kill people, although Robertson isn't running the graveyard shift this month."

Anderson had been very quiet. Marjorie nudged the Sergeant, who was standing beside her, pointed to Anderson and shrugged. "Frank," said the Sergeant. "You ain't sayin' much. What do you know that we don't know?"

"Don't know anything much but here's what I think: I am the CEO of Robertson Group International, and my senior vice president in charge of the corporation's Canadian operations comes into my office and tells me they are having issues with local and national politics at one little mine in the middle of Ontario. I spend some time looking at personnel and facility production records and notice an internal report from a month ago that the birdbrain my VP hired as general manager allowed a drug smuggling operation to get out of hand, based out of RGI property. I send in Thomas, one of my best fixers who shone brightly on several tough gigs in South America and stayed out of trouble while on a three-year pre-retirement gig on Vancouver Island where his wife's family lives. I tell him to go to this Awan Lake place, clean it up, tell the government to get lost, get the expansion underway (it's a small one anyway) and get out of there."

"Okay, CEO Anderson," Marjorie said, "Fixer Manville is in place, but nothing's working. In fact, it's getting worse because people in government are being incredibly stupid and causing trouble, there are unexplained deaths, and some other folks are getting nosy. Now what?"

"I was getting to that, Board Chair Webster. I look at the latest reports and talk around to some people I know and realize that Fixer Manville is operating like he used to do in South America but this ain't South America and he's using bully tactics instead of management strategies. Then I hear that six or seven people have died around Awan Lake and I realize he has let the whole thing get out of control. So I tell my fixer to use Project X, which will get rid of unwanted people, re-set the media stories, allow us to lay off our workers, collect enough insurance to re-new the facility and pay for lost production, enable the planned expansion, negotiate a massive government-backed business development grant and – finally – save your ass so you can go back to Vancouver Island and be ever-grateful to Robertson Group International, where stock prices continue to rise steadily."

Arnold and the Sergeant were looking at each other in mock-horror: "God, Frank, you would have grown up to be an evil bastard if your mother had let you!" said Arnold.

"Unfortunately," said the Sergeant, "I suspect he's one hundred percent correct, or at least ninety-nine percent. Makes me shudder. Okay, all of you, how do we manage the next ten hours so we can keep the good people alive, stop Frank's Evil Empire in its tracks, and catch the bad guys. Better yet, we need to catch 'em and squeeze 'em!"

Anderson chuckled: "Sorry, CEOs don't do details. You'll have to call a senior specialist. Or... we could just have a beer," and he got up and headed to the fridge.

"Kind of working backward, I have to have a word with a couple of our firemen," Arnold put in. "We absolutely can't take that fire truck out to Robertson Mines tonight. Not with people in danger here, last night's fire still smouldering, and visitors gathering in town who, essentially, have been invited."

"Absolutely right, Arnold. Can't do it," agreed Marion. "May have to cool down some hotheads. It may be a good idea to take the keys, or at least have the fire-captains hold them."

"Frank, you have that video clip on your computer, and on a disk or something?"

"Thumb-drive."

"Good, can I have that?"

"Of course."

"I fear that Super George – or others up the chain – may want Sam's computer, video, microphone and cable components taken into evidence, especially if this case kicks into national and international significance. He likely won't be thrilled."

"We'll patch something together for him in the meantime. He won't mind. It was me who suggested he get it in the first place, and come to think of it, it may still technically be mine because I still have the bill. But of course I didn't pay the bill yet. Crap!"

Anderson paused, then turned to Marjorie: "What kind of fish do people drag across a trail to confuse trackers?"

"A red herring. In literature, anyway. Not sure what people use away from the ocean!"

"That's it. John, this may be a red herring, and it certainly won't help us this weekend, but as we now know, Manville was last posted to Nanaimo, where I know there is a nearby RGI facility because I rode on the plane with a guy who did IT work out there. He said their security was extraordinary for a mining operation. I'm just wondering if Manville might have a star security thug out there who he might have hired to fix the Horowitz problem."

"Geesh!"

"I'm just saying. Something we might want to remember on Monday."

"I'll make a note!" And he did. "But, how do we handle tonight? On the video he says he'll be picking up Adamson and Austin at the company boathouse, which means they'll be headed out there sometime soon – likely around suppertime, and won't be doing much until the end of the swing shift. Do we need to plan to intercept them on the water?"

Anderson paused again. "Well, I hate to say this, but I have a hunch that he'll be picking up Austin, but not Adamson. I expect Bob Adamson will be adding carbon to the hottest part of that fire with a bullet hole in his head that you'll never find. He's too low in the pecking order to keep around if he knows too much, which by now he does. Bob's just a family guy with a wife and kids in Spirit River, so he is a liability to Manville and the bosses, and Austin is almost certainly under orders to lose him. Remember, they've let this get so big and complicated that if things go sideways, if any lose ends are left flapping, RGI will be in deep trouble, quite possibly facing criminal charges and civil suits but certainly rattling shareholder confidence, causing losses that could get into the billions."

"Again, you're probably right. So we absolutely must stop this from going down, or we'll lose a well-meaning rather naive guy who doesn't deserve to be lost. Which means we need to get in there before the end of the swing shift."

"Got a S.W.A.T. team within reach? And, do they have a way of blocking all wireless communication for, say, a five-mile radius?"

"Not sure about the communication block, especially if Manville and Austin are using satellite phones. But yes, I can get S.W.A.T. in here by chopper, but I'd better start that ball rolling now, and I'll need to take this to George."

The Sergeant stood up. "I'm going to head into the Falls. I'll phone in along the way. Let's none of us forget that the one thing Manville is not counting on is this piece of video and audio that Sam collected, and it's the one thing that takes down Manville and maybe RGI too, so I'll be sending out the IT guys to pick that stuff up from the Zoo right away. Frank, will you warn Sam please? I'll be in touch again very soon."

"Wait just a minute – Manville is still hanging around here somewhere, and he's smart enough to catch on to someone pulling video equipment out of a place he has just held a meeting. Maybe tell those guys to hold off? I'll talk to Sam, of course."

"Good point. Just tell him not to touch any of that stuff or turn off his computer until our guys get there."

"Let's go and see Sam," said Anderson. "I need a burger anyway."

"You and Marj have a good burger. I need to go back to the shop for an hour."

"Marj, I'll go back to the shop with Arnold," said Marion. "Tell Anderson what we learned from walking through the campsite. There was one really interesting conversation!"

***

As soon as Anderson and Marjorie had arrived at the Zoo, he spent five minutes in the kitchen telling a very cooperative Sam about what would be happening with his video surveillance equipment. Sam assured Anderson that his bookkeeping program, emails and other important stuff was all backed up on "the cloud" so as long as he could get another computer somehow, everything would be fine.

Anderson rejoined Marjorie and they ordered their burgers. "So, you had an interesting conversation with a camper, apparently?"

"Certainly did! There is a nice young mum – Mexican or Venezuelan I expect – who brought her young daughter all the way here from New York City to hear Dr. Horowitz. Her name is Marita Juarez, she works at the Global Conservation Society, and she's out there with her beat-up old car and a tiny Walmart tent."

"Geez, that's dedication! And she's going to be some cheesed off that Horowitz isn't gonna show!"

"Well, of course we didn't tell her that yet, but no, she won't be very happy. Interestingly, she shared some misgivings about her employer... thinks they may be questioning Horowitz's findings – and opinions – on fresh water conservation. She was also frustrated that GCS appears to have been shifting its focus away from fresh water and wetlands toward climate change and caring for oceans and ocean-based critters."

"Yeah, I guess that's the easy way out... much less conflict with governments and industry who can all blame 'international forces beyond our control'. And the corporate and government grants can keep pouring in."

"I wonder if we should find out from John how much we can share about Horowitz, and maybe get Marion to gather the ABC girls and visit her. At least, while she may be disappointed not to meet Horowitz, she will not be enraged! And, with Priscilla, she may find a new ally. Do you think it's safe for the ABC gang – and Flo – to get out of protective custody?"

"For sure not tonight, but probably first thing tomorrow. Depending on how things go tonight, by morning it should be safe for the girls. And yes, we should talk to John about Horowitz, although by tomorrow we'll have to tell folks he is missing even if we don't talk about possible reasons."

"Did you mention to that RCMP sergeant about your suspicion – maybe we should say speculation – that Manville could have ordered a hit?"

"No," said Anderson with a wry grin. "I am sure that many things I say to friends have them questioning my sanity, but I'm absolutely positive that if I said that to the RCMP sergeant, she would write me off as a paranoid nut!"

"Ah... so you actually do worry about black helicopters, because you've seen them, right?"

"Exactly!"

"But even if you've seen the black helicopters, don't you think she ought to know?"

"Agreed, but I think I could avoid being fitted out for a straitjacket if I asked John (or maybe even Super George) to talk to her first."

"That makes sense. And maybe not right away... I have a feeling the OPS gang is up to their ears, just dealing with the immediate future. On another topic, did you get a chance to finish your notes for your introduction tomorrow?"

"Yes, I did. I may have to wing it, to some extent, depending on how Wendy organizes things, but I'm sure it'll work out. If not, I'll talk about black helicopters."

18:45 August 12

Frank Anderson, OPS Superintendent George Daniels, OPS Corporal Marie Beauchemin, and citizen Marjorie Webster were headed west at six knots onboard *The Beaver*, Anderson's workboat. They were headed toward the marshes where Awan Lake spills into the Spirit River, but they would not be keeping to the Spirit River channel. Their destination this evening was actually fifteen miles in the opposite direction so their course tonight would take them south through the many islands south-west of the village, then toward the south shore before approaching Robertson Mines on the east shore. They would be running without lights the last six miles, and as close to the east shore as they could to avoid being seen. They were also hoping for cloudy skies tonight because the moon was only four days past full.

Earlier in the afternoon, Anderson had re-fueled *The Beaver* and helped Cpl. Beauchemin set up a rack of radio equipment in the boat's claustrophobic forward cabin, wired to additional antennas temporarily clamped onto the navigation mast. The workboat would provide forward communication between OPS headquarters in Maple Falls and the officer in charge on the ground at Robertson Mines, including the S.W.A.T. team whose arrival would be timed for fifteen minutes before the end of the mine's swing shift. Sergeant MacLeod had hastily located and detained two off-duty members of Robertson's core staff, interviewing them to better understand end-of-shift procedures and where team members could best gain entrance and remain undetected in the machine shop, garage and office area. The mine workers had been cooperative, if surprised by the nature of the questions. They were thanked, and fed a steak supper, but would remain in custody – without their cellphones – until after the take-down was over.

Marjorie was at the wheel, a role she had enthusiastically adopted except for close-quarter manoeuvres which she happily left to Anderson until she had more experience. In the four scant weeks she had known this boat and its owner, she had grown to love the position of helmsman, and Frank Anderson was only too pleased to share that task with his new friend and lover. He was proud of what she did, and pleased to be free to manage and assist with other aspects of the boat's operation.

Sometimes, that was sipping coffee and having a smoke with the client. In this case, his client was the provincial police service, represented by a former Coast Guard colleague and now Major Crimes Specialist George Daniels. Anderson took a slurp of coffee and asked, "Has John mentioned anything to you yet about the Horowitz disappearance?"

"He did, this morning before we started planning this operation. He mentioned you considered there might be a connection between the RGI boss – Manville – and the guy's disappearance on the coast, and I agreed it was worth taking to the RCMP. He was going to reach out to that sergeant – Mankowski? – and talk to her about it, suggesting she should maybe contact you as well. Since then, things got busy around here – and it is Saturday in Mankowski's Ottawa office – so we may not hear more until Monday."

"Probably so. Although she may actually be in touch with Wendy tonight or tomorrow morning with some wording to explain things to the public at the event. I am certain she expects a deluge of media enquiries immediately following the event, wanting clarification or updates. I don't envy her that... all we have to do in response is give reporters her phone number, but she has to deal with them!"

"Well, she could have remained a corporal running a detachment of two in a small town in northern Alberta. She's a big girl now!"

"Such sympathy!"

"None. Empathy. We've all been through those choices... I often look back very fondly to my days with the Coast Guard, where things seemed much simpler."

Marjorie called from the wheelhouse: "I'm close to that waypoint you set. Is it time to turn south?"

Anderson peered off the port side and responded: "Sure. Turn due south and let's see what that looks like."

The Beaver made a slow ninety-degree turn and steadied on a new course. Anderson went into the wheelhouse, kissed Marjorie fondly on her neck and peered forward through the windscreen. Ahead and to his right he could see the beginning of the cluster of small islands that were home to so many of the summer cottages, and to his left was open water. "Bring her to port about thirty degrees."

"I'm not very good with degrees. Just tell me when," and the boat started a lazy turn away from the islands.

Anderson waited about fifteen seconds until he felt they were on the right course and said, "That looks good. Let's set that into the autohelm and you can relax. I'm going to work on the GPS for a couple of minutes to place a waypoint where we want to hide along the east shore."

It didn't take him long. There was already a waypoint set for Robertson Mines, and he set another about halfway south between the mine and the point where the Spirit River flows into the lake. They had passed some light boat traffic to this point, people going back and forth from their cottages to the village and a few fishers heading for the edge of the marsh, but by now there was only one sailboat on the lake ahead of them, and it was a couple of miles off, headed back toward the islands and – unless it tacked – would not be anywhere near their course.

Anderson nudged the throttle forward until the GPS registered eight knots, put his arm around Marjorie's waist and together they stepped out onto the deck. "George, I bumped her up a little. We're in open water now and we might as well make sure we have extra time to play with once we start coming north along the shore, nearer the mine. It's almost 20:15 and the sun will be going down in about fifteen minutes."

He poured Marjorie a coffee and topped up his mug from the big thermos beside the wheelhouse door. "How is Marie doing with all those radios?"

Daniels had been sitting on a folding deckchair, answering emails at first then taking a number of phone calls on a satphone. "I think she has it all working now. I've run out of cell service and emails, but of course the satphone is working fine. We decided to avoid any other communications than cell or satphone until we are in place and the actions starts, in case those guys have fairly sophisticated scanners. I kind of doubt that, but we can't be sure."

***

Over 2100 miles west of Spirit River, at an acreage residence outside Abbotsford, British Columbia, it was just after five o'clock on Saturday afternoon. Andrew Jenkins, a bus driver for TransLink in Vancouver, had just finished his Saturday shift and was three days late cleaning up and putting away his eighteen-foot fishing boat for another two-week run of daily shifts before he could get another long weekend. When he had returned from a fishing weekend on Vancouver Island, he had been running late so he left the boat and trailer in his driveway, hooked up to his rebuilt 1972 Chevy pickup, and used his wife's Focus to commute to work.

He had his garden hose ready to wash the salt water residue from the decks, seats and bilge of the aluminum boat, and started peeling off the canvas cover at the bow. He was greeted with a particularly unpleasant smell, and wondered if he had left a couple of fish to die in the live-well. When he pulled the cover back to the transom, he realized the source of the smell was more than a dead fish or two. Mere seconds after he threw-up in the hedge beside his driveway, Andrew Jenkins called 911.

Andrew's home was outside of Abbotsford city limits and within the jurisdiction of the Langley detachment of the RCMP. A police cruiser and two officers were stopped on his driveway in eight minutes, and were about as astonished as Andrew was when they realized the source of the smell was a fully-clothed and very dead man, probably in his sixties, sprawled on the bottom of the boat just ahead of the motor well.

There were questions, and there were answers. After the

usual questions: "did you put him there?" and answers: "no I did not!" everyone got serious and started to work out the time lines. Andrew had crossed from Departure Bay on the 08:25 ferry Wednesday, and driven straight home from the Horseshoe Bay terminal. He had not opened the boat cover since Tuesday evening when he put it on, and he had not stopped anywhere since except to get on and off the ferry.

In due course, the dead stowaway was removed from the boat and taken for an autopsy. The RCMP unhooked the boat from the pickup and took it away for more detailed forensic investigation, and Andrew was driven to the detachment office, questioned politely but repeatedly, fingerprinted, and returned to his home and family.

The officer in charge at the scene had retrieved a billfold and credit cards from the right-hand internal pocket of the victim's light tweed sports jacket and a cellphone from the left side pocket. The cellphone battery was dead, and the name on the B.C. driver's license was Sebastian Horowitz. There was no easily-apparent cause of death, but the officer, a Sergeant with fifteen years' experience on the force, wondered if the victim's neck might have been broken.

***

It was 22:42 in Spirit River, and the ABC girls – Wendy Webster, Anita Antoine and Priscilla Morgenstern – had joined Florence Dubois in the lounge at the Spirit River Inn half an hour before. Their plainclothes OPS watchdog had joined them under the guise of being Priscilla's brother from Toronto, but true to his task had been drinking tonic water over ice.

Every person there had their cellphone on the table, but it was Saturday evening, after all, so none of them was ringing. Except Wendy's.

"Hello? Yes, this is Wendy. Sergeant Mankowski? Of course. I just didn't expect to hear from you at this time of day. How's that? No, of course it's alright. How can I help?"

There was a pause. Wendy had already stood up and moved into the Inn's lobby where it was a bit more quiet: "Oh my God... really! Being treated as a suspicious death? Okay. Can I say that publicly? Okay, I get it, no more than that. Thank-you Marianna. No, it's not good news but it is helpful for us to know. I assume the family knows? Okay. Thanks again and good night, Marianna."

Wendy clicked her phone off and went back inside to their table, where conversation stopped and the others looked up expectantly. "Not good news," she said and sat down.

Wendy finished off her glass of wine in one swallow and held it up with a nod to the bartender. "That was the RCMP, telling us officially that Dr. Horowitz is dead and his body has been found, near Vancouver. The RCMP is informing the family as we speak, and it is being treated as a suspicious death."

"So let me get this straight: Horowitz's car was found – wrecked – over the side of a highway in the mountains in British Columbia, but his body was found maybe a hundred miles away near Vancouver. Suspicious death seems a bit of an understatement?"

"I know, Priscilla, but we shouldn't really talk about the car at the moment, at least until we get it from a police source. That was confidential information to help us understand it was unlikely that he'd be here tomorrow. Now that his death is public knowledge, and considered suspicious, we can say that at the meeting, but no more."

Anita was visibly angry. "Horowitz didn't just die because he stole some kid's lollipop... those bastards at Robertson got him, sure as hell..."

"I'm inclined to agree with you, horrifying as it sounds, but we certainly need to know more. We do know there is a police action going on tonight out at Robertson Mines, the second one in three days, and it involves Anderson and my sis, which is a bit scary and the whole thing is also highly confidential. I think I'm glad I don't know more, at least until they're back safe, but I do wish we could get this information to Sergeant MacLeod."

Their plainclothes watchdog's name was Andy, and at this point he piped up: "I can fix that for you. Let me get it straight too: Sarge needs to know that Dr. Horowitz has been found deceased near Vancouver, and his death is considered suspicious. Correct?"

"Exactly," said Wendy. "Can you reach him?"

"Not directly, but through the police radio to my detachment. I'll step outside and make that radio call privately... don't you ladies go anywhere!" He got up to go, then stopped and took out his cellphone: "This will be less obvious – and quieter – than my radio. I'll just call in to our special line from the lobby."

***

It was 21:35, and *The Beaver* had been holding her position about 100 yards offshore and two miles south of the Robertson Mines facility until about fifteen minutes ago, when Anderson had suggested they creep forward at one or two knots. The only lights the workboat showed was the soft glow in the wheelhouse from the radar, GPS and sonar screens.

The light breeze that came with every sunset had quickly dissipated and the lake was flat calm. The half-moon was still low in the eastern sky, so there was little ambient light this close to shore but ahead over the trees they could barely see the glow from the mine and smelter. With twenty-five minutes to go until the end of the last shift this weekend, the swing shift crew would already be phasing back the plant operations and preparing to go home.

"Frank, I think maybe we should take her up to 3 or 4 knots. We want to be right on point when John sends in his team. He just called and said they were almost all in position. There is at least one person in the office, but the team can't get close enough for an ID."

"Okay George, we'll add a bit more diesel to this outfit. Marj, how's that sonar reading?"

"It shows us over a fairly flat bottom with 25 feet under us."

"Let me know if it goes under 20 feet. In any case, I think we could now change course maybe 30 degrees offshore and add another couple of knots. We want to be outside Manville's boat – if indeed he shows up – and not inside. If he's aimed his boat in to land at the boathouse, or even if he's there already, he'll have his attention on the office and there will be less risk of him looking out onto the lake and seeing us. That'll be even more so if he's alone – let's hope he is!"

"Corporal – and Frank and Marjorie – our boating holiday is almost over: it's definitely time to put on your body armour and strap on the side-arms. I have laid the carbines out on the port side of the wheelhouse, inside by the door. They have full clips with nothing in the chamber. Extra clips are in a box against the aft wall and two big flashlights and a couple of sets of cuffs are on the floor there as well."

Cpl. Beauchemin came up out of the forward cabin to put on her armour: "Sir, folks, that was Sergeant MacLeod on the satphone. Says to tell you all that the RCMP found Dr. Horowitz's body near Vancouver, almost certainly murdered. Cause of death is unconfirmed but appears to be a broken neck."

"Thanks Corporal. Isn't that what you kind of expected, Frank? Are you psychic, or what!"

"Crap... yes, I expected as much, but no, I'm not psychic. I think we can point the feds where to look for the perp, though. Robertson's facility outside of Nanaimo, where this bastard Manville was last posted."

"Well, good hunting folks... let's hope we can nail him tonight!"

After putting on his own body armour and making sure Marjorie's was properly adjusted, Anderson had been focusing his time – and his eyes – on the two radar screens while Marjorie managed the steering and throttle: "I've had my eyes glued all night to that new high-definition radar, and it's getting so I'm seeing spots before my eyes."

"Got something against leopards?"

"Not really, but I do prefer redheads."

"I'm not really a redhead, Frank!"

"Well, when it comes to hair colours I'm just a man and don't know nothin'. Whatever you are, I like, and I don't see any spots so you're not a leopard... oh crap... stop the boat! Hold your course, go back to neutral and stay quiet everyone. We have a blip on the radar, just to starboard of our course and about a mile out from the shore." He quickly grabbed a light blanket from the navigation table seats, opened it up and draped it over the GPS and radar screens. The silence onboard was broken only by the steady hum of the idling engines. He peeked underneath at the new radar screen for a half-minute and stepped back.

"Range is about one mile, and the boat is moving fairly fast toward shore. It's moving steadily, so perhaps he hasn't seen us. Let's hope."

"Let's hope indeed," said the Superintendent. "In fact, nice job, I think... pretty well perfect planning and timing!"

"Folks gotta get lucky sometime!" Anderson grunted as he got an elbow in the ribs for that.

"I heard that, Ms. Webster! You can't kill him yet, we got work to do!"

"I'll behave! Tell me, am I supposed to follow that boat in or just hang out here, stopped?"

The Superintendent could hear Marie giggling at her radio perch in the forward cabin. "Okay kids, time to get serious! Hold your course for a minute or so then slowly turn in behind him. Agree, Frank?"

"Yup, that should put us about 25 or 30 degrees off his starboard quarter. We don't want to get too close yet, though – we're still about a mile offshore. Maybe just follow him dead slow until we learn more about what's happening on shore."

"Agreed."

Anderson had taken his binoculars off their peg behind the helmsman's seat, lifted the starboard windshield and was staring forward, thanking himself that he had spent a bit of extra money on the Steiner brand of 7 x 50 marine binoculars – they let in a lot of light and they are heavy enough to be steady on a moving boat. He was instantly able to pick out the all-around stern light on Manville's big and fast boat, and realized that the heavy chrome wakeboard arch had given *The Beaver's* radar a sufficient metallic surface area from which to bounce a sure signal, showing them a blip on the screen despite the boat's low fibreglass hull.

He swung the field glasses up to the office area of the Robertson facility, the building component closest to the shore. He could see clearly enough through the south window to see a person moving around, then – for a moment – two people. He then panned north toward what he knew was the first-floor main entrance, and he could see a number of vehicles turning on their headlights, backing up and turning toward the parking lot exit. Each one paused a few seconds as it was checked out at the gate.

Anderson had been giving a steady description of what he was seeing. He stepped back for a moment and spoke across the wheelhouse to Marjorie: "Okay, time to put her in neutral. He's just landing his boat and tying up... and he appears to be alone. There are lots of lights dancing around in the parking lot right now and there's still the loud hum from machinery, so that should distract him until he goes inside, or more likely up the steps to the parking lot."

The radio in the forward cabin started squawking and

the Superintendent darted forward to the companionway from the wheelhouse into the cabin so he could hear more clearly. Apparently three of the S.W.A.T. officers were strategically hidden in place in the machine shop and office area, and one was on a third-floor catwalk overlooking the parking lot. He would call in three more team members along with Sergeant MacLeod, who were parked out of sight several hundred yards south along the narrow road that went around the entire perimeter of the facility, which had originally been an open pit operation but was now underground in two shafts. For the moment, until most of the vehicles had left the parking lot, everyone was in holding pattern.

The radio squawked again, with a report that two men had come out an internal door from the office to a catwalk overlooking the massive machinery shop. The men were carrying five-gallon jerry cans which they emptied back into the door then along the catwalk to steps in the south-west corner. Anderson could hear one officer clearly on the radio: "The second guy down the stairs has grabbed another jerry can and is dumping gas or diesel – probably diesel long the floor to a big wheel-loader unit and emptied the rest under the engine. Crap, here comes the other guy with a small plastic jerry that he's just splashed under the hood and dropped on the floor. The men have backed off toward the door about 30 feet and are talking."

Sergeant MacLeod's voice interrupted, clear and urgent: "Time to go go go. Keep a guard on the parking lot... the rest of us are about 60 seconds out and we'll go in the main door. Get those guys in the shop – remember we want them alive and cuffed! Ignore everyone else... send them out of the yard. If they cause trouble, just cuff them to something away from the building in case it starts to go up."

Marjorie did a little dance with the wheel and the transmission to keep the workboat from getting closer to the boathouse, and facing straight in. "Do you want the lights up yet?" she asked.

Before either Anderson or the Superintendent could answer, there was a loud "boom" from inside the building. Less than thirty seconds later the entire facility went black, and ten seconds after that the office windows started to glow orange.

"Might as well turn 'em on now," said Anderson. "Everything except the wheelhouse and afterdeck so we can still see what's going on in there. Doesn't look like anything much is going quite as well as planned!"

"No, it sure as hell doesn't. Those idiots didn't waste any time getting that fire going... I guess they don't care if the other mine workers get out of there or not... that swing-shift is less than five minutes over!"

"And we're only five minutes away from a front-row seat at one hell of a big fire," said Anderson. "D'you think it's time to move in and crowd Manville and his boat? He won't wait long for his man... he may just try to get away and save his own ass."

"Yup, move in close. Marie, Frank... load up those carbines."

"Marj – you know what to do. I'll be right here to help but I'm gonna load up a carbine too. I'll just park it by the dashboard where I can grab it. Move in at about half-throttle and be prepared to stop just off the dock."

"You have great faith," Marjorie muttered, almost under her breath.

"No worries, M'am. Just keep on doing what you do!"

It took the workboat less than two minutes to reach the end of the poured-concrete wharf where the blue-and-white motorboat was tied, facing out onto the lake. The two minutes had been punctuated by a number of explosions from fuel drums and tanks exploding from the heat inside the workshop area of the building complex. The hum from the machinery had groaned to silence when the power went down and had now been replaced by what sounded like the roar of a thousand blow torches along with the sounds of cracking concrete, twisting steel, exploding heavy-equipment tires and falling debris. The office windows had burst and were serving as a chimney for the fire below, forcing thick black smoke and orange flames almost to the shoreline at the foot of the dock ahead of the workboat.

"Someone's coming out!" yelled Daniels. His left hand held the microphone for the boat's loudhailer: "Come to the end of the dock and we'll pick you up!" he called.

"Gun... he's got a gun!" That was the corporal.

"Drop your weapon and come out on the dock. Drop your weapon, now!"

Anderson was working one of the two floodlight controllers and swept the unsteady beam down the dock to where it flashed on the man hurrying to untie the motorboat. The response was immediate: Manville used one arm to raise the TEC-9 he was carrying and fire a short burst in the general direction of the floodlight.

The floodlight stayed on, but Anderson felt a hundred angry bees attack his left cheek and a sharp pain in his left arm at the shoulder. He was already on his way to the floor with Marjorie pinned underneath. "Stay down!" he yelled, scrambling back to his feet and pulling the boat's transmission into neutral before he grabbed the OPS carbine from where he had knocked it to the floor.

"Sink the boat... sink that prick!" yelled Daniels and he began firing at the engine cover and the hull near the waterline. *The Beaver* was slowly swinging sideways to the dock so Anderson came out of the wheelhouse onto the well-deck and raised his carbine to fire down into the motorboat just as Cpl. Beauchemin shifted her aim to Manville who had jumped back onto the dock and was aiming his machine pistol.

***

Why did he hurt so bad? No, he had been kicked by a cow once but that wasn't the same. Highway accident... where's Marjorie? No, the boat's running. Crap my ribs hurt. He opened his eyes, but it was dark, well, almost dark – that was George Daniels leaning over him.

"Hey old man, you're back with us, I see!"

"What the fuck happened?" He started to roll over so he could sit up. "Where's Marjorie? Where are we going?"

"In order of importance, you took one round from a TEC-9 right to the chest. You can take that piece of body armour home with you. After all it saved your ass, if not your ribs – two or three of which, in my experience, will be cracked. Marjorie is at the wheel and we're headed back to the village with one royally pissed-off prisoner cuffed to a cleat in the stern with a bullet through his knee. Marie got him, and last I looked, that wakeboard boat was still at the dock but her gunwales and waterline are now at the same level. Let's have a look at that shoulder, then I'll get your Marjorie for you."

"What happened to my arm... it hurts!"

"One of those first rounds Manville fired at the floodlight missed the light but went through your windscreen, then your shoulder."

"I sort of remember that. I remember it stinging my face, too."

"When we get back to the village, you are under strict orders to go to the Co-op and buy a lottery ticket. You're one lucky bastard, Frank – one bullet from a really nasty machine pistol took you square on the breastplate, which held, and the other round gave you a flesh-wound nine inches from your heart. On it's way by, it sprayed glass in your face but none went in your eyes."

"Everyone else was at least as lucky, I hope?"

"Nobody else onboard – except that idiot chained in the corner – was hurt."

Anderson got unsteadily to his feet. "I'm gonna go see my lady, and she can tell me where we're going."

"Yeah, okay Frank, but then go sit down in there... I'll bring in one of the deckchairs. If we had an ambulance out here you'd be on it already, so take it easy. Very easy."

Marjorie was very focused on getting *The Beaver* back to the village, but she sensed him coming up behind her: "Oh my God, Frank. Am I ever glad to see you walking around! George assured me you were alright but you would be really sore, so I guess a hug is out of the question!" She did take his hand and supplied a long kiss, however, before saying, "And you look like hell with a bandage on your arm and the left side of your face looking like you skidded along a gravel road on it."

"I love you too!" Anderson laughed. "I see you've taken over the job of skipper... where are you taking us?"

"We're about two miles off the east shore and I am aiming to pass just east of our island, then straight to the village. That's the part of the lake I know best... but of course I do have the radar and the GPS still on – there was no damage done to the antennas or the wiring – just the windshield. I got some of that in my hair and some pieces in the top of my head but you were in the way of most of it."

"I'm going to get us some coffee and a smoke. I'd really – really – like a cigarette!"

"No, I'm getting the coffee and smokes. I'm putting this

thing on autohelm for a couple of minutes and you can sit here watching the radar screen while the wheel goes lazily back and forth!"

"So what time is it? I have no idea where my cellphone is."

"You would say it's zero-one-thirty."

While he had been waking up, and talking with Daniels and Marjorie, Anderson had heard Cpl. Beauchemin on the radio, and in the background he thought he'd heard Sergeant John. "George, what's been going on at the mine? I see a big orange blob behind us, so I gather it's still on fire!"

"Oh yeah, it'll be on fire for a very long time. They're a bit worried about the fire spreading offsite and getting into the bush, so John has ordered up a couple of water bombers – choppers, actually – and they'll be on standby at the Spirit River field in an hour or so."

"So we got Manville... what about Austin and Adamson, and the others?"

"Pretty tough in there: bad news, some good news I guess. It appears that Adamson and one of our S.W.A.T. officers – a lady – never made it out of the machine-shop after that first explosion. One guy - Austin apparently – tried to get out through the office and fired on our guys. They took him down immediately. It would have been helpful to have him alive and in custody, but from what I gather, he's not a big loss to humanity in any case. At least we have the big boss. We gave him some morphine, so he's not in too much pain from that knee and we don't have to listen to him until we need to... he's sleeping it off back there."

"How about the rest of Austin's bunch?"

"They're all being picked up tonight – John managed to find a couple of them near the mine, and we know where the others are. A couple of the Americans slated to be deported are still in Maple Falls and will be arrested as well."

His memory was coming back. Anderson got to his feet, wincing at the pain in his chest, and walked across the wheelhouse to the three steps down into the forward cabin where Cpl. Marie Beauchemin was still busy with the radios. "Marie..." She looked up and gave a quick smile. "Marie, I don't remember much, but I do remember you taking Manville out of the equation. That saved my life... thank-you!"

"Right place, right time!" she answered.

"Perhaps. But you were there. Much appreciated!"

"Glad you're up and around. Now go sit down before you fall down. Three weeks ago I was where you are, and I know it ain't pleasant. Mind you, you don't got boobs!"

Anderson grinned at her and laughed: "Don't even

wanna think about that!" and he went back to his deckchair.

Ten minutes later, he had finished a very enjoyable cigarette and was sipping the last of a mug of coffee, gazing at Marjorie who's attention moved constantly between the blue-black water ahead, the pulsing radar screen, then shifting occasionally to the engine panel then the GPS screen. He could not deny the love he felt for this special person who had only been in his life for a month. He also could not deny that he needed to sleep, which he did with a quiet smile that belied the adrenaline-high from which he was descending.

07:45 August 13

Anderson opened his eyes and went to roll over. His eyes slammed shut in pain: *Crap, what the hell...* then he remembered: he'd taken a 9mm slug to the body armour that protected his chest, and he had a shallow but messy bullet wound in his upper arm.

Marjorie had brought *The Beaver* home to Spirit River and landed at the dock at 02:45, where paramedics and an ambulance were waiting. They prepared Manville for transport to hospital, shackled his ankles and cuffed both wrists to the gurney. A couple of the paramedics bandaged Anderson's arm, looked over his chest and told him to come in for chest X-rays in the morning. They also spent a few minutes picking glass from his cheek and from Marjorie's scalp before leaving in the ambulance, with a constable riding shotgun and one following in a marked cruiser.

This morning he could hear voices on the porch – women's voices – so he clenched his teeth, rolled over and sat up. He gingerly opened a bureau drawer and took out some fresh jeans and a well-used light blue coast guard shirt. He was successful at getting the jeans on and buttoned but he was having a struggle with the shirt, so he hung it off his right shoulder, poured a cup of hot coffee, grabbed a cigarette and headed out onto the porch. It was a beautiful morning, and there were four very pretty women out there: Marjorie, Wendy, Anita and Priscilla.

"Hey, Priss, you gotta get a shot of Uncle Anderson for the newspapers!" giggled Anita.

"Don't even think about it... not in your dreams! And what's this 'Uncle Anderson' bit?"

"Florence calls you 'Admiral Frank' but we find that too formal," Wendy offered by way of explanation. "Marj, can't you get him a more comfortable shirt to wear over a bandaged arm and a sore chest?"

"Okay, 'Uncle Anderson' it is. But just help me get this thing over two shoulders and buttoned up. Remember, I have to be on stage in four hours to introduce our entertainers: Tony Barker and the Balance Sheets. I'll need help getting my cowboy shoes on!"

"Cowboy shoes?" asked Priscilla."

Marjorie laughed as she gently eased the shirt over his left shoulder and the bandaged arm: "Yes indeed, he has a really nice pair of cowboy boots he got when he lived out west. Twenty years ago, but they still look pretty sharp!"

"And indeed they should look good... I won them in a

knife fight at the Calgary Stampede! So, have you folks heard from George, or John – or even that RCMP sergeant – this morning?"

"John said he'd be here at about eleven.," said Wendy. "Actually, he called us about an hour ago and said he was pulling off our watchdogs because you folks nailed that really bad dude last night, so we were all safe. It felt like being let out of school! Anyway, I don't suppose John got much sleep last night!"

"Marj, did you talk to Priscilla or Marion about going up to meet that lady from New York at the sports ground?"

"Damn. No, forgot. Do you think all us girls could go?"

"What's up? What lady from New York?"

"Sorry, Priss, I must still be half asleep. Marion and I strolled through the sports ground yesterday afternoon, just to get a reading on the folks who were coming in for the Love Our Lake event. One gal is here from New York with her little daughter... she works for the Global Conservation Society and she really came here because she wanted to meet Dr. Horowitz. She was afraid the GCS was out to get him and she wanted to talk about it... of course yesterday we only knew he was missing, but now we have worse news for her."

"Has anyone talked to Dave Bradshaw yet?" asked Anderson. "I guess one of us should let him know before he finds out from someone on the street."

"Right. I'll call Marion right now to see if she called him, otherwise I will. And maybe, ladies, if it's okay with Marion – and with you folks – I'm going to stay back here with Frank while you visit with our New York visitor. I know we have stuff to figure out and clean up this morning. I'll get some 'quiche of the day' for an early lunch for us all, around the time John gets here."

"That'd be perfect, Marj. I know that Marion and Adumbi have everything pretty much in hand for this afternoon, and the local volunteers are all set for food. I think they were putting out the chairs last night and the sound guy from The Falls will be here with his equipment at about noon, so I think we're ready to go."

"Perfect. Apologize to that lady – 'Marita' I think – that I'm not there... I'll catch up with her at the event.

***

Jeanette Benson insisted that Sundays – and in particular Sunday mornings – were family time. Their children had long since grown up and moved off to university, so now family time meant that her husband Harold, whether or not he was the Chief Executive of

Robertson Group International, was to be shaking hands with other members of the congregation at First Baptist Church in their suburban Virginia community outside Washington.

This morning, Mrs. Benson was not pleased. Harold had received a call on his personal cellphone at eight-thirty, from a certain Charles Morrell, the RGI Operations Manager at Awan Lake in Ontario. And Harold was also less than pleased: "Yes, Mr. Morrell, this is Harold Benson. I don't think we've met, but you say you're calling from our facility at Awan Lake in Canada? And how did you get this number? Ah, from Thomas Manville. Where is he?"

There was a long pause as he listened to a his caller explain there had been a fire at the RGI facility that took out the office, equipment repair shop and destroyed much of the headgear on both shafts. Benson was not surprised, although he didn't share that knowledge. Neither was he surprised to learn there was an unconfirmed report that Robert Adamson had died in the fire, but he was indeed surprised when Morrell told him that Thomas Manville was in hospital and under arrest.

"Any idea if there have been charges laid? Okay, keep me informed. Mr. Morrell – Charles – you're in charge out there at the moment but I'll have someone on their way to give you a hand as soon as I can, hopefully by tomorrow morning. This is a terrible incident, and you must avoid talking to the media or the authorities, including the police. Re-direct all such calls to me at this number. I apologize for not asking sooner – you were not hurt, I hope? Ah, you were home when the fire started because Adamson had said he'd stay behind to close the shift? Makes sense. Thank you for the call... we're all family here at RGI and obviously this is a massive setback for all of us, including your operating staff who are facing layoffs."

Benson hardly got started on his poached eggs when his cellphone rang a second time. This time the call was from Jeremiah Lawrence of the Global Conservation Society. He had heard of the fire, but did not have any details. What he had called to say was that Dr. Horowitz's car had been found down a cliff in British Columbia and that his body had not been found. What he had called to ask was if Benson himself had any information about that. The tone of Lawrence's voice implied that any involvement in Horowitz's disappearance would be a deal-breaker: "I could be in a potentially difficult situation if our society is actually seen to be muzzling scientists, and you know full well that Horowitz is due to speak at a highly-publicized anti-mining protest at Awan Lake this afternoon, so it would be appreciated if – under these new circumstances – you did not allude to this matter at all, for the foreseeable future. For your information, I have maintained a record of our emails, phone calls and meetings, just to ensure security for both of us."

Jeanette Benson recognized the signs and knew when she was licked. She exchanged her Sunday-go-to-Meeting summer dress for slacks, grabbed her purse and the keys to her new Audi Q8 and announced she would be spending the day with their youngest daughter at Roanoke, where they had finally convinced her to attend Hollins University after almost a year of traipsing around France, Spain and Morocco.

Harold Benson stared down at the remaining poached egg, which seemed to stare back – as cold and sullen as he felt. He scraped the plate into the kitchen sink, put a dark-roast pod into the Keurig and went to the wet bar in the dining room where he poured a double shot of Jefferson's Groth Reserve before returning to sit at the kitchen table. He was fully prepared for the fire and had already jotted down speaking points for a potential media release. He was not, however, prepared to have Thomas Manville in the wind, alive but badly injured and above all... arrested. There were suddenly far too many places where this could go, and none of them were good. The Horowitz thing was an unwanted complication: he should have told Manville to leave that alone until after the Awan Lake mess was cleaned up.

When the Keurig wheezed out the last drop and clicked off, he brought the cup to the table, took a hard swallow of bourbon from the glass, and dialed his stockbroker.

***

Marita Juarez and her daughter Roberta were having a bowl of cold cereal and a cup of hot tea at the old wooden picnic table outside their small tent when the four women drove up in a grey Honda Accord. She felt a chill down her spine until Marion stepped out and ran over to give her a hug, then signaled Anita, Wendy and Priscilla to join them. Wendy had brought coffee and cookies, and Priscilla and Marita immediately began to talk about New York and – soon – about the Global Conservation Society where Marita worked and Envirowire, where Priscilla worked.

Wendy was the one who had been elected to bring the bad news about Dr. Horowitz. Marita became very silent, staring down at the table, unspeaking. Her daughter knew her mother: she went to her side and put a hand on her shoulder. After a minute or so, Marita looked up, squeezed Roberta's hand and smiled quietly at the others: "I should say that I am shocked, but perhaps I am not surprised. Living so many years in America as one of the unwelcome ones, I am used to the undercurrents of danger that seem to follow wherever I go, and I sensed that same language of exclusion whenever Dr. Horowitz's name was brought up at GCS – not because of where he was from of course, but because of what he stood for. His scientific perspective on the state of global fresh water seemed to make them all uncomfortable, and I was instructed to flag his name and pass anything about him up the line to the CEO. That is mostly why I came up here, to talk to him and see for myself."

"You are passionate about water?" asked Priscilla.

"Yes. I have seen the photos of my mother's hometown of El Callao in Venezuela, where a beautiful part of the world, and a loving community, have been devastated by decades of unregulated mining. There is so much poverty in South America, and nobody wants mining or oil and gas extraction stopped – or even regulated."

"Well, if it's any comfort," interjected Anita, "do you see that smoke across the lake over there – and the big ball of flame last night? That's the last of our copper mine, for awhile anyway!"

"Oh my God, I saw it and wondered what it was. How did it happen?"

"We're not at all sure," said Marion. "But we do aim to

find out. We think there was bad stuff going on and bad people doing it."

"So, is the Love Our Lake event going to go ahead without Dr. Horowitz?"

"Yes, it certainly will, and we think you will be pleased by the speaker who will fill in. His name is Dr. Tony Barker. He is a friend of ours, and he lives out there on an island most of the year. He has a PhD in Accounting, a couple of honorary degrees, and is also the author of a prominent book on applying auditing principles to environmental costs and liabilities. He is a fan of Dr. Horowitz and they had even talked a few times in the last couple of weeks."

Marion pointed out that she needed to go back and keep preparations on track, and as they got into the car, Priscilla and Marita traded phone numbers, agreed to talk again after the speeches were over, and also to meet up in New York later next week.

***

Back at Anderson's house, Marjorie had put the orders of quiche into the oven to keep warm and a case of beer into the refrigerator. Arnold had been worried about his friend and sat with Anderson sipping a beer on the porch until

Wendy and the ABC girls returned, followed within a few minutes by the Sergeant in a police cruiser: "We've pretty well burned up all the detachment staff over the last twenty-four hours, so I'm doing crowd control this afternoon. So, damn it, I can't join you in the beer until later, but you'll be happy to hear I did bring dessert." He put a large box of Tim Hortons donuts on the counter.

"Frank, you look okay for a guy who had the crap beat out of him last night. How do you feel?"

"Sore in a few spots, but I'm okay. My chest feels like I did eight rounds with Anthony Joshua!"

"Yeah, and your face looks like you went skiing on a rock slide. I'm just glad to see you up and around. George says hello... he's got a morning full of inter-agency protocols to deal with, mostly RCMP again. He'll be out later."

"You still got folks out at the fire?"

"Yes... forensics. We found one body – almost certainly Adamson – in the machine shop area and we are still missing one S.W.A.T. officer in there. Charlie Morrell was out there this morning early, and he's like a lost puppy. His chain of command is either dead or arrested under guard in the hospital, and he said he tried to call the office in Toronto, he thought, but wound up speaking to the CEO in Washington. He said that wasn't a big help... the only thing he got out of him was a promise to send out some help Monday morning. Charlie's pretty shook up... I don't think he liked Manville very much but he and Bob Adamson were good friends and neighbours. I went with him to talk with Adamson's wife. That was a tough one – she's a wreck, and of course we don't even have confirmed ID yet."

"Any more word on the Horowitz file?"

"Not exactly, but now we're all on the same page with the RCMP. That Sergeant Mankowski – Marianna? – is being really helpful at this end, and is coordinating the flow of information all the way back through Hope, Abbotsford and Nanaimo. And, thanks to you Frank, they will open an investigation around the Robertson facility there."

"And the video file?"

The Sergeant chuckled. "Yeah, that's the biggie. Of course the OPS tech guys picked up the equipment from the Zoo early this morning, so it's secure. We showed the file to the RCMP, and we had already dumped Manville's phone and found calls to Washington. The minute we showed them that, the RCMP reached out across the border to the FBI and together they are trying to figure out next steps. Actually, I wouldn't be surprised if they seized the CEO's phone this afternoon and likely took him into custody, then went after RGI's head office in the morning. That seemed like the initial plan, anyway."

"Cool. You're going to be one really busy sergeant for awhile. Let's grab some food before these ladies eat it all up!"

By the time they had a quick lunch, and arrived behind the tent at the Spirit River Sport Grounds, it was close to twelve thirty and there was a growing crowd. Marion and her gang had figured for 100 people, but in fact there were closer to 175, and there were already runners going home to get more ribs out of the freezer and more beer for the beer garden, although it wouldn't open until after the speeches were over.

Dave Bradshaw came over to Anderson immediately. "Holy cow, man! You really took a shit-kicking, didn't you! You guys have had quite a week... all things considered, it's amazing we're still doing this thing. And hey, brilliant choice to get Tony to replace Sebastian. He'll do a great job, and I'll just do the birds and fish discussion and talk about some of the water testing. The University asked me to pay tribute to the kids who died, which I will do, but I need to ask Sergeant MacLeod what I can say about how they died."

"Thanks Dave. Marj, could you introduce Doctor Dave to Priscilla? She'll want to interview him, I am sure."

***

It was late in the evening of August 13, and *The Beaver* droned sleepily northwest across the lake on her way back to the village. The sun had just settled below the horizon, and the normally blue waters of Awan Lake were like mother-of-pearl. There were six souls onboard, full of excited chatter when they started out, but now all seemed lost in their own thoughts. It had been a long day.

Considering all the drama surrounding the planning stage of the Love Our Lake event in Spirit River, the event itself went off without a hitch – and with rave reviews from the nearly 200 people in attendance. Willy Antoine had opened the program, standing with his granddaughter Anita to remind the audience that the waters of Awan Lake had brought life to his ancestors but now had brought death to so many people: "May this gathering of so many good people restore the spirit of Awan Lake and bring new life instead of death."

Wendy, as master of ceremonies, keyed off Willy's invocation to talk briefly about several deaths in the community over the last two weeks but especially the very recent and mysterious death of Dr. Sebastian Horowitz, who was supposed to be here to give the keynote speech but would be replaced by Dr. Tony Barker, a highly recognized proponent of environmental accounting and auditing.

After Dave Bradshaw had spoken about the local water conservation committee and the interns and volunteers, two of whom had lost their lives doing research, Anderson provided the introduction to the keynote speaker, whose speech was passionate and detailed and very well received.

After the program was over and people flocked to the barbecue and beer-gardens, Priscilla asked Marjorie if she and Anderson could take her to the mine-site for photographs. One other free-lance reporter and a network television team also asked to participate, so with Marjorie's help, Anderson spent an hour checking engines, finding a temporary replacement glass for the windshield, and topping up fuel before boarding their grateful passengers and heading for the east shore.

On the return trip, with their passengers sitting quietly on the deck, Anderson and Marjorie were alone in the wheelhouse. She took his hand and looked into his eyes for a long moment: "Is it over, Frank?"

He leaned forward and kissed her gently on the tip of her nose before turning away to stare out the window for a few moments: "No, it's not over. Let's hope the dying has stopped for awhile, but in reality, we have only just begun, and tomorrow isn't even here yet."

ABOUT THE AUTHOR

Peter Kingsmill is the author of the Awan Lake mystery series. Peter is a recipient of the Governor General's Conservation Award (Canada) and the founder of the Redberry Lake (UNESCO) Biosphere Reserve in Saskatchewan. When he is not writing novels, he serves as publications editor with the Alberta Society of Professional Biologists and works as a consultant on regional development projects. Peter joined Crime Writers of Canada as a Professional Author Member in 2018.

Peter has been a frequent writer and editor since leaving high-school in Montreal and college in Vermont. He recently retired from many years as a riverboat captain and owner of a small-waters marine services business, and has worked at an eclectic mix of tasks which include logger, trucker and cattle farmer. He is passionate about Canada's rural spaces and has served two terms as Mayor in his home community of Hafford, where he lives with his wife Valerie, an artist and the author/illustrator of the *Redberry Tales* series of gentle children's books.

Other novels by Peter Kingsmill:
SUNSET at 20:47
Learn more at:
www.peterkingsmill.ca

Made in the USA
Middletown, DE
24 April 2023

29010195R00243